Bleed More, Bodymore
Ian Kirkpatrick

**STEAK HOUSE
BOOKS**

First publication in the USA
Steak House edition published in 2021
Copyright © 2021 by Ian Kirkpatrick

Paperback ISBN: 978-1-7368870-0-4
Hard Cover ISBN: 978-1-7368870-9-7
ebook ISBN: 978-1-7368870-1-1
LCCN: 2021905782

Our books may be purchased in bulk for promotional, educational, or business use. Please contact your local bookseller to order.

Cover by Samuel Johnson
www.SpoopySamuel.com

Printed in the United States of America.

31   10   21

1

CONTENTS

The author would like to thank her family. Thank you to those who took the time to edit this book. A special thank you to her writing partner and creative partner, Samuel Johnson for the beautiful cover and the unending encouragement, support, and love that helped get me through the rough spots and doubt. You are the best.

ONE.

"You sure pick the best places to break down, don't you, Way?" I say to myself in the cab of a Bodymore tow truck as I pull to the west entrance of the park. My phone sits in the cupholder. Wayland still hasn't messaged me back with where he's parked and finding him in the dark is going to be a bitch and a half. Of course, Wayland waited until the sun went down to call for a tow in the Baltimore body dumping ground.

This time of year, it feels like the sun's out all afternoon until suddenly it's not and you don't see it coming. Sometimes it feels like things don't exist if the streetlights aren't shining over them; the lights at the park's entrances are unreliable and by the time you reach Dead Run, you're lucky if anything is still lit. Tonight is one of those nights where my headlights are the only thing keeping the streets bright.

Downtown illuminates the horizon beyond the trees and it feels like a different world than the one in this godforsaken park. City Hall. The town center. West Baltimore. The airport. Parts of this city betray the rest of it.

3

Leakin Park isn't even so bad until the lights go out, then tree branches droop, leaves turn gray, the water turns black, and the stink of rot and death rise out of the mud. The maps call it Gwynns Falls or Leakin Park, but locals call it something a little more honest: Murder Park.

The windows are up and the air conditioner's on full blast like it'll push the stink out of the cab. The night's cold, but the heater would just make the smell spoil faster. I can turn the heat back on when I get out of the park. This isn't a problem during the day; I don't know what it is; maybe the sunlight disinfects the ground and keeps the burials at bay.

I drive all the way through Franklintown until I hit the east entrance and have to turn around. Wayland said his car would be obvious. Donny said his exact message was: "you can't miss it," but I still miss it until I do a third lap across Franklintown and I blame it on the park's shoddy lighting.

A white SHO Taurus sits on the shoulder by the east end, nearer to Gwynns Falls and the manor parking lot. Now that I see it, it should've been obvious the last two laps, but I'm sure it wasn't there before. I pull up to the shoulder in front of the car and stand, holding onto the inside of the cab for balance.

"Wayland?" I'm leaning out of the truck door, hanging on the step for a higher vantage point. "You there?" I'm watching the car.

Nothing moves.

I get out of the truck and close the door. None of his lights are on, inside or out. The only lighting we have now is a mixture of my headlights and the street lamp down the road—and that one's flickering.

The trees feel like their rustling quieter. A gust blows through.

I pull my hoodie over my head. My tongue flicks across the ring going through the middle of my lip.

"This isn't funny, Cross!" A buzz and the streetlight

4

down the road shuts off, probably hiding whatever asshole's using the darkness for his drug deal or selling electronics from his trunk or dropping off another pit that's outlived its usefulness. This city's a thirst trap for blood, everyone knows it. Wayland's probably better off with the lights out, avoiding bringing attention to himself, alone, in a pretty decent car, but standing in Murder Park under the mercy of the moonlight really isn't a great alternative.

I walk over to his car. My knuckles knock on the glass. "Way? You in there?"

The windows are up, the glass isn't shattered. Nothing moves inside, but there's also no sign that anything came out of the bushes and grabbed him—or if they did, they didn't break the windows to do it.

I try the doors. They're unlocked. No one's hiding inside. Something moves around in the trees off the side of the road.

I go around the car to stand in the grass. Darkness covers the trees, leaves, bushes, everything, distorting the forest to make it a stranger in the night. But I swear I see someone out there. The ground sinks in where I step and something winds around my leg, hooking into my clothing. Jagged vines like fingers or teeth press through the thin layer of my skinny jeans and stab into my skin. I kick them off and curse at myself for being a pansy.

I survey the ground for whatever it was, just a bunch of weeds, and out in the trees, the movement is gone.

"Wayland Cross, if you make me yell for you, I'm going to charge you extra," I growl under my breath. The next time I say his name, I'm whispering into the darkness, hissing, really. The falls in the distance are more than enough to murmur over me. When my voice echoes back, it feels like I'm disturbing the leaves and I deserve the bullet that's bound to come my way.

Toward the falls, a couple of trees shift, a stick cracks, definitely someone stepping around out there. My jaws tight, my hands tighter, I'm thinking of getting the bat from the cab. "Wayland. Cross," I hiss. "If you don't get out here in the next thirty seconds, I'm taking off with your car and the badges will have to pick up your body tomorrow, sorry."

I'm already turning around before I finish the sentence. I climb back into the cab and lock the doors. I don't even want my headlights on if I'm the only one out here, but I shut them off for a second and I feel the cold seeping into my pants and under my hoodie like invasive hands. Fuck, I hate the dark. I grab my phone out of the crusty cup holder and go to my messages.

JOEY	This is evidence now.
JOEY	UR WITNESS.
JOEY	If I die, I'm @ MP. Wayland Cross is :knife: :blood_drop:
BIG D	Sum1 killed Cross?!
JOEY	No. Asshole's getting *me* killed.
BIG D	Oh.
BIG D	That's some kinda loss?
BIG D	Save some wages.
BIG D	Insurance money maybe.
JOEY	Lose your best mechanic, but alright.
JOEY	I see how it is.
BIG D	jk.
BIG D	Love you, Joey.
JOEY	…Don't ever say that again, Donny.
JOEY	Just
JOEY	If I'm not back in 45, call in a body crew.
BIG D	Starting the clock now.

I toss my phone into the passenger seat. I turn the cab lights off and look around the darkness, waiting to see Wayland come running out of the trees now, shirt soaked in sweat, maybe his jacket torn from getting caught on some sticks, maybe he fell into the river, maybe a bit of blood would stain his stomach where he was stabbed while someone with a knife comes running out of the trees, maybe he got hit by sharp branches or bullets shot by squirrels. I don't know how people die around here, all I know is that it happens all the time and the bodies show up when the sun goes down. I told Donny never to send me to this godforsaken place after dark and yet, here I am. He holds these jobs for me. Just solidifies I'm getting him a blowup doll with a hole in it for Christmas.

I take another look outside. The trees sway with a slight breeze, but they look more like shuffling shoulders of a bunch of tall men wearing the same color suit. I really don't want to go out there, but I don't have much of a choice. I can't go back without Wayland's car. I'd never hear the end of it from Jag.

I turn the cab light back on and climb out. The keys in the ignition keep the lights on, but the doors are locked and the extra keys are in my pocket. I get to work moving Wayland's car onto my tow and if it gets scratched in the process, well, oh well. I climb into the car to check it's in neutral. I've only just got the door open when the smell hits me. The air's thick, even just sitting down in the driver's seat, I feel like it's pushing against me. Oil, maybe sulfur and something else, something familiar. Maybe the rotting mud from the park ground?

Fortunately, the car's in neutral and it's just the parking brake engaged. At least Wayland got that right before taking off. Before I get out, I check the back seat one more time in case I missed him curled up on the floor.

It wouldn't be the worst plan.

When driving through this park, you pass by the busted-up brick well someone was literally burned alive in a couple weeks ago. Candles. Wax. Chalk markings. Salt. The badges said it had nothing to do with Satanists while sliding a burned Satanic Bible into a plastic evidence bag.

"You back there, Way?" I reach between the seats, feel

for the floor. Something wet and cold touches my fingers. I yank my hand back. For a second, the image of him laying back there, dead, bleeding, cold, and that's the smell.

I climb out of the car, slam the door, and reach to get my phone, but it's not there. I go for my keyring instead. There's a small, barely legitimate flashlight hanging from it. I flick the light on. The light throws my reflection into the window. My eyeliner's smudged, but that's all there is to see in the dark and it only stands out against the brighter whites of my eyes. I open the front door, hit the locks, and open the back. I shine the light in the backseat.

There's nothing there. I close my eyes, take a breath, let go, and lean in. I can't believe it until I'm inside the backseat and reaching around the floor when I mutter, "there's nothing there." I climb back out of the car and shut the doors, pocketing the keychain light. I reach for the cigarette box in my back pocket but leave them.

I can't light up until I'm getting out of here.

The car's hooked up and the tow's growling sounds like a roar in the night silence. I'm waiting to hear crickets or an owl or the stream, but even that's gone. Closing my eyes doesn't make any of the park sounds come back.

Now I'm hoping for a car stereo blasting some BS beat as it drives by thirty miles over the speed limit, but it's like I'm in a sound vacuum and the city lights shine on the outskirts of the park more than the stars overhead.

I pull the keys out of the lift when the car's positioned on it. I'm on the lift, securing the tires when I hear movement in the trees again. It's not swaying leaves or branches, but the crunching grass I'm afraid of. It's fast and it's echoing in a way that sounds like it's all around me.

I don't have time for this.

I repeat the words in my head until I'm miming the words on mute lips. "I don't have time for this." My heart's racing, pounding louder in my ears than the movement in the trees. My hand's underneath the back passenger tire with the strap. Something wet splashes up my arm to my elbow.

I squeal and draw my arm back. It's cold water at first, but after a couple of seconds, it feels like a boiling heat. My hoodie sleeve clings to my arm. The wet parts grow hotter, more painful. I rip the hoodie off and toss it down on the truck flat. The cold air nips at my bare arms. Encouragement to move quicker. There's still a soft sting on my skin, but I can deal with it; I can ignore that until I hook up the car and climb into the cab.

I secure the other tires and when I'm done, I'm looking off into the woods towards Gwynns Falls. I almost call for Wayland one more time, but I think better of it at the last second and bite my lip ring instead. The leaves rustle. Something cackles from somewhere. It sounds like a bird, but it's odd enough, maybe it's not a bird. "Cross!" I hiss under my breath, scanning the trees for any movement.

The cold air stings my arm, but not as much as whatever residue Wayland's car splashed on me. I swing my arm through the air in an attempt to cool the burning sensation.

"If you're out there, stop being an ass and get in the truck!" My teeth are together. Another scan of the trees, the bushes, the grass, and the park.

Nothing.

"Last time, Wayland!" I jump off the truck flat. I grab my hoodie, but keep it held out.

Looking for Wayland in the trees is my last concern. He's had enough warning. I'm hungry, I hurt, and now I'm cold. The headlights are flickering when I reach the driver's door. By the time I open the door, they, and the cab lights, flicker off. I climb into the cab, locking it immediately. Something smacks into the truck somewhere in the back. I glance through the rear window expecting to see a face or a knife or even a gun. Nothing. I grab my phone from the passenger seat. Battery's dead. I could've sworn it was at 40% when I picked it up last. I maneuver my cigarettes from my jeans' pocket and light one. I turn the keys, the car reignites without a problem. If Cross's hiding in the trees, too bad, he's finding his own way back.

When I get back to Bodymore, Donny says, "I was about to send the search team looking for you."

"No, you weren't." I toss the keys onto the counter, making my way to the back of the shop.

"You're right, that's kinda pricey… Sorry about that," Donny says.

"No, you're not." My arm's still burning with pain from whatever came out of Wayland's car. When I pick up my hoodie, the sleeve is hard, dry, sticky, and it smells a bit like sulfur. In the light, my arm looks swollen, puckering, irritated, blood veins seem brighter than before. Red and blue lines travel up the underside of my arm.

I go to the sink in the back of the shop and flick the water on. I hiss, breathe in hard to stop myself from making any other sound, and pull my hand out of the water. The cold feels like acid against my skin. I turn the water to hot and wait for the pipes to heat.

Donny's yelling across the shop, "you find Cross?"

"Nope. Looks like MP got him."

"Shame. Guess we wait to see if we can sell his car? How long would you give it?"

The water's only lukewarm now. "You really think he's dead?"

Donny mumbles something, I'm not sure what.

"You try calling him since we got his car back?" I say.

"What, didn't you?"

"My phone died while I was out. *Sorry.*"

Donny groans. "I guess I could give him a call then."

It wasn't the sound of Donny realizing something he didn't know. It was him thinking about having to get off his ass and push a couple of buttons to do something. I get it; it's late, it's almost eleven and we both want to go home because we both know we open early tomorrow. The busy season's starting with people waiting to get their winter tires on before the snow hits and somehow, everything else is wrong with everyone's car from all the appointments they put off during the summer and the last three years, because they wanted to ignore the lights on the dash or the smoke coming from the hood or the smell coming from their gas cans and *it could maybe last a little bit longer—it could last until the summer,* they're sure of it and they had something better to do than spend Saturday sitting in an auto shop or in their living room at home, waiting. The water's still not hot yet and the redness on my arm isn't going down, the sting isn't going away. "You need to get the pipes fixed, Donny!"

"What's wrong with 'em now?"

"The same thing that's been wrong with 'em for three months. You need to get them fixed!"

He grunts again. I pull away from the sink just enough to peer into his office. He's got his phone pressed to his shoulder. At least he's doing that. If I had to call Wayland and actually got him on the phone, I don't know if I'd be able to hold back every last profanity I've learned over the years, including the Italian ones I got from Donny.

The smell of Leakin Park is back, filling the garage now. I follow the scent back to Wayland's car where it's set up on the first hydraulic. The decrepit, rotting mud is caked onto his tires and the bottom half of the car. There's a dent in the side of the back door, and thick, stained handprints over the trunk. Mud or something. A little brown, somewhat red. With the light of the auto shop, I open the car doors to take a peek inside the front seat and back.

Despite having checked already, I'm still expecting to see something on the floor. A body, a garbage bag, maybe a bag with a body in it. At the very least, dirty laundry, but the backseat is empty. I go around to the driver's side to pop the trunk.

The putrid smell fills the garage immediately. The same dirty, wet, sulfuric, and muddy flavor from MP, but now there's a much more metallic element to it. Blood.

11

My heart's pounding and I don't realize I'm shaking until I reach for the popped trunk lid to push it up. I double over with vomit at the first glimpse inside. I run to the sink and empty the contents of my stomach. Donny hears me and says, "you're not pregnant, are you, Joey?" but then after another moment, the stench must have reached him because he says, "what in the fresh hell is that? Someone forget to flush again?" He comes out of the office holding his shirt to his nose like it's going to help. I'm gripping the sink's edge for stability. The smell follows and wraps around me and is suffocating like hands wrapped around my neck, fingers pressing on my throat. A hand smacks into my back and I jump from it. Donny's staring at me like he's asking what's wrong, I've gone crazy, get it together.

"You smell that, right?" I say.

"Yeah. What the hell is it?" Donny says.

"Look in the trunk."

He does, but his only response is, "shit."

I wipe my lips with the back of my arm and return to the car. Rolled up in the fetal position is a body, a corpse, face mangled beyond recognition, cut up, bloody, the eyes destroyed. He's naked with skin darkened by fire or some other kind of damage that left him raw. The trunk's stained with blood, some pooling underneath the body along with some thick, silver water. My arm pulses looking at that water and something sends a shock wave through me. I go back to the sink, the water's still running, steam's coming off it now, so I thrust my arm under it.

Silver water sticks to my hand like poorly applied fingernail polish. The heat burns, but I grab the washcloth from the edge of the sink and scrub my arm, hard. The burning slowly soothes, and my veins sink back into my skin or whatever you'd call it. The bright reds and blues aren't drawn so close to the surface anymore.

When I've cleaned my hand, I rinse my hoodie so I can skip the laundromat for at least a few days more. By the time

I'm done, Donny's got the phone against his ear again and he's giving our address. "Yeah. Big sign. Bodymore Body Shop. There's an arm coming out of the tire on the sign. Ironic, but this isn't the normal kind of job we do. Right. Right. Yeah. We'll be here. Ring the bell when you get here."

I turn the faucet off.

He's standing outside his office, leaning against the frame. "You didn't have any plans tonight, did you?" he says, but it's not really a question as much as an opportunity to make a joke.

I'm thinking about home, the burnt smell of dad microwaving some frozen mac and cheese a little too long, but he doesn't care if the edges are a little black. He likes the crunch, and it goes down fine with some Barton's. The smell sticks to the dishes piled in the sink and God knows where those come from since he uses paper plates and disposable dishes for almost everything anyway. Shaking my head, I rub my eyes. I want to go home and hit the mattress, but I know better than to think I can. "Nope. I'm all yours."

"Good. The badges are gonna wanna talk to you when they get here."

"It's gonna cost you overtime and something of a bribe." I lower my hand. The tips of my fingers are black with smudged eyeliner.

"How about a half bag of Doritos?"

"Throw in a pizza and I'll consider it. I'm starving and I promise I can't complain if there's something in my mouth."

"Hm…" Donny's walking back to his office. "Maybe that'd work better if you weren't like a daughter to me. I'm not into that shit."

Still, he's dialing his phone and I hear him call for a pepperoni pizza and whatever else they make him buy to get delivery. I go back to the sink and wash my arm a second time. The prickling and stinging are gone, so I just leave the lukewarm water to massage my skin instead while I try to replay the scene from the park in my head. The details were fading before the badges got here, but I told them everything I could remember. Then I went home with half a box of pizza and an unanswered text from Jag saying, "come over when you get off."

TWO.

Dad's still asleep in his armchair in the living room when I wake up the next day. Two-liter bottles of Barton's lay at his feet. The TV flashes between commercials, illuminating his face. Drool drips down his cheek, it doesn't look like he's shaved in a couple of days. His dark hair's a mess and his glasses hang crookedly off his nose. I pull the half-eaten tray of mac and cheese from his lap. He's carved out all the burnt edges and mixed around the rest with a plastic fork. I throw the fork into the sink to wash later and stick the mac and cheese in the fridge. I don't know if it's still good, but I don't want to get into it again after dad's 'forced to take his lunch out of the trash because I'm inconsiderate.'

I grab a bag of Pop-Tarts from the cabinet and shove them into my hoodie pocket. On my phone, there are three messages from Donny and one from Jag. Donny's say, 'sleep well?' 'badges're back,' and 'get here ASAP.' Jag's says, 'thanks for leaving a mess last night.'

JOEY   sry. I'm traumatized.
JAG   Excuses.

JOEY   I almost died.

JAG   Yea?

JOEY   For real. Car shot something at me.

JAG   Scared of a little grease?

JOEY   Oh, fuck off.

JOEY   Someone in the bushes.

JOEY   MP @ Night. You do it next time.

JAG   Been there, done that.

JOEY   Alone.

JAG   Yeah, and?

JOEY   Find a dead guy instead of car trouble.

Jag isn't quick to text back this time.

JOEY   So, badges…

JOEY   I hate them hanging around.

JAG   No one likes it.

JAG   Shoulda dumped the body somewhere.

JOEY   Where?

JAG   Anywhere.

JAG   You were at MP.

JAG   Find a spot. Drop him. Call in a tip.

JOEY   Before opening the trunk?

JOEY   How would I have known?

JAG   The smell?

JAG   I could smell this guy from blocks away.

JOEY   Fine. Next time we get a night call,

JOEY   I'll call you. You go.

JOEY   If you're sleeping? Too bad.

JAG   Deal.

JAG   And if I don't scream, you owe me something.

JOEY   Like what?

JAG   Haven't decided yet.

JAG   Will let you know.

I roll my eyes while shoving my phone into my pocket. I grab my skateboard from the wall in my room and head out.

There are three cop cars, a black van, and two news vans outside Bodymore. A man and a woman from separate vans approach me at the same time. The flags on their mics say they're from different companies, but the plastic preparedness of their appearances makes them look like they came from the same machine. Her with the shiny, straight black hair, long lashes, darkened skin, and a smooth voice like she practices her vowels in the mirror for hours. The dress she's wearing looks more appropriate for a cocktail party than work with a deep V in the front and nowhere near her mid-thigh. She walks with ease like she's wearing tennis shoes, though her pumps give her four more inches. The guy has gray hair, fashionably gray, not old-age gray. His suit's blue-gray with pinstripes and a darker blue button-up and black tie because bright hair and dark clothing are trendy right now. They say, "hey, do you work here?" at the same time like they're connected to the same brain or the same radio tower, I guess. I push past them, but they still say, "I want to ask you a couple of questions. Do you have a minute?"

"Nope. Can't. Sorry. I have a real job to get to." I know I shouldn't say anything to the mics, but I didn't sleep well last night and I'm irritated and the only thing I want to hear is running water, a coffee pot, metal against metal, and our shit radio trying desperately to hold onto a signal.

"Were you the person who found the body?" they say.

I'm making my escape fast, but the shop door doesn't open. I grab the handle again and pull it harder.

Locked.

I smack it with my fist. The door rattles in the frame. "Open up!" barely gets out before the door opens and Jag's standing on the other side. I slip in, he locks the door behind me. I tuck my skateboard and hoodie behind the counter and follow Jag into the shop.

A couple of badges hang around the lobby. They look up when I walk by but say nothing. The garage smells like coffee instead of oil or gasoline. There's a coffee pot I don't recognize in the break room, bigger than our usual 10-year-old Mr. Coffee.

"How are we so lucky?" I'm walking toward the counter it sits on.

"Don't get too attached. Donny said it's going back when the badges are gone," Jag says.

"Then I guess we'll have to hide it then so he can't." A couple of cups sit on the counter beside the pot. I grab one from the stack and fill it with the remaining coffee.

"If you take the last of it, you have to make a fresh pot, that's the rule," Jag says.

I'm pursing my lips, arms crossed, turning toward Jag. "You were waiting for me to take it…"

He shakes his head, grinning. "I'd never." He didn't shave this morning and his jawline is covered in short, dark hair up to his brown hairline.

"Whatever. I'm used to lazy boys." I take a sip of the coffee to taste it. "Is this new coffee?" There's a small box of sugar packets on the counter and some flavored non-dairy creamer. "CoffeeMate? Wow. We're really moving up in the world."

"He was hoping it'd get them out sooner."

"How's he feel about the mics out front?" I toss the coffee filter into the trash and give the tray a rinse.

"If they're not bringing in customers, he doesn't want 'em."

"I thought any publicity was good publicity. It's not like *we* killed the guy."

"Though there's been some speculation."

"You're lying." I turn from the counter.

"Nothing substantial, but they've been talking."

"I didn't kill him. They need to take *body shop* a little less seriously." I open the coffee cabinet to grab the canister.

Beside the Folger's is a shiny red bag that reads PREMIUM and MERRIER and ARTISAN and CHERRY WOOD. "Donny got *real* fancy for the badges, didn't he?"

"I told you, he wants 'em out."

"He sucking 'em off behind the shop too?"

"Joey—"

"I just don't think making them cozy is the best way to get them to go. That's all."

The water's in the pot and the feeling of coffee fills the room. It's not bitter and muddy like the Folger's, but something a little more pleasant and light and it doesn't make the air feel thick. The scent of stale crackers, dust, and a sandwich gone rotten in the back of the fridge are gone. The cup in my hands is warm. As much as I thought I'd never get *that* smell out of my nose last night, I'm having a hard time remembering what the body smelled like right now.

The image of it floods back to me. Nude, punctured skin, burns making him look like a cranberry, and his face scratched so raw, he was unidentifiable. His hands were gone, cut off clean at the wrists, and laying between his legs, a black garbage bag tied shut. "Did you see him?" I take a sip. "The body."

"Badges had it gone by the time I got in this morning," Jag says. When the coffee's done brewing, he immediately makes himself a cup. Black.

"What about the car?"

"They took that too."

"So… what the hell are they still doing here?"

Jag shrugs. His breath pushes the steam from the coffee he's holding. His hair's messy, uncombed by anything but fingers, but that's his usual. He has dark bags under his eyes and they're a little red. His sleep was probably just as good as mine and I only got two hours of it. My arm was burning like it was on fire. Lotion did little to subside the pain, a couple of ibuprofen muted it after a while though, but what's his excuse?

"Stay up too late jerking off?" I say.

"You should've come over when you got off last night."

"Lonely?"

"I'm not gonna say worried, because then you'll get a big head."

My heel bounces against the floor. "I had to check on my dad."

"Your dad can take care of himself—"

"Joey!" Donny's calling from the garage. I'm not even out of the break room when he's yelling my name in my face, followed by, "oh, there you are."

"Yeah. I just got in." I take a step back to put some space between Donny and me, but I end up stepping on Jag's steel toe. "What do you need?" I say to Donny.

He eyes the cup in my hand. I'm waiting for the comment that it's coming out of my paycheck, that it's not for me, what kind of favors will I give, or "that overtime just got paid for." Instead, he lowers his voice and says, "the badges wanted to talk with you about what you saw—"

"I talked to them last night!"

"What was out there. What you did when you got there. They want to know everything."

"What I did when I got there last night? What's that matter?"

"I dunno, Joey. You brought in a body; they're getting info—They don't think you did it or anything, but they want to know everything you know."

I'm going to argue, but I know it's useless. Nothing I say will get me out of talking to someone about last night. It shouldn't be the badges though; I know them well enough, and BPD isn't exactly known for being efficient or ethical.

One day you're sliding down a rail outside the courthouse, the next you're standing before the judge as he says you admitted to robbing that corner store. When you say no, the judge asks if you talked to the badge and when you say yes, they take you talking to the badge as admitting to guilt you never had.

I don't know if it's Baltimore or if they're like this everywhere else, but the badges here aren't interested in justice.

Though I feel my mouth moving and I hear my voice, I don't really know what I'm saying to the badge until he asks me what happened to my arm. It's puffy, swollen, only mildly discolored compared to my other arm though. "You keep scratching. Are you alright?" one of them says and when I follow his pointing hand, I'm wondering if my arm's been that red all morning. I tell him about the splash of liquid from the car, maybe it was acid, I just didn't know from where and it didn't *smell* right. "Did you see anyone at that time?" the badge says.

"No." I'm sucking on my lip piercing.

"Where were you when you were splashed with the substance?" the badge says.

"At the park."

"What did you do when you realized it burned?"

I point him to the sink where I washed my arm. I didn't know they were going to take it apart and swab it. When they disconnected it from the walls, some bit of thick, silvery water puddled on the floor, dripping from the pipes, still liquid, but thicker than water. Maybe like blood in various stages of clotting, but it's silver, or white, or clear pending on how much it's pooled.

"Is this what you washed off?" one of them is saying. He has to say it a second time before I actually hear him and nod, but I'm not sure how to answer. The badge slips on a pair of gloves and gathers the globby bits from the pool of water. He drops it into the evidence bag, takes a swab, mops up the water with that, and drops that into the evidence bag too. More of it falls out of the pipe and more of it is solidified like Jello, wiggling when the badge picks it up and drops it.

"What the hell is that?" I say.

The badge doesn't answer me. Another badge, this one wearing pressed slacks, a neat, tucked-in shirt with no stains, and a black silk tie tucked into his shirt approaches and asks the same thing, and the first badge says, "don't know, but it feels like flesh."

"Like human flesh?" My hand covers my mouth, covering a soft burp. I sip the coffee hoping it might make the sickness back off, but the sugar tastes bitter and feels like sand.

"Don't they use other words if it's not human?" Jag says from beside me. I don't know where he came from, but I kinda wish he wasn't standing next to me because it feels like he's waiting to rub it in that I'm not feeling well.

He doesn't say anything though.

I distract myself with my cell, checking the messages for anything from Wayland, but the last message is still from three days ago.

The badge with the tie comes to me. He's got a badge on his belt not too far from his gun. "Morning," he says, pauses, waits for me to say it back, I don't. "I'm Detective Stone Grant. What's your name?"

I don't say anything. I feel Jag's eyes on me. I still don't say anything.

Stone slowly nods, smiles, pushes his graying brown hair back. "Alright… Would you be willing to come to the station to give an eyewitness statement?"

A laugh surprises me. I purse my lips and step back. "No. I'm not going to the station. I didn't *do* anything but find this treasure chest of horrors for you. So, you're welcome. Consider that my public service for the rest of the year, but that's it."

"We're not accusing you of anything," Detective Stone says, and I know he's trying to be reassuring and that's what they do and there's really nothing to be mad at in his voice, but it feels patronizing and I need more coffee. "We'd like to take some photos of your arm, sample it for evidence. Did this substance get on anything else? Shirt? Pants?"

"No." I glance at Jag, then around the room looking for Donny, hoping, for once, he'll say something like *you can't leave, need ya to stay here for a while*, but I have a feeling he'll side with the badges. "If you want a sample or something like that, you have the car. Look for it there."

"We will do that," Stone says. "But—"

"*But* you wanted to get me to the station for some kind of bullshit reason, lock me in a room, and ask me questions until I say something that doesn't make sense with something else because I'm tired and hungry and want to go home. Get your pics. Get your whatever, and then leave me the hell alone unless you come back with a warrant. Thanks." I stick out my arm and wait for them to collect their samples.

It doesn't take long; they're ready in seconds, taking pictures, running a swab of something cold on my arm. It stings and smells alcoholic. They rub a couple different sampler cloths on me before they say they're done.

Stone takes out his wallet. A small, brown business card comes out and he holds it to me. After a moment, I take it. The front side reads DETECTIVE STONE GRANT in gold lettering on dark brown, recycled paper. On the backside is a phone number scribbled under the precinct office number and he says, "if you think of anything else you'd like to say."

"Don't you think you're being kind of bold, *Rocky*?"

"Excuse me?" Stone says, his voice is smoother and more controlled than I was expecting it would be.

"I know your kind," I say.

"My kind?" He fails to hold back a chuckle on purpose.

"There are only two kinds of badges: the absolute corrupt or the absolute drunkard. Some of you guys get your kicks by putting innocent people behind bars because it looks good on the books. The rest of you are miserable, lonely workaholics who either chased away your wives working all nighters or they died in some tragic accident, probably a fire, and now to deal with the heartache and loneliness and the emptiness of your existence, you drink. You drink and desperately claw your way forward saying, *this time* you'll catch him. I've seen the movies." I lean in, give a long, hard whiff. "You don't smell like booze, so that leaves only two options: today's a good day or you're absolutely the most corrupt badge with the BPD. Tell me, Rocky… Which one is it?"

"That's an interesting assessment, but mostly wrong," Stone says.

"I've. Seen. The. Movies."

"This isn't a movie." His head cocks to the side.

I cross my arms. My tongue flicks my lip ring. "Uh-huh. Gotcha."

He thinks it's working, but I know better. The manipulation tactics, the badges in real life who will determine an ending and chase any evidence they can get to verify *that* story. Not what really happened, but what they want to have happened. Everyone puts on a mask to get what they want and making up the reality around that mask is only part of *chasing the dream*. "But for the record, and you *can* put this *on the record*, I don't have anything else to tell you that I haven't said already, alright? Last night and this morning, what you know is what I know, so I'm not going to call you. I'm not going to need your number." I hold the card out for him to take, but he doesn't. Instead, he turns his back to me and acts like I didn't say anything.

He's talking to the officer by the sink, they mutter between themselves to the point I can't hear them and if I move even a step closer, their voices actually sound further away.

I'm standing still just to wait for the silence to seep in and amplify their voices. Instead of silence, there's a wild drum beat quickly growing faster and louder than before.

My chest's throbbing. My fingers are numb. Everything around me fades so one color smears into another like some mid-century painting.

There's no coffee left in my cup to wet my throat and I'm blinking a few times just trying to breathe, but it's hard.

My tongue bounces against my lip ring.

I grope my pocket, my phone, waiting to feel it buzz.

It stays quiet.

My vision comes back the same time the drumming disappears, and I feel the wet coffee through my canvas sneakers, seeping into my sock and the detective's making sounds again when he talks. I bite the inside of my lip hard enough to taste blood. "Hey, I have a question," I say to Stone.

I feel stupid for saying anything, but something being stupid never stopped me from doing it. I don't think I actually expected Stone to pause his conversation and turn to me. He says, "what's that?" with his eyes and full attention pointed.

I mutter something that sounds like, "thanks," but I'm hoping it's lost in everything going on in the room.

The radio in the back corner.

The Beatles playing on some throwback channel Jag can't get enough of.

"I don't even know if you can tell me this, but I…" To stop my voice from trembling, I pick up the coffee cup I dropped at my feet. "Do you know who was in the trunk?" Detective Stone doesn't say anything, so I add, "You don't have to tell me *who* it is, but can you at least tell me who it *isn't*? Was that Wayland Cross in the trunk? Do you know or is that something that's still being figured out?"

Detective Stone actually turns to me. I want to think he's thinking I'm stupid for even asking. There are enough TV shows that go over some level of police procedure and that's not counting stuff like *Live PD* and *First 48*. I don't watch any of it, but dad's got random shit on every time I pass the living room. Mostly game shows, sometimes the history channel. He likes stuff about aliens and pyramids and crop circles, but not as much as he likes *Cops* and *The Price is Right*.

Detective Stone walks toward me, I take a step back, but force my legs stiff after the first step. "The person in the trunk was not Wayland Cross," he says. "We don't know where Cross is at the moment. If you hear from him, we're urging you and your colleagues to give us a call."

"Is he in trouble?" I say before even thinking the words.

"There was a mutilated corpse in his trunk. We don't know who did it, but as the owner of the car, the longer he's missing, the worse it looks for him," Detective Stone says. "He was the one who called in for the pickup? There aren't many more ways for this to go."

"I…" My jaw's clenched as the thoughts roll over in my head. "Don't know if he actually called in the job. I didn't take the call. I was just given the assignment."

"That's in our documents, but your boss has verified the person who put in the call identified himself as Wayland Cross," Detective Stone says.

"And you're sure it was him?"

"Number, license, name, account, car. Do you have reason to believe it wasn't Mr. Cross calling a tow for his own vehicle?" Detective Stone reached for his back pocket. A notepad comes out and a pen from his pocket.

My skin's hot. I can't really think. "I don't get… if he had a body in the back… why would he call someone to come get the car? Or… why wouldn't he be there with it? He was so careful with that car, he didn't eat in it, he didn't like picking up groceries in it, and he never let anyone *borrow* it, but… What if—"

"He also asked if Jagger Locke was working that night," Detective Stone said.

"He asked for Jag?"

"Is that odd?"

I'm pursing my lips, head shaking, before I say, "no.

Just… nope."

Detective Stone writes something down on his notepad. I try hard not to think about what it is, but I can't keep my mind from going there.

Wayland wasn't friends with Jag; he didn't care about Jag. Any time he came around here, it was to see me and Jag wasn't a concern. He rarely even came up in conversation except for when I complained about him after a particularly bad day. But I look back at the detective who keeps flicking his eyes up at me, pretending he's not writing, but looking over notes, and I know I'm being too optimistic. He's thinking there's something about me. They always do. Between his clean, ironed suit and tucked-in shirt, he looks at me like all the other badges look at me with a skateboard, ripped jeans, smeared eyeliner, and a lip ring. My hands are still stained with yesterday's grease and there's more discoloration on my skinny jeans from jobs long past. He has every reason to not trust me, the badges always do; we play for different teams.

"Do you have anything else you'd like to add, Josephine?" Detective Stone says.

I'm startled when he addresses me. It feels like it's been years since I heard that name. My mouth's dry, I'm licking my lips to prove myself wrong by wetting them, but my lips remain dry. "No," I say.

He closes the notebook.

"But," I stay paused, even as he watches me until he tosses the notebook open again. "It's Joey, not Josephine. No one calls me that. Got it?"

"Understood." He writes something down, closes the book, and pockets it. "I'll remember that next time."

I'm standing there idly after he turns away to tend to his friends in the background, looking at whatever's still in the pipe or sink or drain. I thought they got all the nasty stuff out, but they're still swabbing the pipes and the drain.

I take a couple of steps back with my eyes trained on

Stone, waiting for him to say my name again and tell me to wait, he's got more to say, he's already talked to his super and they want me down at the station, but I reach Donny's office without the detective's attention turning back. I knock on the frame and enter. Donny's got the blinds over his window tugged back with his finger so he can peer outside. "Five news trucks down," he says. "CNN is out there."

"God…" I groan. Crossing my arms, I lean against the door. I close my eyes to imagine the parking lot, a circus where the reporters are the animals and the badges are the tamers telling them to stay behind the tape, stay out of the way, stop asking questions, you're not getting answers, this is an ongoing investigation, and people actually work here, you know? People with lives and bills and booze to buy, you can't just take up the parking lot and close the garage because *you* wanna get paid. But the badges wouldn't say half of that to the journos and the journos wouldn't listen to them anyway.

Getting out of here's going to be hell.

I only hope they don't know who all works here yet and that none of them show up at my house. If they do show up at my house… I wonder if the home insurance might cover it if the trailer catches fire. "Donny… today was my day off," I'm saying slowly to gauge his reaction to what he knows must be coming. He's never been one to express his rage until he's punching holes into the wall or beating the blood out of a waiter's face for messing up his dinner one too many times, but until he's pushed to the edge, Donny's temper is almost nonexistent. Sometimes, it feels like he doesn't have regular emotions at all and he just smiles to get along with the rest of us. "Is that still a thing? Can I go?"

"If the cops are done with you, yeah, you can go." The blinds snap back into place when he lets them go. He takes a seat at his computer with a sigh. The open schedule spreadsheet lights up his face with appointments waiting to be canceled and customers that needed to be called. "Ask them. And while you're at it, ask 'em if they can put in a good word with the news crew. Commercial grade stuff, not anything that'll scare people off."

I laugh. "Donny, haven't you heard? Macabre is a service all its own now. You can get customers who just want the opportunity to lick the floor a serial killer once walked on."

"We don't have a serial killer and we're not having another body," Donny says. He stares at me a moment then points at me hard. "Don't bring back another body, kid."

"You can only say that if you don't send any of us to pick up at MP anymore." I wave, walking out of the office.

"After this, I just might do that," is the last thing I hear from him before I'm out of the body shop. I grab my skateboard and hoodie from the service desk and sneak out the back of the store in hopes of avoiding the newscasters parked out front. It doesn't work entirely, but they can't catch up to me when I put my board down. They're still hopeful that they'll see the badges remove something front page-worthy from the shop that they don't try to chase me down the block. I'm hoping the disappointment is enough to send them all home and put everything back to normal by tomorrow.

THREE.

I'm supposed to leave this kind of thing to the *professionals*, but since when do the badges have a good record for solving crimes? I remember dad passing out to some documentary a while back called *True Detectives* and it said badges solved maybe 40% of murders in Baltimore on a good year. That number's probably a hellova lot less since they never find the bodies in the first place. People around here just disappear. We don't know if they've moved, if they're hiding out in a presumably uninhabited building, or if they've died. We just accept the disappearances as part of the city life cycle and if the next time we see their face is on a nightly news report as a body found?

No big surprise.

I should've worried when I hadn't heard from Wayland in a couple of days, but it's so normal and I've been waiting for the day when he realized he was so much better than me that he'd never talk to me again anyway.

In the daylight, Leakin Park looks completely different. The trees aren't men in dark suits standing in lockstep, but leaves and thin branches in fall colors. I don't know what

I'm expecting to find if I go back to where I picked up Wayland's car. Maybe a badge is stationed on the lookout, but somehow, I knew even that would be a little too much for what the city would donate to this case.

The spot where I picked up Wayland's car is clear while visitors to the park drive by with their bikes and families in minivans toward the parking lots on their way to a picnic or the visitor's center and the Orianda House or to take pictures of the falls or jump on one of the many trails in the park as if the whole thing doesn't reek.

I know I'm being unfair.

Hundreds, if not thousands of people enter this park on the daily and nothing bad happens to them. But you'd be an idiot not to know how dangerous this park is.

I'm walking through the brush with my skateboard under arm, looking over the road, looking into the bushes and weeds and leaves and trash for any sign that Wayland climbed out of his car. Blood, crushed sticks, anything. A log with the word HOPE carved into the side lays in the middle of the clearing between trees. A crushed Pepsi can, a plastic Gatorade bottle with the label pushed inside, a bunch of cigarettes, a condom wrapper.

I'm too far away from where I picked up Wayland's car. I check my phone to see if he's tried contacting me yet.

Nothing.

It's been nothing for four days.

A text message pops up.

I'm excited, but it drops as soon as I see Jag's name. He asked, "where are you?" I tell him, then he says, "be right there." Before too long, his Mustang's parked at the side of the road and he's calling my name. The trees whisper it back in a way you really don't hear unless you sit in silence.

I meet him at the road.

"What the hell are you doing?" Jag says while I'm approaching him. He's wearing stained jeans, torn in one knee, and the black shirt he's normally got on at work. He wears the scent of oil and grease like it's perfume.

"What's it look like I'm doing?" I open the backseat of his car and slide my skateboard in.

"Make sure it's on the floor," he says.

"Oh, God!" I grab my face. "Jag—please forgive me. The wheel caught on the seat and—Oh… Oh no! Is that dirt?" I grab onto the car's open door and pretend to wipe my shoe off on the bottom of the car. "And I totally didn't realize I stepped in something while I was out there in the trees and woods and gook and now it's all over the seat too. Oh my god! I'm so, so sorry, Jag! It's probably gonna stain if you don't clean it off, like, yesterday."

"You didn't…" he's saying it like he doesn't believe me, but he's still coming toward me quickly, brushing me out of the way, glancing over the back seats. He shuts the door when he's satisfied to find that I was lying. "Why the hell are you out here, Joey?" He hits the lock on his car, so he's got my skateboard captive.

I make my way back into the trees where I heard the sounds the other night. The howling, the whistling, the bell. There was definitely a bell now that I think about it and… moaning waves of a voice coming through the falls.

"What's it look like I'm doing, Jagger?" I glance over my shoulder at him but keep going into the brush. "I'm looking for Wayland."

"If he's still out here, he's in a bag."

"Shut up—"

"If he's not in a bag, he's the fucking psycho, Joey. You really wanna spend your day off looking for either a dead guy or the dead guy maker? He's front-page news for the wrong reason!"

"I said shut up, Jag."

"There are more killers in this city than we know what to do with. What makes you think Cross didn't crack and become one of 'em? Even I've thought about it once or twice. Felt the fissure of insanity or whatever it is… And if there's anywhere to get away with that kind of thing, it's here. Well, here or California—"

"Jagger. Ashley. Locke." I turn around. I'm not stepping away. "Wayland is *not* a killer, so would you please shut up?"

Dry twigs snap underneath my sneakers. My breathing hitches, tension's tight in my shoulders and chest. Again, my arm throbs at a familiar smell, something metallic and sulfuric from the other night and my body remembers it. I feel sick to my stomach.

I swallow hard to push myself through it. "If you're not here to help me look for him, you can leave. I don't need you getting in my way, thanks." I turn back around. "Weren't you on shift today, anyway?"

"Yeah, but between the badges and the camera crews, we aren't seeing any cars today and Big D doesn't want to pay anyone for doing nothing, so…"

"Great. So, you're bored…?"

"I'm going to make sure you don't make tonight's news as an encore. Killers return to the scene of the crime, you know? Donny showed me your texts from last night." He's following me slowly. The leaves crackle beneath his step.

I think about running for it, but not yet. "I've been taking care of myself since way before getting a job at Body, so, thanks, but I don't need your *adult* eye."

"Whatever you have to tell yourself."

I slip a cigarette from the box in my back pocket and light it up. "I'm not just talking out my ass here, Jag. I've got life under control. And if you think Way planted that body in his trunk just to give us a call, you can get the hell out of here. I'm not searching for guilt; I'm looking for a missing person—" My foot falls through the ground and I'm off balance and reaching for anything to keep me up. My dropped cigarette's gone. My right leg sinks into a muddy hole and it's sucking me in rapidly. "Jag—Help!" I'm past my ankle now. Thick, smelly water floods my sneaker and seeps through my sock. My foot burns, cold and warm at the same time. Rotten eggs, sulfur, the smells getting stronger. I hold my breath, sit down beside the hole, and use the ground as leverage to push out of the muck.

Jag slides his arms around me saying, "I've got you," and pulls.

I groan, snap, "stop!" and he does. "It's stiffening when you do that—I think you might break my leg if you pull too hard."

"There's a swamp here?" Jag says.

I shake my head. "There shouldn't be."

"Cement burial?"

"I don't—I don't know what it is. Feels like a bunch of hands pulling me down and they're on fire."

"So, a burial." Jag laughs.

"Just help me get out of here—please." I push off the ground a little at a time, trying to ease my foot out, but whatever's holding me is like concrete. Hot, liquid fingers cling to my leg like it's a lifeline out of Hell.

"Don't panic—We'll get you out."

"I'm not panicking, Jag." I'm breathing hard. "It's just getting really hot."

"Hot?"

"Like fire."

"Okay, stay put a sec—" Jag is running back through the brush, heading toward his car. The heat's intensifying far beyond what I felt last night when Wayland's car sprayed me. Maybe it's because I hadn't been submerged last night or maybe it's all in my head and the ground isn't hot.

Jag comes back to me with his water bottle from the car. He uncaps it and pours the water at the ground, soaking my knee and part of my exposed leg. "How's that?" he says.

"Are you retarded?" I don't know what expression I'm making, maybe nothing at all. Jag's saying something, but I don't care.

I tap my foot on the ground on the other side of the hole, looking for solid ground. In the trees, something's shaking, there's a hiss somewhere far off, but I feel it in my ear. The leaves rustle and a big raven hops out from between the trees. He only takes enough steps to become visible.

There's a whistle.

It can't be him, but it's coming from *him*. Above him, sitting on the branches, two more of them, not nearly as big, but all of them watching me.

The heat reaches my bone. My legs ache. "Jag—" I grip the grass with one hand and reach out for him with the other. I'm going to tell him to help me, get me out of here, do something, but instead, I say, "do you hear that?"

"Hear what?" Jag says.

"A whistle? A whisper? Anything? I don't know."

"You're freaking yourself out, Joey."

My face burns with embarrassment and I hold back a snarl. My hands grip my thigh and I reposition my free leg. The ground holds tight, snaps around me like a mud mask to the skin. I feel the earth through my pant leg, right against my skin, maybe my pants aren't there anymore. Something moves along my heel, my arch, it's definitely fingers. I yelp.

"Joey—"

"It's nothing, Jay, just—Stand back unless it sucks me in." I'm pulling my leg and the ground is slowly letting it go. I don't know why.

I feel like I'm being watched.

A peak up.

The bird's still over there, watching me, it's not moving at all. Its head is cocked to the side and obsidian eyes are just watching like it's waiting for something. Waiting for me or this hole in the ground to do something.

"That. Do you see that?" I nod toward the bird.

Jag follows the nod. "It's just a raven."

"But what about behind it?"

"What the hell are you talking about?"

A purple light flashes between the trees. Like a stream from a lighthouse. Just a second, and it's gone. "What about the light. Did you see the purple light just now?"

"There's nothing there."

"So, I guess you're blind in addition to being helpless." My leg's released halfway down my shin and then to my ankle. Roots like a hand wrap around my foot and a solid yank tugs me toward the hole. "Holy shit—!" I brace myself with my free foot. Jag's got his arms around my body and keeps me from falling in. After the yank, it's like the mud turned back into water. Jag pulls me back and my leg slides right out this time.

I fall onto my back as soon as Jag lets me go. I'm breathing hard, dizzy, leg still burning.

"What the hell is that?" Jag says.

I open my eyes. My leg's covered with stuff the consistency of wet nail polish, a mixture of silver and water and it's definitely where the sulfuric smell is coming from. It's like the stuff I washed off my hand, the stuff from my hoodie, the stuff from the pipes. It's not mud, but it didn't look like this in the hole. The hole looks like dirty, muddy water. The stuff clings to my pant leg up to my knee. It coats my sock. My shoe's gone.

"That's the weirdest mud I've ever seen." Jag bends over to get a closer look. The stuff doesn't reflect the sun but absorbs its brightness. "What the hell is that?"

"I don't know, Jag." My voice shouldn't be whiny and I'm mildly ashamed that it is, but the pain's getting to me. I unhook my belt. "The blood of the damned? All the bodies of the dumping ground, just, fell into the earth or something. Cult rituals. Deer meat. A portal to Hell?" My skinnies are rolling down my thighs. I try not to touch the wet part, using the dry fabric as a glove. I kick the pants off and then use them to pull off my tainted sock. My teeth chatter between the cold air and the adrenaline.

"Wow—"

"Wow, what, Jagger?" I don't mean to sound angry. My tongue flicks my lip ring. I ease my cigarettes out of my pocket and stick one into my mouth, unlit.

"Your leg is hella red, Joey."

"Damn. And here I was hoping it'd match my arm."

I dig out my lighter. The first breath helps to warm my body, but I'm still shaking when I exhale. I take a couple more hits in quick succession before letting my eyes drop to my leg.

Without my pants, my leg's in full view and it's red and throbbing and raw-looking, not like a burn from fire, but like layers of skin have been removed. The lack of hair is from much more than shaving. I pinch my cigarette between my lips and gently run my fingers over my shin. Pressure spikes immediately into an acid-like burn. I exhale through my teeth, groaning. "Jag—"

"Yeah?"

"You got a garbage bag back in your car?"

"What for?"

I take a couple of breaths through gritted teeth. The cigarette doesn't provide enough soothing. I need something stronger, at least eighty proof. At least the cool fall air gives me a mild relief. "Can you go get one?"

He nods, then says, "yeah," and heads back to his car. I look back toward the trees where the raven once stood, but it's gone. So are its friends. So is the whistling. I'm thinking about sliding further away from the hole, but my heart spikes at a fear that I'll fall into another hole if I try, even as I watch Jag reach his car, showing me everything's fine. The muddy hole bubbles, like air bubbles reaching the surface. Strips like fingers break the surface and fall back in, flashing a hand like Nessie sticks out of Lock Ness, only long enough to make folk stories, but never providing evidence of anything.

That's enough.

I struggle to my feet and stagger back. My heart's racing. I grab the dry part of my pants. Jag's behind me with a box of garbage bags in his hand and saying, "I didn't know how many you wanted—" and before he can go on forever, I say, "this is good, thanks."

I yank one of the bags out of the box and swing it open by flying it through the air a couple of times. I pull the bag around my arms, pick up my pants, and flip it outside-in. The top tightens, I knot it shut.

"What if it burns through the bag?" Jag says.

"I guess we'll see if it does before we get back to the car, huh?"

I'm moving away from the hole. The fabric's been fine even if the water messed with my leg. I'm moving quickly to get through the chilly air. My teeth chatter from the cold against my bare legs. Glancing back at the woods, I look for the hole in the ground. I can't see it from here. Something moves in the branches. Another cackle, the whistle is soft between the trees. I think I misheard something. I hold my breath to hear better. The whistling's gone, but the source remains. Feathers upon feathers, wings upon wings, standing on the branches, I count three ravens. "You see those, right?" I'm walking toward Jag at the front of the car, reaching for him blindly, my hands seek his face, pinch his chin between thumb and index finger, and turn his face toward the birds. I don't want to take my eyes off them, even to blink as if they might disappear if I stopped looking for even a second.

"See what?" Jag says, pretending he's looking past me at the trees.

"The birds. You ever see ravens around here before?"

Jag shakes his head and says, "don't think so, but… I wouldn't be surprised. They're carrion birds. This has gotta be a feasting ground for them." He's still looking at the trees. I follow his eyes; he's not looking at the birds.

"They're what?"

"Corpse eaters."

"You're joking."

"Look it up. Bet they've got something to do with the

afterlife too. You know how many mythologies talk about ravens and souls and death?"

"Why would I know that?"

Jag shrugs and doesn't say anything more about it.

My hands drop from his face. I turn away and make my way back into the brush. I keep an eye on the ground as I move just as much as the trees and the birds. They're big, fat, hard to miss. Their little black eyes, even in the distance, reflect a pool of infinity in their little heads, a pit you could fall into like the hole in the ground. A bundle of sticks cracks under my foot. The biggest raven of the three had been watching me before, but that got the other two to stare with it. They cocked their heads in unison. "There." I point to one of them. "And there." I point to another.

"Ah," Jag says in a way that tells me he's still not seeing them.

"Are you blind?"

"I think you're stressed out, Joey. Stressed and cold and half-naked in Murder Park. Let's go." He grabs me by the arm and pulls me back toward the car. I yank my arm from his hand. Still, I come back to the road from the muddy forest floor on my own.

Hitting the concrete feels like landing on solid ground after being on a boat for months. My legs shake and chatter, not just from the cold, but instability, the mild throb, the adrenaline still going through me. Jag pops his trunk open. In an instant, the lid's yanked up and the garbage bag's tossed inside. We give it a moment to see if the pants will melt through the plastic, but they don't. Water doesn't even spill from the open seal. My fingers curl around the edge of the trunk lid. My thumbs tap and I glance back toward the forest, the trees, Dead Run, the spot where Wayland's car was parked last night, and the spread of police tape already blown loose by Baltimorons who couldn't give a shit about the boys in blue or another missing person.

To be fair, I'm surprised there's even the residue of torn

police tape and a grease stain charading like someone existed yesterday who doesn't today.

No.

I shake my head like it'll get rid of the thought, erase the phrase, pretend the idea never even came.

"We need to go, Joey." Jag takes the trunk from my hands and slams it shut.

A hard gust carrying the smell of mud and the Murder Park decay that only comes out at night rushes toward me. My nose crinkles. I turn to Jag, he's got the same look on his face. He pops the trunk again and carefully inspects the interior until he's satisfied, even going so far as to lift the bag.

"No spillage?" I say.

"Surprisingly."

"Great." I look back to the woods. The ravens are gone.

"You ready to go then?" Jag says.

"You in some kind of hurry, Jay?" I'm walking toward Jag slowly, hips swaying more than I'm sure he's used to seeing because he's looking down at them and at my face and down again at my black boy short undies.

"You know… You could get something lacy every once in a while," he says.

"What? You don't like 'em?"

"They look like what my brother wears to hide his shit stains."

"Thank God I'm not your brother."

"Anyway, let's go. If you're okay with standing around MP in your panties, there's something wrong with you—"

"Wouldn't you save me, though? If someone pulled up right now, popped the door open, and tried to drag me in…" I grab the center of his shirt around the collar. Jagger's got half a foot over me, him being a little bit over six feet tall. He's got muscles developed from working on cars, lifting tires and engines, and pushing cars around to get them where they wouldn't drive.

"What? You wouldn't kick their asses?" He cranes his head.

"Sure, probably, but wouldn't you come to my rescue if I needed it? You're out here right now, aren't you?" My tongue flicks against my lip ring when wetting my lips. The cold air makes them feel dry.

Jagger licks his lips after, then he's leaning forward into me.

A chill goes over my skin, a gust of wind rustles the trees, and something shoots off in the forest.

A bunch of birds flee to the sky.

A couple of pops, an engine revs down the road.

Tires screech.

Something that feels like heat comes toward us; it's whatever the feeling of a car speeding toward you feels like if it had a feeling.

I'm stumbling back, eyes closed, pulling Jag with me by his shirt and still walking—I don't know to where. His hand slips around my waist. The revving engine and tires squeal past us as someone in a black sedan speeds past and peels out of the park entrance.

My eyes are open once the sound passes, but it's only then that I notice how hard I'm clutching Jag and how he's clutching me back. He's closer than he was before, holding me like he's trying to keep me from flying away in a tornado and we stand in the grass off the side of the road. I release his shirt. He releases me. I step back.

He says, "how'd I do?"

I don't know what to say at first and I want to be snarky or sarcastic and pretend Jag can't keep up, but I'm the one struggling to find anything at all to say. I pat his chest twice and step back again, this time putting space between us. "I'm still standing here, so, I guess... pretty good." I swallow, reach for my ass pocket to get a cigarette, but I've got no ass pocket and my cigarettes are in the bag with my wet pants. "Let's get out of here." I climb into the passenger side of the car.

Jag takes me to my house for a new set of pants. Dad doesn't notice when I come into the house. I get back in the car and Jag mentions taking the pants to the badges. I can't help the laugh, I ask, "why?" like it's an apology.

"Evidence?" Jag says.

"Since when have you become a best friend to the badges?"

"I'm not, but you want to find Cross faster?"

"Giving the badges my jeans isn't gonna make them find Cross any faster or even at all."

"Fine, then don't turn them in."

I wasn't going to. My foot taps fast and hard against the floor until the growl builds up and I say, "fine. Take me there."

The burning water at the park doesn't have anything to do with wherever Wayland went and even if it did, the badges were calling him a murder suspect now and they couldn't care less about finding a missing murderer. All they want is a name so they can close the case. If Wayland showed up dead, better for them, less paperwork, but still, I take the pants into the precinct and drop them off with the clerk sitting at the counter pretending it'll mean something.

"Rocky might want this," I say to the woman. "They're covered in the shit they swabbed me for this morning. He'll know what I mean—How the hell am I supposed to know what it is? It burns and it's sticky and it tried to suck me into the ground, alright?"

I know I've said too much when the clerk is staring at me with a mild tilt of her head and thin, judgmental eyes, not unlike my art teacher from eighth grade when I made a bloody couch out of clay. Feet stuck out between the jagged-toothed cushion mouth. I told her that in Bodymore, the dead don't die, they just try to find a way to escape this Hell and go to another one. She said she didn't realize I was religious and then asked me straight, "you believe in Hell?"

and I said, "I kinda have to. I mean, I live in it."

The police station clerk asks me who Rocky was. I say, "detective guy," but I can't remember his name. "Stone something?"

"Detective Stone Grant?" she says.

"That's it."

"Would you like me to get him for you?" she says, phone already in hand.

"No. Just give him this. Tell him I'm from the body shop. He'll know what to do." I wave at her and get out before I hear her talking on the phone. Everything of value's already been pulled out of the pants and I don't really want to get caught talking to a badge. It was bad enough I walked into the tank on my own.

I get out the doors and Stone's coming up the stairs with a brown bag in his hand.

"Hey, you come to talk?" he says.

"Nope." I don't stop but run for Jag's car. He peels out of the parking lot before I'm even buckled in.

"What do you want to do now?" he says.

"Turn on Buffy, order three pizzas, only eat one, then pass out."

Jag asks me to come over, but I tell him, "I'm not gonna be much fun while Wayland's missing." Jag says, "sure, but you don't have to hang at home," and I say, "yeah, I kinda do. Sorry."

At home, I only order one and I lock my bedroom door after bringing it in so my dad can't take any of it from me.

The next day, I'm woken up by my cellphone buzzing erratically on my side table. A piece of half-finished pizza sits on my chest. I wipe the grease and saliva from my chin, grab my blanket, and wipe my arm off with it. Three missed calls and another one incoming. It's Donny and he's telling me the badges wanna talk and if I don't come in, he's gonna give them my home address. I tell him to do it and hang up.

I'm dressed and running out the door with my

skateboard before I can secure the pizza somewhere my dad won't find it. I guess I'll trade the half a pie to my dad so he can deal with the badges. He's always been pretty good with that anyway. He's probably going to shit himself when he realizes they aren't there to talk to him about *him*. Then he'll shit himself again when he tries to think of everything he's gonna have to do for himself while I'm behind bars.

I'm not getting arrested for anything, but he doesn't know that. He's been expecting me to do something terribly illegal since I was ten. He used to think I was selling myself, though I don't know what gave him that impression. I never had boys over, but then, I never had anyone over. I didn't wear lipstick or girlie clothing. I think the last skirt I owned was when I was four and it was the dress mom made me wear to church the one time we tried going. The prostitution angle kinda died when he saw how little money I had and assumed I was giving it away for free.

"Fix that," was his casual business advice.

I stopped trying to correct him a long time ago. He's drunk and lives outside of reality and you know what? When someone's in a self-induced psychosis, it's easier to just let them believe whatever they want than to get into a fight with them every time they toss a bottle at your head or break it on the couch and cut you down the arm because "this is how you actually kill yourself." I've seen him on the floor in a puddle of his own piss with his muscles deteriorating and his cheeks stained with tears he shed in the dark when I couldn't see him and the smell of death hanging off him like a corpse already buried and brought back.

He was always depressed, but a while ago he really changed. Became angry instead of suicidal.

I'd like to say my dad isn't that bad and I'm just making stuff up, that there's some kind of warm feeling still from when he gave me a train or a ball or a Barbie Doll for Christmas forever ago and he wishes me happy birthday around the vaguely correct time of year, but I don't think he remembers dates anymore.

I'd like to say I'm focusing too much on the *dramatic moments* dad has, that there really aren't *that* many and that the good make up for the bad, but that's not the life I have. You can talk about leaving, but then you hear his voice say, "you're just like your mother," and next to him, that's the last person you want to be.

Both of them are human, so you do everything you can to avoid the fate of turning into either of them. When he grabs you hard enough to leave prints, you tell yourself it's only gonna be a couple of seconds of fight; he doesn't have it in him to last long, and even while you're bleeding, you can wait it out. When he forgets what he's doing or let's go because he's reaching for a weapon, you run and lock the door and you wait until midnight when he's asleep again to clean up the broken glass, not for his sake, but so you don't cut your feet when you try to take a piss in the middle of the night.

I could leave, but then wouldn't I be just as cruel as him? All I can imagine is the trailer catching fire and the badges showing up with the fire depo and apparently, a spark lit the place up and the scattering of mostly empty bottles acted like igniter fluid around the house, expediting the issue and since my dad was asleep watching TLC, knocked out in another drunken stupor because he stopped eating, stopped caring, stopped getting up at all… he's dead and it's my fault.

I walked out *just like her, you bitch*. If I walked out, it would be my condemnation of him. I would be the reason he gave up and put a gun to his head and fed the blood-lusting mud of Bodymore. I don't know what it is about this place that makes people desperate.

Desperate for a future.

Desperate for money.

Desperate for someone else.

It's always everything we don't have that's going to solve

that desperation.

If only we could get it.

Things would be a hellova lot better around here if people just accepted you get what you get and if you've got shit for expectations, it's hard to be disappointed, you know?

FOUR.

DEATH IS PARADISE is written in bulby letters across the cement wall, blue with white outline, a little too upbeat for the message. GET YOUR KEROSENE COCKTAIL is written beside it with a martini of gasoline and an umbrella on fire. LIQUOR AND EVIL ARE THE DEVIL'S DRINK OF CHOICE someone says in orange. FALLING INTO THE ABYSS AND I LIKE IT reads red and black cursive lettering. Underneath in black block letters reads YOUR MOM'S AN ABYSS and under that in white reads FUCK YOU. Then on the opposite wall is a zombie with one of its eyes hanging out of its face and fingers sticking out of its mouth. A bloody, broken heart with a nail through it accompanies the phrase, HORROR IS WHAT HAPPENS WHEN EVIL OVERTAKES THE HEART. Beside that, in loose black lettering is, AND BALTIMORE IS THAT HORROR SHOW.

The walls of Fort Armistead are a kaleidoscope of the Baltimoron mind. Thoughts uncensored, responding to each other with little fear of judgment or repercussion. It's the most honest any Baltimoron would ever be as long as no one's watching them write.

I roll up to the edge of the cement loading platform and look down at the muddy path to the catacomb entrance. I ride back to the gun platform steps, jump down them, and flip my board.

Fort Armistead is an old military base now returned to the earth and the scum of Baltimore. Okay, not just *scum*, but if we're talking used heroine needles, garbage-lined corridors, semen-soaked condoms, and immature assholes trying to look badass by writing 'fuck' on a wall in the dark, then, yeah. I don't have a better name for that.

The place is made up of an above-ground building and a connected underground catacomb with a never-ending echo of dripping water and feet splashing like ghosts live on the inside. There are no doors, windows, or window frames; the only broken glass laying on the ground is from broken alcohol bottles. But there are plenty of plastic Jim Bean and Barton bottles around here too, don't worry.

The fort isn't dangerous all the time, just like Baltimore isn't dangerous all the time. It's only dangerous *at the right time*. Sunlight scares off the ghosts and creepers and dealers. If you don't think about what could happen in the dark caverns of the underground catacombs, it's really not that bad.

I've skated here more times than I can count, alone and in a group. Between the stairs, the platforms, and the old buildings, it's one of my favorite spots to waste time. And best part? No badges.

Take that how you will.

For the last couple of years, the average number of murders in Baltimore has been over three hundred—and it's been going up. Mind you, that's only whatever the badges count as *official murder,* and believe me, there are people that don't count when they die. Black garbage bags are dropped around the city like geocaches waiting to be found and opened. Fun fact: more crimes are committed on Monday than any other day of the week because everyone does actually hate Mondays.

I sit on the gun platform's steps, my skateboard leaned back and my phone in hand. I'm scrolling through old messages from Wayland because he hasn't sent me anything new yet. The bottom of our texting chain is just me for eight messages and I'm only mildly ashamed that I look needy.

I know he didn't kill anyone, but the longer he stays quiet, the more I think he might be in one of those smelly bags by the river that you're pretty much 70/30 pitbull or person. Maybe the numbers aren't that high, but every plastic bag on the side of the road gives me pause and I'm never prepared for it to be filled with abandoned clothing, shoes, or assorted garbage that still, somehow smells like rot and death.

I look over the screen again. My finger hovers over the green 'call' button for the tenth time today, but it slides away.

I hate using the phone.

That is, I hate talking on the phone.

I avoid it at work by dunking my hands in whatever I can to grease them as an excuse not to answer when it's ringing. It doesn't stop Donny from calling on me to answer.

"Your voice is nice," he says. "People like to hear a girl when they call a number. Doesn't matter what it's for. Unless it's a wife that found out about your girlfriend," and then he laughs.

I'm sucking in the ring going through the middle of my lip. My tongue flicks it from side to side. I don't notice I'm rocking. My heart's pounding. I've been in this position maybe ten times today already. My head's saying, 'wait, just wait, just wait, just wait,' but my thumb plunges down.

Ringing softly comes from the earpiece.

It's two, then three times before the phone's at my ear.

Two more rings and it goes to voicemail and I say, "call

me when you get this, Way. If I'm phoning, you know it's really fucking important, right?" and then I hang up. I slide my phone away and get back up.

Someone's voice is coming from the parking lot.

I grab my board, drop it, and get on. I slide into a jump to grind on a rusting guardrail. A couple of people come through the trees with cameras around their necks.

They seem surprised to see me.

They look like they're from Virginia. I don't know how to describe it, but when you live so close to another state like that, you can get like, this smell or this look when someone comes from your *neighbor* state. Virginians don't belong in Maryland for the same reason Marylanders don't belong in Virginia. When we meet, it should be in DC where everyone is the same kind of nasty: feds.

I step on the deck and watch them move awkwardly from the trail through one of the bigger doorways and out of sight. They whisper to each other as they disappear. Seconds later, their cameras are clicking and murmured voices echo off the cement walls.

I step back on the board and jump over a small ledge.

White paint on a magenta background reads DESTROY WHAT DESTROYS YOU. An arch reads KEEP ONE ROLLED. The wall says FINNA, then another wall closer to the ground says the same thing. Then another wall beside the arch says BE EVIL with an upside-down smiley face painted above it.

I'm listening for the couple.

They aren't clicking pictures anymore.

They aren't whispering, but I didn't hear them walk away either.

I peek around the main structure where I last saw them.

The couple goes down the steps together; I think I hear them saying something about the catacombs.

It's none of my business if they go in and I shouldn't get involved.

I'm dealing with enough.

I check my phone to see if I missed a message from Wayland, but there's still nothing.

The trees around the fort rustle with a short gust of wind. Something sounds like a caw or an inhuman cackle, but when I look around, I'm alone.

Down the steps, black hair bounces, a head, a thin arm, rolled up sweater sleeves past the elbow, a gray pant leg. I wouldn't think it's Wayland, but for a moment, I swear he turns his head and I see his profile, his brown eyes catch mine through his glasses. He startles and hurries down the steps faster. It all happens so fast; my legs are cemented to the ground even though I'm telling myself to run after him. My mouth fights against me to say anything, not for fear that it's not him, but what if it is?

"Way?" The words make their way out, though it's a weak whisper and I curse myself for it. I don't recognize my own voice from just how scared it sounds. "Wayland?" I say again, stronger this time, but still shaky. "Is that you?" I edge toward the steps, knowing better than to just run down them. If it's not him, it could be the kind of person I know I don't want to run into alone here.

I tuck my skateboard securely under my arm. I stare down the steps, no one's coming.

The bushes aren't even moving.

The only assurance I have that maybe someone *is* around is more crackling sticks, but you know, Leakin Park isn't the only place in Bodymore that's got something wrong with it. I swear to God, ghosts make up half the city's population. Sounds follow you around like they're shadows, muttering warnings and making up stories about how they died just to see if you'll run, slamming doors until you're paranoid and locked in a CVS at midnight when all you went in for was cough drops and a pint of ice cream.

The caw comes again. This time, there are three ravens sitting on a branch above me. Behind me, two more sit on the fort. Then five more sit on the large, cement courtyard outside the old mess hall.

"You wanna stop following me?" I say to them.

The ravens don't look toward me; they act like I'm not even there.

I turn back to the stairs. "Hey?" my voice shakes a little. I clear my throat. "You guys down there? Was that your friend?" I pause. "Wayland?" My voice echoes back from the stone walls.

I'm not following my own advice and I know it.

Mind your own business and keep yourself moving isn't just advice for living in Bodymore, it's advice for keeping your head on anywhere you go. Getting involved with anyone causes problems.

The stairs down to the base of Fort Armistead are sturdy but partially crumbled from age. Grass, moss, and weeds shatter other bits of cement, forcefully reclaiming the hill no longer occupied. The iron door is a mouth into the abyss-like darkness, unguarded, unlocked, but also uninviting. Graffiti paints around the entirety of the twelve-foot doorway. Dripping water and splashing puddles escape from openings, betraying whatever secrets the fortress is trying to hide.

I never understood where the water came from, but the fort has always been flooded, the ground's a mixture of garbage and what has to be sewage. I pretend it's brown because it's really dirty and not full of piss, but the smell makes a convincing argument otherwise.

I peer into the doorway down the long cement corridors going in opposite directions. Both end in complete darkness.

"Hey, you in there?" The darkness doesn't return my voice but consumes it this time.

Something makes a sound behind me.

A can smacking the cement, a cackle.

I turn around to scan the nearby trees.

Maybe that couple didn't go in. They didn't even have flashlights, but I guess they probably had cellphones. They'd find their way out. It wasn't like the building was that big; it wasn't like there weren't multiple entrances in a row.

"Hello?" I lean into the cavern.

The stone's colder than I'd expect it to be when I touch the wall. A chill goes down my body. I'm waiting to see a druggie hiding in the dark distance or a thug running toward me with a knife and a demand for whatever I've got. I grip my skateboard tightly, preparing to swing it if necessary, and walk-in. Stacks of old, soggy paper and Styrofoam cups sink under my foot. The nasty water fills my canvas shoes. Something splashes somewhere down the dark cavity. I glance back at the entrance. The light streaming into the fort mirrors the door's long shape and looks like a portal to another place. Despite the size of the door or the amount of light let in, the darkness devours it quickly.

I grab my phone from my pocket and open the flashlight app as I move further into the corridor.

I can't see the entrance anymore. My flashlight reflects off the water puddled in one corner and beside it lays an empty, used crack needle. There's a spot where the cement's busted out of the wall with something that looks like a small, square drop that goes somewhere. The opening disappears into darkness though you'd think it'd be shallow. Graffiti over the hole says TRY ME and running down the side of the hole says SRY COCK TOO BIG.

Graffiti's always full of cocks and profanity, tits, and nightmare fuel or LSD trips. Sometimes it looks like stained glass with patterns on top of patterns, shapes on top of shapes, but most of the time, it's someone who thinks they're an edgy boy, tagging their name or dick size somewhere in public; a lot of losers treat tagging like they're celebrities or comedians leaving a signature behind because all it takes to be funny nowadays is a dick joke, any dick joke.

"Wayland?" I raise my voice, but it's not as loud as I had

expected it to be. "If you're down here, tell me. I'm not talking to the badges, I just—I've been looking for you. Where the hell have you been?" I wait to see if he'll say something back, but nothing returns. "They found a body in your trunk, Way. Why?" The next words catch in my throat: "Did you do that?"

Stupid questions don't deserve answers, I know. Anyone with half a brain wouldn't straight up admit they killed someone and stuffed 'em into their trunk. Wayland's the kind of guy I cheated off in school to get a steady stream of Cs and Bs while he got whatever there was above an A. He was smart, he was from a good family. He had a future and the abilities to get there. But... even smart people do stupid shit sometimes, right?

I'm moving through the cavern and I haven't seen one of the entrances in a while.

Water splashes behind me.

I turn around immediately.

There's more splashing in the other direction now.

Something touches my back, then grabs my arm.

I'm screaming as I swing around, my skateboard smacks into something, the pressure on my arm releases. Light flashes over a face, it must've been a face, but I'm running before anything registers in my head. The flashlight on my phone flickers—I've never seen it do that before.

The water's up my pant legs and none of the entrances are showing up. I should've passed at least one by now. The splashing follows me. My skin's slick with sweat and moisture and I'm freezing.

Where did my skateboard go? I don't remember ever putting it down, but it's not under my arm anymore. I'm running faster. Whatever's behind me is keeping pace and it sounds like it's catching up.

"Wayland! Tell me it's you or I swear to God—" My phone light flashes over graffiti on the walls; none of it looks the same.

I don't see the hole or the COCK and instead, I'm seeing stuff like fire. Bold letters say SHALLOW WATER in loose, diagonal writing. The next time I put my foot down, the water comes up to my knee and I fall forward. The light from my phone reflects against the surface of the water, now up to my elbows.

The splashing steps echo nearer.

I grab my phone without much time to question how or why it's still working when it should be waterlogged. The light stays on and I need it and that's all that matters.

The water's halfway up my calves when I stand. It's too high to run and the floor is almost too slick to even walk.

I don't remember this part of the fort, but I guess it'd be a little hard to anyway when everything's so dark.

To the left, plain, black letters read along the wall YOU WALKED IN THE CORRIDOR. Once that ends, YOU CHOSE THE DARK is on the right. At the end of the corridor, the wall's caved in. Cement crushed and leaning against cement, but there's a gap big enough for me to squeeze through.

"Wayland! I'm going to kill you for this!"

I slip through the collapsed corridor. The tight space grows tighter as I go deeper. I'm going to get stuck and whoever it is—probably not Wayland, probably the guy who killed Wayland and stuffed a body in his car, probably pissed I smacked his head off—is going to pull me out and do to me what he did to his last victim.

The rocks don't finish at a dead end, but the hole looks too small for me. I tuck my phone into my pocket and feel my way through.

On the other side, something grabs my foot.

I growl to stifle a scream. "Get off me, you fuck!" I kick the thing as hard as I can. I don't hit a person, but a jagged rock.

Maybe the thing won't fit through the gap.

Maybe I can lose him on this side.

There's only one way to go now, so I follow the otherwise empty corridor. There's less chaos on the wall, an area where bored kids haven't made it yet. The water's back at my knees again and I think the wall has to end at some point or turn in some new direction, but all I see is darkness. At least I hear nothing behind me. The footsteps are gone.

Dripping water echoes around me.

Something glows in the distance.

I turn my light downward and gain on the glow until I'm standing beside the word FEAR written in small, but glowing green print.

On the opposite wall, the word's bigger and orange, and looking at the wall ahead, the word repeats in neon color, changing shape and size with FEAR in black flattening on top of the otherwise glowing colors.

My heart's racing and with every beat, I can't stop the feeling I need to run. The water splashes rapidly as I try not to slip. Loose, wet pieces of paper wrap around my sock.

The corridor never ends.

FEAR consumes the entire wall and lights the path to the point I don't see the need for my phone light anymore.

"This isn't happening. This isn't happening. This isn't happening," I'm muttering to myself as I go. "You bumped your head running from that thing, Jo. That's all. You bumped your fucking head."

The temperature drops and I see my breath in every pant.

My toes are made of ice, but the water's not frozen.

I grab my phone.

I've got no service.

Great.

I slip, smack into the wall and fall.

My phone flies from my hand. The phone light spills through the water and fills the corridor more than it should. The last thing I see is the phrase I WAS WAITING painted across the ceiling.

Darkness surrounds me.

My head throbs.

The cold is under my skin with icy water plastering my clothes to my body.

All around me are the dead: skulls and bones stacked into walls watching me fall. I don't know where the floor has gone, but I'm falling and reaching to touch the walls. No matter how close they are, they're just out of reach. The soft glow of paint is visible above, rapidly growing dimmer. Music plays far away, at least it sounds like music. Maybe chanting, like a choir, the kind you hear outside of old churches during a funeral. While my skin's ice, the inside of my body's on fire. The heat eats its way out of the pit of my stomach until I'm screaming from how painful it is.

My vision goes blurry, flickers black and back and black for longer intervals until I can't see anything at all.

I'm not screaming anymore, but my voice echoes back to me, distorted, deep, and filled with terror beyond anything I've heard from myself.

The nothing I feel after is a relief against the backdrop of everything else.

FIVE.

An organ's playing before I hear anything else. Not like, a church organ, but it's what I imagined a box organ would sound like, from, you know, one of those organ grinders that used to hang out around circuses.

The sound amplifies around me as if I'm sitting in a room of speakers.

The ground's against my back. Cold. Hard. Feels like gravel.

I open my eyes. The sky's violet with small black specks appearing far from one another, acting like stars. The moon—or what I can only assume is the moon—is large and black and somehow glowing in the dark sky. Light from an iron lamp post washes over me.

My clothes are heavy, my body aches.

It's like every one of my muscles is trying to hold me down.

I push myself from the ground. My wrists hurt, maybe a sprain. The ground is made of brick patches going from buildings that look like they're made of black licorice and bones.

I don't know how else to describe it.

The streets are slim and the buildings tall, covered in reflective, dark windows from top to bottom. The place looks like the Old Town Mall with older buildings of different sizes squeezed together, buildings that look like they were designed at least 150 years ago. The brick path between some of the buildings is made of bone and kept together by the squishy, muscle-like substance between them.

It reminds me of tendons.

What little room it looks like there is between some of the buildings is consumed by darkness I wouldn't trust to walk into.

The courtyard is slimmer than the true Old Town Mall, but maybe that's because there are more people here than I've ever seen dare walk down the mall path. Chairs and tables sit in the street outside of a row of bars. The rounded building that should've been *Kaufman's* reads THE BIN and all the windows are opaque. The red building that should've been *Trend Setters Hair Salon* only reads SALON. All the metal gates that should've been over the doors are gone.

No security.

No broken windows.

Everything's open and lively. Conversations flit through the air with ease. The smell of piss and abandonment is nonexistent, but instead, there's a kind of cinnamon or something like incense.

The couple I saw running into the fort stands in front of me, hand in hand. They're both pale and I feel like I can see through them. I rub my eyes. Again, I'm looking at them and I'm sure I'm looking through them somehow, but my senses tell me that's not possible even though I'm seeing the ground and buildings through their mildly translucent forms.

"Hey," I say. The two don't hear me or, if they do, they don't turn around. "You hear me, yeah?" I come up behind them. The couple dropped their held hands before turning to me.

"Yeah," the girl says. "That's a dumb question. You supposed to be invisible?"

I bit back the snark I feel on my tongue. "Sorry if this sounds weird, but weren't you just at the fort?"

The girl tilts her head slightly to the side. "The what?"

"Fort Armistead. By Chesapeake Bay."

The both of them look clueless.

"In Baltimore. Maryland."

The couple look at each other before looking back at me. "We've never been to Baltimore," the guy says.

They're lying to me, but I don't get why. I know I saw them around the fort taking pictures. I never forget a face. She's wearing the same jeans and t-shirt and jacket from American Eagle. He's got the ball cap, jeans, button-up, jacket from Zumiez, though he obviously doesn't skate.

"It's a public park. You don't have to lie about being there," I say.

The guy reaches for his girlfriend's hand again. "Who the hell are you calling a liar? Get lost." He pulls her off.

I don't bother following them.

They disappear into a nearby crowd gathered outside of the bar with a sign reading POST MORTEM. Crowded tables sit gathered on the porch lit by small red and white bulbs. Beer fills bottles and mugs and spills into the air. Glass crashes somewhere inside, but there's only cheer coming out from the door. Music streams into the streets with electric guitar overtaking the organ and choir I once heard. Someone at one of the tables smacks down a hand of cards and cheers at his win. The outside of the bar is plated with bones from arms, legs, and chests, all human. Pillars made of skulls line the edge of the outdoor seating and become chandeliers inside.

I don't know if they're real, but they don't look plastic.

Rib cages make the backs of chairs. The barstools are

plush, red, but held up by long bones instead of steel. The couple from outside has disappeared into the crowd. It's not like every inch of visible floor is taken or that people are packed shoulder to shoulder in here, but there's a sense as I watch someone get up from a table and walk away, they disappear like they're going into an invisible fog.

Still, the bar's full and lively and nothing like I've ever seen in the Old Town Mall.

Everyone's laughing, maybe there's a fight in the back corner with a small group of people surrounding the two men going at it, pushing them back at each other, but the energy in the place is high and infectious and it's getting into me.

My foot taps to the music.

I reach for my back pocket.

My cigarettes are wet.

My mood burns.

I go to the bar.

Before I can say anything, the bartender lays a mug of beer in front of me and says, "hey there, new face." She has wavy chestnut hair, curled only from being tied up in a loose bun all night. She looked exactly like she had the last night I saw her. Heat rushes to my face, I suck on my lip ring. My foot won't stop bouncing.

"Mom?" I say, my breath is stuck in my chest.

"Is that what you see?" she says.

"What… the hell do you mean by that?"

"Well… And this is always the hard part…" She grabs a beer from under the counter and sips half of it down. "I'm not your mom. I'm sort of your companion here in the afterlife. You know, so you don't have to sit around dead all by yourself—"

"Dead?"

"I take on the form of whoever you've wanted to see most to sort of ease the process."

"Oh, fuck off." I roll my eyes. "I don't want to see my

mom. I'm looking for someone named Wayland Cross."

"If you prefer." She picks up the beer bottle and finishes it off. She tosses it into a bin behind the counter. At the same time it crashes into another glass, she looks like Wayland. It wasn't subtle or a transition, it was just… suddenly Wayland was standing in front of me and I don't remember a moment when he wasn't.

My heart's racing. "Holy shit—go back. Go back!"

"You sure?"

"Yes!"

She bends down to grab another bottle of beer and comes back up looking like my mom the last time I saw her. I don't like looking at this either, but a fake mom is better than a fake Wayland. "Better?"

"Not really, but you… can… just stop."

"Alright." She fills another mug of beer. This time, she slides it down the counter.

I sit down like I'm on automatic.

"Anyway, you can call me Sol. Welcome to the rest of your life."

My fingers wrap around the beer mug she set in front of me. I take a swig; the taste of cinnamon cider lingers on my lips. "What do you mean?"

The band at the back of the bar drowns me out so that I can't hear my own voice, but Sol still seems to. I would have walked away, but the pants she's wearing have a hole in the knee and smears of red and white paint on the pocket ass. That was from Wayland; those pants were mine from Junior year just before I dropped out. She turns around saying, "Huh? What was that?"

Okay, so maybe she didn't hear me. "What do you mean by the rest of my life?" I say.

She laughs and leans against the counter. "Haven't you figured it out?" She patiently waits, her head rocking gently with the music, her shoulders sway. She bites her lip with a soft, subtle smile. "You're dead and this is the afterlife."

"Dead?" My throat's tight. "Like dead-dead?"

"I… don't know if saying it *twice* makes it *more*, but… yeah, I guess, dead-dead."

"You can't be serious. I was just in Baltimore. I was just at the fort. Everything was fine and I'm talking to you right now. I can't be dead."

Sol leans back, holding onto a pole behind the counter. Her head drops back with a sigh. "The first stage of grief is denial. The quicker you get it out of your system, the quicker you can get on with the rest of your life."

"Stop saying that. What *rest of my life*? If I'm dead, this is the end of the line, isn't it?"

"This is Cavae Mortem, the city of the dead, so yes. There's no going back to the way things were. You can only move forward and forward from the living is coming down here to the end. Do you need me to say it one more time before you get it or are you good?"

"I'm not dead." I smack my hand against the counter.

"Ah, c'mon. It's really not that bad." She stands upright and gestures around the bar. "Music, drinking, friends, you never have to sleep, you feel no pain, no fear, nothing—"

"I don't think that's true. I'm feeling a lot of something's right now," I say through a stiff jaw. Irritation bubbles inside of my chest. I drink the cider to stop myself from doing something stupid.

"Really? That's weird. You shouldn't feel anything—"

"Cool, so that's two things that are broken down here. Next?" I growl into the mug's neck.

"Oh, please. Just… give it some time. Death comes with a kind of anesthesia. I guess sometimes it works slower for other people, though… I've never seen this before. But everyone here's been through what you've gone through. Gone through all the stages, still going through some of them maybe. It only hurts you the longer you sit in the stages of grief. Like, denial won't bring you back; anger won't bring you back; bargaining won't bring you back—

you get the picture. Hurry up and process your issues so you can join the rest of the community."

"Stop saying that—I don't want to *join the community*, I want to get the hell out of here." I thrust out of the barstool. My hand smacks into a full mug of beer, the glass falls over. It empties, but it's not spilled. The liquid rushes over the surface of the counter but stops at some invisible wall along the edge. Just as quickly as the glass fell, the liquid falls into the table like it's made of a sponge. I touch the surface. It's solid like any hard wood. "What the hell?"

"I'm telling you, Josephine, you're not on the living plain anymore—"

"How do you know my name?"

Sol crosses her arms. Leaning back, she rolls her eyes, mutters something to herself that sounds like, "I hate this part, every damn time," then her eyes lock on mine. "Look—"

"Stop lying!" I don't give her the chance to say anything. I yank the glass mug off the counter and chuck it at the wall of booze behind the bar. Bottles with labels of gibberish names and brands of alcohol probably from a Russian off-market line the shelves. Like the couple when they came into the bar, the mug disappears into a clear mist, never colliding with the shelf.

Sol reaches under the counter and places another mug of foamy cider on top. "Have a seat, Josephine. Let's talk."

"I don't *want* to *talk*. I want to get the hell out of this fun house."

"Fun house?" Sol says, smiling.

"What else do you call it when everything's made of freaking bone?" I pointed to a table near the bar. Its legs are made of either arm or leg, I don't know enough to label them specifically beyond being human. The bar's lined with rib cages, stacked and organized in a half-hazard pattern.

"It's utilitarian," Sol says. "Humans put them in the ground. What else are we supposed to do with an abundance of dead? Let's just be completely honest here: you eventually run out of space underground, plus, this keeps everyone connected to their home lives—even if they don't remember them."

"What do you mean *don't remember*?"

Sol pulls back as if surprised. Her lips twist into an odd, crooked smirk. "Well, do you know where you came from? I bet you don't."

"Baltimore. I told you, I was at the fort." I'm standing up, ready to walk out again.

"The fort?" Sol leans against the bar, the smile melts from her face.

"Fort Armistead." I don't know why I say it like I think she'll know what I'm talking about. "The old military base on the south side?"

Sol stares at me for a long moment. With a towel in her hand, she wipes down the inside of a mug she gave me. She fills it with the tap, sets it down in front of me, and leans in. "You're making that up."

"Making *what* up? The fort? Everyone knows about it. Especially for parking lot blow jobs and shooting up."

Sol crosses her arms over the counter. Her head falls to the side with a small shake. "Take a look around. There's no such thing as *the fort* here. If you take a look around—" Sol leans back. She's the only person behind the bar, but she looks around as if checking with someone else. She leans into a door behind the bar, waves, slips out from behind it, and comes up beside me. "It'll be easier if I show you."

"I'm talking about Baltimore—not whatever this place is." But against my better judgment, I follow Sol outside.

We move through the animated tables stacked around *Post Mortem* and into the busy courtyard. People spill in and out of The Bin with bags looped around their arms. There's something off about their eyes though, and I'm not sure what it is. Had the couple looked like that?

The sky does nothing to make the street darker or lighter.

The lights, however, held up by bone stands with black licorice cages around the light source keep the path bright, but moody. Sol leads the way to the edge of the Old Town Mall where the sidewalk should've turned into Volin and Orleans. The tall, brick Fire Museum doesn't have a clock at the top, but it has been converted into a lighthouse whose beam shoots through the purple fog around the block. National Rubber Footwear's massive brown building across the street looks more like a hotel in a red-light district. Red lights fill small, glass panels lining the side of the building. An empty valet desk sits outside of the front door, a red and black velvet canopy hangs over it. The billboard which normally offers a lawyer for auto accidents says YOU HAVE IT ALL instead. The guy on the billboard points at me and looks like my fourth-grade gym teacher, but happier. It's impossible to see what's become of Peter's just a little further down the street as the dark mist obstructs visibility like static on a television.

I'm walking further down the street without Sol leading me.

There are no cars.

The pavement looks fresh and smooth without cracks or litter or cigarette butts obstructing it.

The closer I get to Peter's, the more I hear it.

Rushing water, splashing falls, the whistling trees, and leaves in the wind, a soft caw. It sounds a lot like Leakin Park, but that's not possible.

The end of the street is cut off by an overgrowth of forest, with grass and weeds breaking through the closer sidewalk edge. The trees are black, the bark black or something dark with highlights of white that appear more like a pattern in wood than a hint to where the light's coming from.

Maybe it doesn't look like Leakin Park, but it smells like it. Something beyond rotten, sulfur, decay, the rot of the night, blood. Muttering anger emits from the trees.

My body locks up and I can't will myself any closer to the tree line. I cover my nose with my arm in a futile attempt to block out the stench, but it permeates everything.

I'm staggering back, reaching out, but no one's there. The cold of the area seeps into my clothes. I feel unbelievably heavy. My socks are cement. My jeans are freezing again from the water I'd forgotten about back in the warm, comforting bar. Everything I feel is echoed by a stranger's voice in my head screaming GIVE UP and LAY DOWN and DRINK DRINK DRINK DRINK.

Everything around me should feel warm and festive.

The music from the mall is still audible over here.

The laughter, the party, the warmth of the streetlights died about a block back.

GO BACK, the voice says.

I'm freezing and I want to curl up under a blanket, maybe check out the hotel, but the smallest part of my mind tells me not to listen to the voice.

"What the hell is going on here?" I'm reaching behind me, thinking Sol's standing somewhere nearby and I'll feel her, but she's not there. My eyes are trained on the trees as I step away and the mist slowly dissolves the branches again. As they disappear from sight, the soft growling, whispering, and whistles go with it. Still, the Fire Museum lighthouse does its best to tear through the violet sky.

"Hey—" I turn around. Sol's on the other side of the road, staying on the sidewalk. She watches me closely. "What's going on here?" I say again, walking toward her now. "Where the hell am I?"

"Cavae Mortem," Sol says.

"What's that supposed to mean?"

Sol glances sidelong quickly then back, then past me again and back. I follow her stare to what should've been a white cloth sign with red lettering that said OLD TOWN MALL, but instead, it was a brick sign, more formal, with festive lights wrapped around its shape and all of them worked and the lettering read CAVAE MORTEM.

"Okay… There's a sign…" I rub my temples. "But what *is* Cavae Mortem?"

Sol takes a deep breath. She blows out with pursed lips. Her hands press together and she flattens them. "Okay... We'll try this again…" Her hands gently clap together. She wrings them out. "Cavae Mortem is the end of the line."

"You keep saying that—but what exactly is *the end of the line*? A nonstop party? Getting drunk?" I'm walking toward the sign. My head's spinning and I need to feel something other than the ground to make sure I'm not residing in some figment of insanity.

"Yeah. That's pretty much it." Sol follows behind me, slow and at a distance. "I know humans spend so much time trying to figure out what's on the other side of life. You fight wars over it and kill each other like the enemies gonna come back and fill in the blanks, but this is it. This is *that* end." When I don't respond, she says, "you're dead, Josephine."

I turn to her instantly. "I'm not dead."

"And that's why this is the hard part." She sighs. "You know, most people, when they get here, they just sort of settle in. They forget ever being anywhere else. It's always harder on the ones who're thinking of some other place when they arrive. Not everyone lets go of life when they die… and that obsession with some other place is going to annoy the hell out of you. So… for your own sanity, it's probably better if you just *forget* about that place you came from and move on. What was it called again?"

"Baltimore."

"Damn. I kinda hoped you forgot…"

"You're telling me there's an *Old Town* of *dead people* under *Baltimore*?" I pinch the bridge of my nose while walking away from the sign. "Why am I not surprised? No wonder the city smells like shit all day, every day. Bloody bodies buried in the dirt, fertilizer made of flesh. But everything it touches just… dies. The city is built on the dead," I'm muttering until I finally sit down on the hard ground. I reach for my cigarettes again, but my pants are too tight from the water and I don't care enough to struggle with them to get the box out.

I lay back on the ground just to make sure I don't pass out and hurt myself as everything spins around me.

"But the only way to get here is to *die*. This, Josephine, is the rest of forever."

I hang my arm over my face so I wouldn't have to look at the sky, at the little dark dots pretending to be stars or the black moon absorbing all the light, the bars, the dancing, the smiling faces and holding hands so unlike this part of town, and the ghosts so disassociated from reality. I hum to myself to cover the music, but nothing I do can block out my surroundings. The hard, brick ground isn't turning into a bed under my back and the jovial music around me keeps going, maybe even louder than before. "Sol… Two things…"

"Yeah?" she says.

"One: I'm not dead… and two: don't call me Josephine. It's *Joey*."

"Are you going to be okay, Joey?"

My arm drops away from my eyes. She's hanging over me, staring down curiously. After a moment, I push myself up to sit. A minor bout of dizziness runs through me, but it's more from getting up too fast than from this fever dream. "How the hell do I get out of here?"

"What do you mean *get out of here*?" Sol says, following me.

I'm moving down the street back toward Peter's, but when the smell hits, I stop. "God—What is that?"

"Caedis Silvis." Sol points. "The forest."

I look back toward the fog, toward the trees, toward the disappearance of details in the mist. I shouldn't care as much as I do about how this place works. Questions get people killed. Wondering if that was Wayland in the fort apparently got me killed, but if questions got me into this, they have to also get me out. "What's it mean?"

"What?" Sol says.

"Caedis Silvis."

Sol shrugs.

"Mm. Helpful." I turn away from her.

My sneakers don't make a sound as I walk back into the mall courtyard. I'm swaying with the music, bobbing my head to guitar and drum and a singer who sounds like he should be cutting himself, not headlining in Hell—but maybe that's how he got here. I watch the people for a second, interacting with each other, acting like they're out in a nice, decent restaurant back home. I sit down against a concrete globe pushing itself out of the ground. It's not made of concrete, but I'm trying not to think too much about whatever it is made of, bone and tendon and whatever.

A young girl, probably high school age, comes out of the old Kaufman's with large plastic bags hanging from her arms. She crosses the courtyard to *Post Mortem*, steps through the doors, and disappears inside. A couple comes out of the bar holding hands, spinning each other to a song that's not playing. Moving fast, they walk past me without a glance and head into the hotel across the street. They stop at the valet station, acting as if they're talking to someone, and take something before they enter. The movements and sounds around me are constant and it's making me feel sick, the world's running on a loop: card games, drinking, televisions lit to look like white screens in windows but people keep stopping to watch them and cheer and laugh like they're seeing something different. Constant movement in and out of the stores that should've been covered in metal grates, boarded windows, and broken glass. No one leaving the mall courtyard gets anywhere near the edge of the fog. They won't even step off the lit path between here and the hotel. A group of three girls enters the old Kaufman's.

Something about them is familiar, but they aren't visible long enough for me to make a connection. "Sol," I say.

"What's up?" Sol says from beside me.

"You said this is the end of the line, yeah?" I glance sidelong at her.

"Correct."

"So… what are we waiting here for?"

"I…" her voice hangs in the air, "Don't know what you mean."

"After this." I wave my hand forward like it paints a picture of what I'm saying and she should know or see it, but she doesn't.

Sol slowly shakes her head with squinted eyes and pursed lips.

"You know, after *this*. Like, if any religion ever was true, there's supposed to be a judgment, Heaven, Hell, angels, demons, something, you know… forever?"

Sol's voice rolls in a hum behind closed lips. "This *is* forever."

"So, is this… Heaven, then? Or should the hotel and drinking kind of tip me off that we're in… the other place? I thought it'd be hotter, to be honest. They always say it's hot down here. Fire everywhere, you know? Screaming and pain and—this just doesn't seem right."

"This is Cavae Mortem, Joey. That's it." She places her hands on my shoulders and gives them a squeeze. Instinctively, I pull away, get to my feet, and step back so she can't sneak up behind me and do it again. "Get it?" she says.

"Not really."

"Sorry. That's the best I can do." She shrugs.

"Well…" I look around, shake my head. A small group passes, making for the hotel. They don't look related to each other. "Why don't we go to the bar? I think I could use another drink." My hands reach desperately for my box of cigarettes and I force them out of my back pocket this time.

Once I get the box out, none of them are wet. I dig my lighter out. The cigarette lights with ease. The nicotine is a nice relief and at least a little bit of familiarity for me to hold onto.

Entering the bar, I'm waiting for someone to tell me to put the cigarette out, but no one does. Sol ducks behind the counter, fills an icy mug with cider, and sets it on the counter in front of me. I glance around the bar waiting for my dad to appear, not because I expect him to be dead too, at least not now, but he'd smell the beer, he'd follow the smell of cigarettes, and he'd have something to say about my ass sitting at a bar instead of doing *something*.

"Your mother wasn't like this," his voice snaps in my head.

"Yeah, well, look what it got her," I mutter with the glass pressed to my lips. I'm sipping the beer so fast; I don't realize when the mug goes empty. Sol quickly takes the glass when I set it down and gives me another. Full and icy and it's back in my hands, against my lips, and disappearing when my cigarette's in the tray on the table. "Compared to her, I made off like a bandit. No college degree. No debt. No heartache or disappointment beyond what I was born into. I lived good enough, I guess. Long enough before I could go to total shit. Who wants to see the other side of twenty-five anyway?"

"That's the spirit." Sol smacks the counter enthusiastically.

I turn around from the bar and lean back against it with one arm. The other brings my cigarette to my lips. Exhaling smoke, my tongue flicks against my lip ring. My head bobs more willingly with the music. It's the only thing that really seems connected in this place.

It's weird to look at the people here.

Their blank eyes make them look anonymous.

Do I look the same to them?

The people nearest to me are seated one over at the bar

---

and neither of them notice when I say hey to them. It's not uncommon in Baltimore.

I've heard about that small town thing where people know each other and say hi to strangers or even invite them to dinner like what's the worst that could happen? But the Baltimoron way is to pretend you don't see anyone if you don't already know them—and even then, you don't greet someone unless you were meeting them. You don't want to be the last person who sees a guy before he shows up on the news and you don't want to be the person called down to the station to identify the killer, the dealer, the thug. The less you know about someone, the better. I can't even tell you who our mayor is. Don't think I'd want to. There's too much dirty money going around the city and you can see it in the ways buildings are boarded up, rotting, probably filled with tetanus, but businesses somehow still run out of them. The city's not going to shut anyone down if they can pocket more money through business licenses and taxes while leaving people to their own rusted devices.

Everyone's minding their own business here, but at least they're happy with no bills or beatings or worrying if the guy in the trailer next door is gonna bring too much attention to the neighborhood. If this is forever, I almost wish I'd slipped and killed myself sooner. All those ollies could've saved me a few years of disappointment if only I'd fallen hard enough.

SIX.

The music's playing slower, softer rock, it's like a concert winding down, but still good, moody, relaxing. Better than anything I heard in person while alive, at least. I'm only noticing now that the musicians don't have faces beyond the lips the singer presses into the microphone. That is, his glossy, dark eyes seem forgettable and if I focus too long, he looks inhuman. The black eyes are normal here; I'm getting used to it at least or I've been drinking too much. "Sol." I move to swing back toward the counter, but she's sitting in the empty chair beside me. She's got normal-looking eyes. I glance back at the stage. How does she look more human than them? "What happens at the hotel across the street? Do ghosts, like, hook up and get married down here or what?"

"Dunno. I don't really leave the bar," she says. "Well, beyond walking down the street with people like you, but that's about it. I've never been in the other buildings."

"Why don't you leave the bar?"

"Because… It's my job. I'm supposed to keep people from getting lost."

I groan. "There're jobs here?"

Sol shakes her head. "Not for you."

"What's that mean?"

"Nothing. You don't have to work. Don't have to worry. Don't have to do anything." Sol gets up and slips back behind the counter, refreshing my glass as soon as she gets there. "You should check out the Bin."

"What is it?" I turn back to her, light another cigarette.

"You can buy anything. Lodgings'll give you a place to store it whenever you want a break too. They've always got rooms open."

"And Lodging's is… the hotel across the street?"

"The one and only."

"Creative name. Kind of surprised it's not called *Eternal Slumber* or something," I say.

"That'd be funny. Maybe submit it to the Cogs. They don't tend to change things, but if you make them laugh, maybe they'll make an exception."

"Sounds like a lot of work," I say, expecting maybe to hear Wayland say, "then no?" but he doesn't.

I grasp for my phone to check for messages from him, but unlike my box of cigarettes, my phone's not there.

Of course, it's not there.

I'm in Hell and why would I have a phone? I don't care how many times Sol tells me this isn't Hell. You get a judgment when you die, everyone says so, and once you get a judgment, you have to get sent somewhere whether it's community service or parole or maximum lockdown or house arrest with an ankle monitor. You can't have souls wandering around doing nothing but drinking and dancing and shopping until the end of nothing, right? For eternity? That's dumb. If this is the end of the line, I'm going to kill myself again in hopes of reaching some deeper level of 'forever.'

Wait.

I turn back to Sol. "Question. Where do people come

78

from to get here?"

Sol closes her eyes hard. When she opens them, she's judging me in her eyes. "What do you mean? People die. They come here."

"Yeah, but die *where*? If they die in Baltimore, do they come here?"

"Probably. I don't know. I don't know anything about Baltimore—"

"You said you greet people when they get here."

"Right."

"All people?"

"All people. It's what I do."

I pull myself partially onto the counter. "Have you seen a guy named Wayland come through here? Wayland Cross? Black hair, glasses, kinda nerdy-looking, and never looks like a slob cause it'll make his parents mad or something? You put on his skin a little while ago. I think at least a little Japanese if that helps."

Sol shakes her head slowly, but only after I prompt her for an answer. "I really don't leave the bar so if he didn't come in here, I wouldn't have seen him."

"You greeted me outside on the pavement."

Sol lifts her hand making a choking sound. "Different cases."

"And everyone doesn't come in here when they arrive?"

"Surprisingly, no." She places another mug of cider down in front of me, but I don't take it. I wouldn't call myself a lightweight, but I've already drank two full mugs. I don't feel even the least bit tipsy yet. Maybe the truth really is that I'm dead and I can't actually get drunk anymore.

My stomach groans, empty.

I reach for the drink thinking maybe that'll help, but in my head, something says the cider, and this whole place is fake. Bubbles push off the sides of the glass and rush to the liquid's surface. My arm snakes across the counter, fingers wrap around the base, not to grab, but to take in the mug's form. A moment of impulse interrupts. My hand lifts and shoves the glass over. The beer rushes across the bar surface with the sound of glass clattering, but no one around me looks up from what they're doing. It's more like no one even notices I'm there. Just as quickly as the beer spilled, the counter absorbs it just like before.

"No wonder I'm not getting drunk…" I turn back to Sol. "It's all fake."

"It's not fake," Sol says. "It's Cavae."

A man laying out cards two tables down grabs a slice of ham off his plate without looking. It finds a way to his mouth. He slaps his hand down on the table. Deep laughter erupts, filling his corner of the room while one of his opponents throws their cards on the table and the other throws his head into his hands. Another roll of meat hits his lips. He pulls the coins on the table toward him. If the bar gives out free beer, what the hell is the money for?

The guy sits back down, the group shuffles the cards, and they're playing again.

This place doesn't even feel current, but like it's from the twenties, yet I recognize the fashion of the patrons. Baltimore, Virginia, Maryland, DC, tourists, and townies. Further down the bar, I recognize a classmate from seventh grade: he died in eleventh, shot on his way to the bathroom. That's what the papers said, anyway. He was just on his way to piss during chemistry when he caught a stray bullet between buildings two blocks over. His mom didn't make a statement about his booming baggie business in the last stall. I'd bought pot from him a few times, but it wasn't great, and he charged way too much.

Another face, thick body, looks like he might've played football in college. He was the guy the badges found in the well at Leakin Park a couple weeks ago. His body had become charcoal, he was burned so bad. If they hadn't put his mugshot on the report, I wouldn't have recognized him, but there's a crazed look in his eyes that's hard to miss. His lips are pulled wide into a grin, half natural, but there's something causing it to twitch on the right edge. His pupils disappear into dark irises. His eyes appear entirely black, glossy, preoccupied with something unpleasant and muted. My classmate has the same look in his face. Both of them are tense, shoulders high, twitching, release, relax, drink another round.

Another guy sitting at a table, another news report. He's stringy skinny, light, pink indentations in his bare arms look like relics of dog bites. They said he was found in an abandoned building filled with cages and dog shit. Pit training. They found a couple of bodies and a car battery in an empty pool out back. They said he had a needle in his arm when they found him.

The Post Mortem door opens and with it, a chilly gust and two men enter with the feeling they aren't like anyone else here. They're opposites in appearance, one wearing all white, fitted slacks, a long coat with fur around the neck, and gloves. His hair's slicked back and platinum, almost white while his skin is pale and his expression dead. The man beside him is a couple inches taller wearing tight black jeans, a black t-shirt, leather jacket, no gloves, messy black hair, and black eyes, less focused than the other man's, but attentive, peering, observant, and interested. There's something familiar about them, but they're so peculiar, I can't imagine not remembering where I might've seen them before.

My eyes meet with the man in black; his brows furrow and the small smile falls from his lips. His head tilts to the side, he leans down and whispers something to the guy in white.

I quickly turn back to the bar and lean forward. With elbows on the counter, my hands tunnel my eyes to hide them from the newcomers. "Who are they?" I mutter to Sol.

She doesn't turn around.

I smack the counter a couple of times, trying to keep it

quiet to avoid attention but to get her to look, I have to slam my palm down. When she turns to me, I ask her again.

"Who?" she says.

"Those guys." I nod my head back to where they stood when they entered, not knowing if they stood there still. "Black and white."

"Black and white...?" she says slowly. She scans the room, gets visibly startled for a moment, but gains composure quickly and leans down to meet me at the counter. She shakes her head. "Dunno. Couldn't tell you, but probably... don't talk to them."

I groan. "It doesn't sound like you don't know."

"They're regulars, sure, they come in and out, but they never order anything, and I don't know what they even come in here for, really." She laughs, nervous. "I don't know anything about them."

"And you know things about anyone here?"

"I talk to a lot of people—"

"But you don't talk to *them*?" I say.

"I told you, they don't stick around."

"What are you doing here?" says a voice from behind me, smooth, flat, unemotional.

I don't want to turn around, but I do it anyway. The man in white stands just inches from my stool, behind him, the man in black is close. I look to him; I can't help it—the familiarity of his face is bugging me and the inability to figure him out captivates me.

"Did you hear me?" the man in white says.

"Yeah. I did—Sorry—Who are you?"

The man in white rubs at his temples. His expression is unchanging, but annoyance emanates from his being. "Will you answer my question?"

"When you answer mine," I say.

"Charon. A reaper. Maybe you've heard of 'em?" the man in black says.

"Val—" Charon says. "Stop."

Val straightens up. Charon's bright, blue eyes return to me.

"Karen?" My hand can't stop the laugh. "Like the bitch who holds up the return line at Walmart every night because she dropped her five-year-old shit in the bathtub and she wants her money back, even if she didn't buy it there?"

"Excuse me?" Charon, staring at me. His face betrays no emotion, but business. Reminds me a bit too much of the badges, if I'm honest.

"Hey." I lean back against the bar. "You're not like other people around here."

"You're right. I'm not," Charon says.

I wait for him to say more, but he doesn't. Instead, he watches me with expectant eyes waiting for me to tell him everything, explain why I'm there like a badge asking why you're smoking by a dumpster outside of the gym instead of sitting in class wishing you could just die as Mr. Handson goes over algebra again while talking about the one who got away in college, and how math and love had something to do with each other.

"I know this will probably sound weird—hell, it sounds weird coming out of my mouth too, but…" I groan, the words catch in my mouth, maybe in my head, they don't even make it to my tongue. I have a vague idea of what I'm trying to say, but it's not translating into actual words. "Look—I haven't been here very long, but I've noticed, alright? Kind of hard not to. The people here—ghosts— zombies—whatever they are—everyone seems pretty… wound about themselves, you know? Like they aren't paying attention to anything outside of immediate arm's reach and honestly, who would? They're dead. So, who gives a shit, right? But that's the thing. Everyone here is just sort of minding themselves and you come in here and it's like you're looking for someone. No. Scratch that. You're definitely looking for someone. I mean, you're the first person that's talked to me that isn't the chick on the other side of the bar. So, whatever everyone else is doing here—you're not… you're not like them, is what I mean. Does that make sense?"

Charon's face is unchanging, but I feel the judgment, words like idiot, questions like 'are you retarded?' statements like, 'you're a dropout,' must be circling around followed by, 'why did Wayland Cross keep you around?' I imagine he's sizing me up and asking who I am and how, out of every other lazy ass person in this bar, did *I* notice him walk in when no one else did. There's something about him that tells me he's used to just slipping through things, unnoticed and unconcerned. I know that feeling.

When he finally speaks, his voice isn't passive, but low, even, and tempered. "As you heard, my name is Charon. I am a reaper. I collect souls and guide them to their next destination."

"Next destination?" I try to catch a quick look at Sol. She's not behind the bar anymore. She's not anywhere I can see. "I'm already here. Sol told me this is the final stop."

"This is not the final stop. Now, tell me why you are here," Charon says.

"Didn't you just say you're the reaper? It *should* be obvious." I get off the stool. "I'm dead. I'm here because I'm dead." I pause. "You said there's more than this. Did you come to take me there, then?"

"You're not dead. So, I ask again, why are you here?" Charon says. Regardless of the words, his voice doesn't change level and his expression is unchanging. It takes me a second to get past his monotone to hear what he actually said.

"What do you mean I'm not dead? I'm here. Isn't that kind of a prerequisite?"

"Yes, it is. How did you get here?" Charon says.

"Fuck if I know!" My lips smack together tight. I suck my lip ring. My arms cross. "One second I'm at Fort Armistead, the next I'm pulling myself off the ground in the

84

SEVEN.

We walk through the mall courtyard with everything around us pulsing with life and chaos and party and an empty echo of joyfulness. I don't know if they can hear that echo, and no one notices us. A couple of girls run out of the old Kaufman's and into the building across the street without even a glance up as they run between Charon, Val, the big guy, and me. The sky glows purple from the firehouse lighthouse. We leave the Old Town Mall and move into the street, passing by a sign reading YOU HAVE IT ALL and the rubber factory turned hotel. We near the edge of the street, where concrete turns to dirt and roots and trees, and the smell of yuck replaces beer and merriment.

The mist parts for Charon's entry, carving space for him and his guests to enter without being consumed. The mud sinks rapidly under foot.

A lash of panic shoots through me and I walk faster with the feeling that I'm sinking into the ground like I had back at the falls with Jag. I run into Val's back, stumble, back away from him. He and Charon turn around to look at me, though they say nothing.

I think about apologizing, but for what?

The ground doesn't get any more steady. The mist and darkness around the forest consume everything more than three feet away. The music bleeding out from the mall goes quiet before the light disappears between the leaves and branches and then there's nothing.

No leaves cracking.

No mud squishing.

No bugs or birds or someone with the radio turned up too damn high so all it sounds like is bump, bump, bump.

"Don't wander off," Charon says. "Don't run ahead."

"Didn't plan on it," I say, reaching for the box of cigarettes in my pocket. Lit up, no one notices or cares to say anything.

A branch crunches under my foot. I feel it, but the sound isn't normal, but more like a bone snapping like in horror movies. I look at the trees. The faintest of outlines is visible between the branches and leaves and bushes, but even without being able to see fully, I recognize everything. Between the purple leaves and near black stumps, the sound of Gwynns Falls rushes in the distance, now keeping the forest from being a dead air of snapping necks or silence. Something reflects like a jewel in the darkness. It can't be eyes; it's larger and there's only one of them.

"I said don't wander off," Charon says louder.

"I'm not!" I say before I realize I'm standing still. I glance ahead to see Charon and Val both looking back at me.

The forest mist is closing in and it feels like little pricks, small, numbing taps against my skin. The guy they plucked from the bar is muttering under his breath, lost in his own world, talking to someone I can't see. "Look. I was following. I thought I saw something." There's no change in the two of them. "Is there something out there?"

"Keep on the path and there will be no problems. Do you understand?" Charon says.

"I understand, but that doesn't mean I don't want to

know what the hell's out there—"

Another flick of something, this time, though, I'm sure it's a person.

This time, I'm sure it looked like Wayland.

Like light flickering off his glasses.

I want to convince myself I'm seeing things and Wayland isn't down here, that whatever stuffed the guy in the car didn't cut off Wayland's head and stuff him somewhere else. But the alternative to Wayland being dead down here is that he is the one who stuffed the guy in his trunk.

I'm sucking on my lip ring, pushing it in and out of the hole with breath and tongue. I bite my lip to keep my voice from coming out, but his name jumps from my lips like a hiccup and I'm saying, "Wayland? Are you out there?"

Val grabs me by the arm and yanks me forward. I fight against his grip, but he holds stronger. My feet slide through the soft mud.

"Get off me!" I pull.

He pulls back. "You can't go out there," Val says. "When Charon tells you to follow, that's what you do."

"I wasn't going out there," I say through my teeth. "I'm just talking." I relax only long enough for Val to trust me and let go of my arm, but his eyes stay trained, focused, surveying, and waiting for me to make a run for it.

I've seen that same look enough times on the badges patrolling the neighborhood. Eyes making judgment calls of danger, risk, and 'can I take them?' I've skateboarded since I was eight and it was only the first time the badges saw me that they didn't think I'd be much trouble, so they left me alone. They learned fast when they saw me skate along stairs, ramps, parks, walls, monuments—near them, not *on* them. I learned fast that badges don't like kids who openly defy the rules. Stay off the grass. No smoking. Don't touch this. Don't talk back. They see a kid with a skateboard the same as a guy in a hoodie with a knife or a rock coming up on a window. The first time they saw me jump a curb and grind the rail of a church, they knew they didn't like me. Which, fine, I didn't like them either. I never liked anyone who tried to use some arbitrary position over me as some authority in bossing me around. They named themselves the authority. It's not just the badges, dad, and teachers, but death, apparently, too.

"What if I saw something?" I'm scanning the trees for movement again, but resisting the urge to run, knowing that if I tried, Val would grab me again. My arm throbs from where his hand used to be, the grip harder than I realized until it was gone. He wasn't a small guy, but he wasn't obviously buff either. Tall, sure, and he looked like he'd gotten in his share of fights, but his disposition is nothing but fearless. It was the animal thing.

A guard dog, stationed and waiting for his master's command. What *is* he?

"There's no one out there," Charon says. "The lost souls in the woods can't be found." I don't know when he turned around, but he's now facing me. I didn't notice it before, but his eyes, too, are inhuman. A pale, steel blue, there's an uncanny valley thing where there's something missing that stops him from feeling like a person. I don't think it's a soul, but what else could be left when our bodies rot in the dirt?

"I definitely saw something," I say.

"I'm not arguing with you," Charon says. "We have work to do. If you get lost in the Liquor, no one will come for you. If you choose death now, there's nothing I can do, but I will not lead you to that end."

"Wait—You mean—when someone dies, they don't always come here? Like, ghosts really *do* wander around on earth or—"

Charon's dismissive in the way his eyes won't focus on me. He keeps checking on his ward, the big guy who seems paralyzed beyond muttering to himself. Though the guy is tense, sweaty, his muscles engaged, he looks like he wants to fight or at least run into the trees, but for whatever reason, he's staying put, completely still with his arms at his sides.

"There are alternatives to being delivered," Charon says. "If they work out for those who choose them, it is not my judgment. I cannot recommend it nor can I recommend against it. I work within an order. If you want to seek a prize outside of that, you do so at your own risk."

My jaw tightens. His words feel like gibberish, vague enough to be confusing, but clear enough that I'd feel like an idiot for asking anything. I feel like I can listen to him talk and never know what he's actually saying. A lot like high school. "If that's true, then maybe there is someone running around the forest? How? I get anywhere near that fog and it hurts, I can't breathe."

Charon pinches his nose.

Val slides his hands into his pockets. He turns his head, his nose scrunching as he looks out and away. "You don't wanna find the stuff that strays off the path, alright? It stinks. Reeks. Rots. Got it? If you say you saw something out there, pretend you didn't. It's not human and you can't help it."

"What *is* it?" I say.

Charon doesn't say anything, but he looks over my face and he must be able to read that I won't move without some sort of explanation. All he ends up saying is, "horror."

I say nothing more and follow Charon's gesture to keep going.

Val moves behind me and keeps watch like he's afraid I'll really run off into the trees despite the fact Charon said I could run off if I wanted to.

Leaves grow darker the deeper we go, but there's still a glow of purple on them around the edges. The soft murmuring sound of the falls and the river are somehow calming. So familiar, but slightly off, I expected car horns and bicyclists passing by somewhere outside the trees. While I feel cracking garbage, aluminum cans, and nature under my feet, I see nothing there. The big guy from the card table is saying, "I wasn't all that bad, you know? I did what I had to do. That's human. You don't punish a man for doing what he gotta do to survive? Send me back, man. I don't wanna be here."

"I'm not in the business of judgment," Charon says without turning around. "If you plan to plead, I recommend you work on your case rather than try to work on me. I cannot spare you and even if I could, I wouldn't."

"Don't say that," the big guy says. "There's always something we can do for each other. If I got one lesson outta life, it's that there's always something you can do for someone else that they can't do for themselves. So, what can I do to make your life better? Just let me know what you need, man, and I've—" the man's begging and pleading turns to cursing when Charon stops responding.

The man's body tenses, his arms raise like he's fighting against a weight pushing his body down and holding him in place. He reaches sidelong to grab Charon by the shirt, but his hands move straight through Charon's form. "What the hell?" the big guy says. The weight on him appears to lessen for a second, he swipes quicker, trying to grab Charon's neck, but his hands go through him again. Then, like paralyzed dead weight caught him again, they fall to his sides.

"You are free to run," Charon says. "But the forest does not allow souls to escape. If your choice is torture for eternity, then I welcome your disobedience. I only sign one form for your loss." Charon's tone was much more chilling than his actual words. The implications mixed with his casual voice should've taken the threat out of what he said, but it only made it worse, lining each word with an experience from the past of someone running away, screaming as the darkness destroyed them and the trees refused to mute their misery.

The mud becomes grimy bricks of glistening bone or

marble. The walls are lit from behind and the river is much wider than the one actually sitting in Leakin Park, but it's similar enough to recognize. The falls are taller, wider, falling farther and splashing up, sparkling in silver mist.

A boat sits against a dock that doesn't exist back home. I near the lake's shore. The sand's a lighter color than it should be, almost white with specks of darker gray throughout. The water shines silver and opaque in the dark moonlight.

Charon leads the man to the boat, where he sits without a fight.

I reach the water's edge. I can't take my eyes off it. The water's smooth, calm, almost completely still. Its surface is like a mirror, reflecting my face, paler than I've ever seen it. Something weighs hard on my shoulders and I feel myself sinking toward the water, drawn in with the desire to touch it. I bet it's soft. My fingers barely miss the surface before a hand grabs my shoulder and yanks me back. I fall on my ass saying, "what the hell?"

Val stands behind me. Charon's at the boat, watching, but unmoved.

"You don't want to touch that," Val says.

"Why not?" I look back at the water again. The sky reflects off it and all the backward, dark stars glow in silver-white specks on the water's surface. I get up and brush my pants off. Something swirls in the liquid but isn't visible above the water. The waves move, not like a fish, but something struggling. The water bounces gently, a vibration of heartbeats or breath or rhythm that the water won't allow to stretch out too far. It's unnatural. A sense of unease makes me step away. "What is it?"

"The River Styx," Charon says. "Be careful of the edges. If you fall in, you will drown on regret."

"What?" I say with a throaty laugh. My skin puckers with goosebumps. I don't believe him, but I feel like I should. I rub my arms to warm them, but the feeling creeps around my shoulders and up my neck.

"You will never get out," Charon says. "If you fall in, you cannot return to what you once were."

The river splashes in the distance. I barely catch what looks like a semi-transparent arm flinging back into the water while drops of liquid flick off frantic fingers. "What was that?" I say.

"What do you think?" Val says.

He comes up behind me but doesn't grab my arm this time. He nudges my back with his elbow and he urges me toward the boat. With a hand on the edge of the ship, I glance back at the forest. The boat's not big, a little larger than a canoe with standing room, allowing the four of us to sit comfortably on short benches. The boat's white. Where my fingers touch, it appears to glow. The front of the boat has a long, curled pole, twisted around the handle of a bright lantern. The ship is smooth other than the symbols carved into the sides. Cylinders, balls, hoops, x's, and bars that look like they belong in a book of magic. "What are these?" I say, tracing my fingers along one of the curling shapes.

"Sigils," Charon says.

The big guy's breathing hard, panting, his hands are stiff and he's rocking back and forth just a little. He's sweaty, down the side of his face, his hair's wet, stuck to his skin.

"Uh, you okay, buddy?" I wave my hand in front of his face.

His eyes are bloodshot, the sweat glistens, drips down his chin, and lands on his sweatpants. He says nothing.

"Is he gonna be okay?" I say to Charon but he doesn't respond to me either. "Okay…" I stand up.

Val boards the ship and shuts the door beside him. I lean against the side of the boat, looking out at the forest, the purple mist is trapped between the branches, none of it comes anywhere near the sandy, white shore, or the bony path. Something moves through the trees, fast. I know I see him this time because he's staring back at me from between the mist, beneath the branches, but not on the beach.

Cracked glasses, light catches and illuminates a part of his face. His short black hair's messy, unlike him, his sweater ripped and dark, covered in something I can't make out from the darkness, but the thought of it makes me sick.

"Wayland!" I grip the edge of the boat. We're already a few feet from the dock, but it's not that far. I can jump and run. I brace myself, lift up.

A hand grabs the back of my shirt, pulls, then grabs my shoulder, and two hands hold me. I'm screaming as Val pulls me back to one of the benches. "Let me go! He's there! He's right there! Let me go!" My elbow slams into him.

Val grunts, but not because I hit him or it's some struggle to hold me. Though he shifts a little when I pull, his hands make it clear just how much stronger than me he is. "Stop it," he says.

"Go back!" I pull away.

Val pulls back.

"He's out there!"

"There's nothing out there!" Val growls.

"Don't play with me—I know what I saw!"

Val shifts our weight and forces me down onto the bench. No amount of struggling works to resist. "There's nothing out there for you. Nothing. Whatever you think you saw, it's not whoever you're looking for—"

"But I saw him."

"You saw an echo."

"Yeah?" I smack at Val's hand. He doesn't even feel it. I push to get up, but he pushes to keep me down. Any time I try to look around him and back at the trees, he stands in the way, too broad and too close to see past. "And how would you know? You don't even know what Way looks like—"

"That is his only reason for existing," Charon says. "He finds the dying."

"The dying?" I say slowly. "What's that have to do with

95

someone I saw in the woods?"

"This is the world of the dead. No one is dying here. If there was a dying soul nearby, Val would know," Charon says.

"What about me?" I shift so my legs are on either side of the bench so I can look at Charon at the head of the boat and Val beside me. I see the shores past him now, but the shadows under the tree are little more than purple mist while the reflection, the glasses, the spot where *he* had been standing is empty now and disappearing fast as the shore recedes. "I'm not dead."

"No, you're not. That's why you stood out," Charon says.

"So how am I here?"

"Perhaps things are not as secure as they should be, but that's not my job," Charon says.

"And your job is… guiding people? Souls?"

Charon sighs. "Do you know anything about reapers?"

"Yeah, duh—but you don't look like any reaper I've ever seen. Sorry. No scythe, no robe, no skeleton—and what is he supposed to be a grim reaper too? I thought there was some kind of uniform. At least he's got the right color—" I'm pointing at Val.

Val laughs suddenly, wide, loud, it echoes off the river surface and is consumed instantly by the water. "No. I'm not a reaper. I'm a raven," he says.

I turn to him, look down to his sharp, polished boots, black denim, studded belt with silver buckle, black shirt, and leather jacket to his face. Maybe he had a more pointed nose, but his dark hair, dark eyes, and human body betrayed his claim of being a fucking bird. "You're not a raven."

"Okay, right," Val says slowly, "I'm a valravn."

"A what?"

"You really don't know anything, do you?" Charon says.

"Oh, I'm sorry." I turn to him. "Did I miss some important part of school where they tell you everything you need to know about the afterlife and that the grim reaper is some kind of wannabe LA model in white who has a raven for a buddy who isn't actually a raven, but a tall stalker in black and does, what? Finds dead people for him? My god. How did I ever miss the unit on that? Must've been one of the days I was out sick, skateboarding in the park. Dear me. How could I have been so dumb?"

Val finally removes his hands from my shoulders. He steps back to lean against the side of the boat. "I think that's where I've seen you before."

"What?" I say.

"At the park," Val says. "You go to the park a lot?"

I purse my lips, cross my arms, and look away. "Which one?"

"Were you at..." He looks around briefly, his eyes trace a circle as he searches his thoughts for something. "Leakin Park a couple of days ago?"

"How do you know that?"

"I thought I recognized you. Yeah. It's coming back now." Val nods to himself.

"How did you know that?" I stand up. "How—where did you see me?"

"I was in the trees. You can't say you don't remember. You looked right at me. I remember that much. Your leg went into the ground. You were with someone?" Val says.

"You... were in the trees?" I stare at him while I replay the memories of the day in my head. My leg sucked into the muck, the burning shit, taking my pants off. Then, I catch on. The chorus of cawing seemed like a figment of my imagination at the time. I thought I was making it up, the murder of black birds with eyes like crystals together in the trees. Jag refused to see them. "The crows?"

"Ravens. I'm a *raven*," Val says.

"What the hell were you doing there? Were you following me?"

"I don't follow people," Val says. "I find the dying." He's

smiling wide, playful, friendly. He licks his lips. I don't know if he knows what he's saying or if he does and he's completely insane.

"It's simple if you think about it," Charon says. "Ravens are animals. Val is led mostly by his survival instinct, his desire to eat and unfortunately, ravens desire human hearts the most. They only consume those of the dying, however. You've heard of carrions, I'm sure." He pauses to give me a chance to respond. I nod like I know what he's talking about. "Ravens have a limitless ability to sense when someone is going to die. They gather and wait for the moment so they can eat. The closer someone is to death, the stronger the scent, the less they can resist gathering. Think of it this way: any time you see a murder of ravens, it is because someone is about to die."

"Alright, smart guy, if he's a bird, then why doesn't he look like it?" I say.

"Because I'm a *valravn*," Val says.

"I don't know what that means," I say through my teeth.

Charon's eyes close. He gently shakes his head and turns around to face where we're going.

I hadn't realized how long this river was until just then. Charon says nothing more, neither does Val and I don't bother. They're like every teacher I've ever had, expecting you to know what they're teaching before it even comes out of their mouths and getting mad when you don't.

Schools are a waste of time.

I learned that way before dropping out. Kind of hard not to when you've got the perfect example of failure in your dad. For all the school he went through, show me, where is his success? Smells like piss, can barely get himself up for a shower every couple of days, alone. School's an unguarded prison while you're in it and the biggest nuke life has to offer if you're dumb enough to pursue it when you're not required to be there anymore.

The boat stops. Charon hooks it up to the dock with a

rope I hadn't noticed on the front. The dock leads to stone steps, more sigils are carved into them, this time, with little tunnels for water to run through them and into the River Styx.

The big guy stands up, his arms swing with a growl. He's livelier than I've seen him since we left the bar. "You're not fuckin' getting me! You got that? You're not taking me!" He throws himself over the boat's edge. A frantic splash echoes around the cavern, like a sea of creatures fighting to escape the water.

"Why do they ever think they can run?" Charon says. He comes to the edge of the dock and peers into the water. Val stands behind him, shoulders hunched and watching over Charon's shoulder.

The water's flinging, splashing, and threatening the shoreline. Out in it, arms, a mixture of bone and flesh and muscle, some burned, some missing fragments, some whole, but none of them bloody, reach out of the water and grab for anything they can get a hold of. The big guy from the bar is screaming while water grabs his arms, yanks him under by the legs, and races to fill him. His every breath is strangled. His voice breaks between gasps and water.

My blood's rushing, heart pounding in my ears. Every muscle in my body seizes, telling me to run into the water to help him while my head says don't be a moron, you stupid fucking idiot. I'm feeling ready to jump in the water when Val's hands find their way back to me. He holds the back of my shirt in one hand and my shoulder in the other. Charon steps in front of me. Arms wrap around the big guy like tentacles, bones bending and moving in unnatural ways. One goes around the neck. Bumbling, flailing, he's screaming in agony, and then he's gone.

I swallow hard. My throat's tight. Skin hot. Heart still racing. I try to force the tension out of me with a laugh, but I choke instead. "You weren't kidding about that, uh… drowning on regret thing."

"I wasn't speaking figuratively," Charon says. "Regret fills the River Styx. For every moment you've had a second thought, you've considered a different option, you saw how things could have been, those moments live in this river with everyone else's. Jump in and they will come to the surface and drag you down. Every human is filled with regret, and that regret feeds on the soul, consuming the body with it. It is a very painful process. I do not tell you to avoid the river for *my* benefit."

The big guy from the bar is gone entirely now and the water's quiet again. It's like the flailing and waving arms flying out of it had been a dream.

Charon turns away from the river and moves up the steps to the larger set of carved doors built into a castle-like house, white, not bone, probably marble. It sits on an island with a small stone fence off to the side, reminiscent of the Orianda House by Gwynns. The windows are closed, curtains hang over them with little light seeping through the cracks. A single tree sits in the grass, undisturbed, but for an apple laying beneath it in the lawn.

"What is this place supposed to be?" I ask, following Charon.

He doesn't say anything as we approach the door. It grows larger, wider, and more overbearing the closer we come. He reaches for the door and pulls at the looped knob. "For most, it's judgment. For you, it is the exit." Light slips through the cracks in the door. He pulls it the rest of the way open and instantly I'm consumed so much by light and warmth, I can't keep my eyes open. Even with my eyes closed, everything's white. Just as quickly as it's come and my ears are ringing, it fades.

The sounds of the soft shore are replaced with rusted water dripping between cold stone. I lower my arm. My pants are wet and I'm standing calf-deep in water somewhere pitch black. I pat down my pockets. Empty. But my phone's sitting on a stone slab above the water just a few feet away, flashlight on.

FUCK and GOT DAMN GOOD are written in graffiti with a 666 underneath on otherwise dark concrete. The fort surrounds me with dripping from unseen sources. Goosebumps line my skin and the chilly fall air clings to my damp clothing. I can't see the exit when I start walking, but I know where I am. It's only two turns before one of the fort's wide openings bleed light over the muddy floor.

Light.

It's not even night.

Maybe afternoon.

I slip outside into the fresh air. The sun warms my skin, even if it's fall, it feels warm compared to the darkness.

My skateboard leans against the steel gate. I grab it and back away from the fort, looking the door down, waiting to see if someone comes out after me, but no one does. I run for the stairs, but my foot catches on something and I fall to the ground. Sitting back, I curse at the twig I tripped on, but it's not a twig. It was the guy and the girl, the ones with the cameras who disappeared into the fort, who were inside the fort, dead. Their faces are mauled to nothing. Stab wounds litter their chests in equal rage. Their hands are bloodied with torn nails. My throat burns with vomit. I lean over and spill whatever comes out on the grass.

It's not much.

As I'm wiping my mouth with the back of my arm, I'm dialing the badges.

"I think you might want to get down here. Armistead. Yeah. I dunno. Maybe if you think a couple of dead bodies are important, but I get it, the BPD has *priorities*. Oh. Fifteen minutes? Great. They'll see you when you get here." I hang up. I didn't want to wait for them, but I think I preferred talking to them here over getting a visit at the house.

EIGHT.

The interrogation room's cold. The badge has asked if I wanted coffee or cigarettes like, eight times, and every time I've told him no. I've seen enough TV to know if I accept, he'll think we're buddies now and he can ask all kinds of questions like what's my star sign, where was I born, what about that bra size, and why did I kill that couple in the park? Beyond asking if I want anything, he hasn't tried talking to me yet. My feet press against the table. I'm leaned back on two chair legs, balanced, arms crossed. Some badge whose name tag says, *Garrett* asks, "how did you find the bodies?" and I say, "what is this? The geology department? Wait. Shit. That's a garnet. Sorry. What was the question?"

"How did you find the bodies?" he says.

"Oh. That." I glance toward the door. My eyes meet me in the one-way mirror. Black dust from my eyeshadow smears down my cheek and makes my face look sunken in more than it really is. It looks like maybe I've been crying, but I haven't. I don't cry. The run on my face is from sweat and whatever sewage goes through the fort. I feel like I should tell Garnet, so he knows I won't crack.

The black-rimmed circle clock in the room says it's a quarter after four. It's been maybe two hours since they brought me in for a statement.

Is this normal procedure?

Walking out the door's an option, but how long until they show up at my house with *more questions*? I didn't like seeing them out on the street, at my store, and I didn't want them being dragged back to my house to obstruct my life unannounced. I get enough shit from the neighbors without them yelling if it's a drug bust and who's getting arrested.

My phone vibrates against my thigh. I'm reaching for it. The interrogation room doors open and Detective Stone walks in. He's shaved this time. I take my feet off the table. He pats Garnet on the shoulder and says, "why don't you take a break?"

"Don't mind if I do," I say without getting up.

The badge looks at me, picks up his coffee cup, and leaves the room. Detective Stone sits down in the other empty chair, closer to me than the other guy was. He's not threatening or anything, but close, trying to be personal, like when someone sits in the back of the badge car with you and tries to get an easy confession.

"Hey," I say. "Let me guess what kind of cup you drink coffee from. A *tumbler*, right? Because your... name is Rocky. So... you got a rock tumbler. Get it?" I point at him with a finger gun.

"We should stop meeting like this." Stone slouches, relaxing into his seat.

"Right... It's becoming a habit." I suck at my lip ring. "Isn't two times a habit? Better stop before it gets any worse. Badges are all about shitty habits, yeah? Smoking, drinking, beating your wives..."

"Hey, I only know a couple of guys like that." Stone laughs.

"Isn't it the end of the month? How's your parking ticket quota going?"

"Falling a little short, but I think we'll be able to pick up. You remember what your plate number is?"

"I don't have a car." Crossing my arms, I lean back.

He mirrors me. "I took a look at your record—"

"Oh, jeez." I groan. I'm looking away, getting impatient. My own stupid face reflects in the one-way mirror. God only knows how many badges are on the other side, waiting, watching, recording everything they can take as a confession for something I never did.

I knew better than this.

Don't talk. It's always so tempting to plead your innocence like you can actually convince someone the bodies you found weren't yours. And the trail that's apparently following you? Also, not yours. I know it looks suspicious, but you don't talk. "Tell me, Rocky, what'd you find?" I say.

"What do you think I found?"

I shake my head. "Nah, fam. Not playing."

Stone gives it a couple of seconds before he crosses his arms to match me more closely. "Nothing much. A couple of fines. A juvenile record. You like to skate where you're not supposed to."

"The city likes to turn a lot of places it shouldn't into no skate zones."

"For safety—"

"For greed." When I look back up at Stone, he's looking at me. My foot's tapping rapidly. I don't know how long it's been doing that when I finally force it to stop. "Look, I already told your guy what I saw. Everything I know. If he didn't write that shit down, it's not my problem."

"I read it," Stone says.

"Good. So, if I leave, you won't come looking for me now, right?" I uncross my arms and sit up.

"Do you think we have a reason to come looking for you?" Stone uncrosses his arms and sits up. "I'm not saying you're suspicious. You're not even a person of interest if that makes you feel any better. Well, okay, that's mildly untrue. You are of interest. You've turned up three bodies now in less than a week. The chance of that happening to a regular person is… pretty low."

"Yeah. Right. I understand it's weird. I didn't ask to find any of them."

"I know." Stone picks up the box of cigarettes from the table. He puts the top of one in his mouth while reaching for the lighter. He flicks the lighter until he gets a flame but doesn't bring it to his cigarette and lets it blow out. He plucks the cigarette from between his lips. "How are you doing with the experience? The bodies were pretty gruesome."

"I pretend they're movie props, so they'll stay the hell out of my dreams. But where do you think we are? This isn't the first time I've seen a body. I can't even think of a kid who'd be surprised at seeing what I saw. We live in Bodymore, Rocky. The status quo is bleeding on the pavement without a pulse." Then it comes back to me. I never actually forgot. How could I forget? But asking anything about them had slipped my mind for a bit. In part, everything I saw in the fort had become kind of distant and fuzzy, like how a dream becomes forgettable within minutes of waking up, but you remember how you felt while you were asleep. The panic or anger or sorrow or lust follows you into the world of the living. "Are you a religious person, Rocky?"

The detective couples his hands on the table. His eyes train on me. I've made a mistake saying anything, but instead of backing down, I lean forward, my elbow on my knee, my back arched, sitting straight to mirror him.

"Catholic," he finally says.

"What do Catholics think about the grim reaper?"

"Well…" Stone let out a deep sigh. "It depends on who you talk to. The church doesn't formally recognize the grim reaper as anything. You might stumble across Santa Muerte if you look into Mexican Catholicism, albeit those who worship her have been disowned by the Mexican Catholic church as being part of a cult."

"What's a Santa Muerte?"

"The saint of death. She became fairly popular with criminals, the poor, those who felt abandoned by the church. With a patron saint of death, what the hell could go wrong, right? In some places, she's even more popular than Jesus Christ. Then, with immigration, she found her way here. Try as they might to deny it, but people love blood, death, and macabre," Stone says.

"I've noticed. Take a nice neighborhood and slather it in a bloodbath? Neighborhood might not price well, but Hollywood's ready to make your street name famous," I say. "Kinda surprising there aren't like, fifteen Bodymore movies yet, rivaling the likes of Jason and Mike Meyers."

"Why do you ask?" Stone says.

"Oh." I sit up instantly, too rigid. Stone's watching me with an empty expression trying to be compassionate and curious. I can't imagine him using the same expression on a guy. At least, I can't imagine any guy in Baltimore opening up about murdering someone because some other guy *tried* to look like he was kind and compassionate. The look of a disappointed father just waiting to be there for his kid. Any random gangster I've seen on the streets would be ready to punch his sharp face.

That look's never been real, and I learned it well enough. When he looks at you like that, it's to get you to talk, so you'll say something he can latch onto and throw himself into a rage. There's no such thing as a look of kindness because kindness itself is a myth. What does everyone want more than to be accepted and to feel loved? Even if it's fake. Even if that love ends in an hour. Everyone I know is willing to stomach the acidic swallow of every bit of burning bile they taste when they lie to themselves in hope that things are different than how they seem.

I reach for my pocket, feeling for cigarettes. The box sits on the table. I take one of those. Stone holds out the lighter, but I take it from him to light the cigarette myself. I take a couple of hits, slow breaths that give me time to mull over what's going on in my head. I glance at the detective over my knuckles. He's not looking at me, but the wall behind me. The one-way mirror. His legs kick out. He's relaxed, smoking for real now too. "If I walk out now, are you gonna have someone stalk me home?"

"Should I?" Stone says.

Irritation moves through my lips. I feel another buzz against my thigh from an incoming text message. "Look, the bourgeois are behind a lot of shit in this city, but I'm not the one you're looking for. Maybe try Capitol Hill instead of Deadwood Trailer Park."

"You wanna take a look at that?" He gestures halfway to my pocket.

"I want to finish up here." I hold the cigarette to my mouth and try to relax.

"Might be important," he says.

"Maybe. And if something happens, who's to blame?"

"The one not answering the call," Stone says.

"Text." My fingers tap against my thigh. I'm looking back at the glass, guessing how many badges are back there and trying to retrace the steps I took coming into this room. How many desks would I have to walk by to get out? Could I get away without an escort? I steal a glance at the detective to see just how much he's watching me. His expression says nothing about how guilty he may or may not think I am. I drop my feet to the floor and get up. The cigarette's not burning anymore, but I'm not leaving it in the ashtray. "I can leave, yeah?"

Detective Stone leans back with a single nod. "You're free to go at any time. You're not under arrest." He smiles. "Yet."

My hands smack down on the table harder than I

expected. Stone's stare turns on me and I'm stiff, waiting out the moment. "Don't *even* joke like that." I drag my hand back, taking my box of cigarettes with it. I pop one out to tuck behind my ear. The box finds my pocket. "And don't let me see you at my house." I'm leaving the room, hand on the knob. "Or I'll call a couple of badges to pick you up." I wink. I'm closing the door, but his hand stops it. I let the door go and keep moving down the hall, fast.

"What're you running from?" Stone says.

"You said I could go." I turn around, walk backwards. He's following fast. I turn forward again.

"I'll show you out."

"Not necessary," I say.

Gray doors in gray walls with black room numbers and bland, brown-gray carpet line the hall. It feels long until I'm at the end and the metal door is locked. I jiggle the knob, hoping, maybe it'll surprise me and loosen up and come unlocked. I feel Stone behind me before he says, "I told you I needed to let you out." He runs his badge over a gray box on the wall. It beeps and the door unlocks. I glance over my shoulder, mutter a 'thanks,' and walk beside Stone until we're back in the lobby. He's saying something generic like, "good to see you again. Give me a call if you think of anything else. You still have my card?" but I'm barely listening as I grab my skateboard from the front desk and get out the door.

I run down the stairs, picking up speed as I cross the parking lot and get down the sidewalk. I'm not running away. I'm just putting some space between that front door and myself to make sure Stone can't watch me through the windows. My heart's racing as I pull out my phone. The screen lock says there are three messages waiting and one of them's from Wayland. When I get to the messages screen, I only see three messages from Jag.

JAG   Hey.

JAG	Don's asking about u.
JAG	Where are u tho, fr?

I go through my inbox again and look for deleted messages, but my last message from Wayland was still from a week ago. First, I send a message to Wayland that just says, 'hey.' Then I go back to Jag's thread.

JOEY	You hear from Cross?
JAG	Where you been?
JOEY	Blasted.
JOEY	Sue me.
JAG	fr?
JOEY	Idk. Something weird happened at the fort.
JAG	Weird how?
JOEY	I think I saw
JOEY	nvm
JOEY	What's Don want?
JAG	You. At. Work.
JOEY	When?
JAG	Tonight?
JOEY	What about the badges?
JAG	Cleared out.
JOEY	Journos?
JAG	Mostly gone.
JOEY	I don't want to work.
JAG	So, don't come in, I guess.
JOEY	Nice knowing you.
JOEY	Be there in twenty.

Twenty minutes isn't long enough when I'm walking through the front doors of Bodymore Body Shop. The place smells like stale coffee. In the breakroom sits a half-empty pot, cold, probably leftover from this morning. The Styrofoam cups beside it are scattered with coffee splattered on the outside of them and the counter surface. A box of chocolate cookies lays open on the counter. I grab one while I clean up the cups and wipe the counter down. In the garage, Jag hangs over the hood of a red Honda Civic someone brought in two days ago. I tap on the doors as I approach. He doesn't look up.

The garage is mostly empty; we usually have at least five cars in here this time of day, but right now it's empty beyond the Honda. I walk around the front of the car where Jag's working. The radio plays from across the room, but the garage distorts the sound so much, all I hear is the drumline and mumbles that are supposed to be lyrics. Every now and then, the lyrics cut off and continue so abruptly, the attempt to censor profanity only makes the missing words more obvious. "Where's all the work?" I say to Jag. "What am I supposed to do on shift tonight? Vacuum the shop?"

"Yup. You know Don's policy. I can't touch the vacuum, but *your* hands were made for it." His tools click against something in the engine.

"Oh, fuck off, Jag." I kick the back of his knees. He bends but doesn't fall. A hand holds up the car's hood, his tools click, and he smiles at me, purses his lips to stop himself, then smiles again. "What?" I laugh.

"So… I kinda lied." Jag sets his wrench down on the edge of the car's fender. The molding's uneven, he's barely turned away when it starts sliding off toward the interior of the engine's cavern. He grabs the wrench and places it on the metal tool tray nearby where it belongs. "Don didn't need you to come in tonight."

"…Are you kidding?"

"Nah—"

"If you tell me you only wanted me in here to clean up the mess in the break room, Jay, I swear to God—"

"That was nice of you, but no. That's not it at all—"

"Then why am I here?" My arms are crossed and I'm thinking of grabbing my board and flying out of here with the speed of a demigod. I'm tired. It's not even dark out, but I don't want anything to do with people anymore for the rest of the day. Between the fort, the ghosts, the badges, and everything else, all I can think about is grabbing a six-pack, a bag of pretzels, some nacho cheese, and locking myself in my room. With a cigarette lit, I'll let the heat rise and defuse it with a cold beer, the lights out, and my dad's TV yelling through the door.

I just want to forget the last twenty-four hours happened. Maybe the last week altogether and wake up to a text message from Wayland and realize everything since he called for his car to be picked up has been some kind of fever dream. Frankly, I'd prefer a coma right now with someone desperately trying to reach into my unconscious to tell me they're about to pull the plug while I'm oblivious to the danger I'm in. Every passing second, I go a little more brain dead until it's too late and then I meet the sweet relief that's nothing. The afterlife. The party. The reaper.

"I was worried about you," Jag says.

"Worried?" I come back from thought. "About me?"

"With Cross missing… We don't know what the hell's going on and you've been MIA all day—"

"It was my day off, Jagger—"

"I was starting to think Wayland got you." Jag leans against the car's hood.

"You don't seriously think he actually did *that*, do you?" My eyes flicker toward the corner of the shop where Wayland's car once sat. There's nothing there now, but I can still see it like the night I brought it in. A little bit of chipped paint on the door, some discoloration on the trunk. Mud splatter under the tires. It wasn't like him. He hadn't ever even got so much as a chip in the windshield.

Jag's jaw goes tight. He sucks in a breath, says nothing, turns away, and laughs like it's going to soften whatever comes next. "You know him better than me."

"Cross isn't a killer."

"I don't know how you can say that—we found a body in his car, Joey. What else is that supposed to mean?" He picks up the wrench, but only to give him something to do.

"We found a body, but we didn't find Wayland—"

"Yeah, which means he dumped the body so he wouldn't get caught. No murderer hangs around with the corpse unless they're stupid or nuts."

"Why the hell would he have called a pickup on his own murder scene, Jagger? Why don't you use your goddamn monkey brain for a second?"

"Why don't you?" Jag snaps with a hand smacking the nearby toolbox and a heavy exhalation at the same time. "Do you even see how far you're going to tell yourself Cross is innocent? The only thing missing from what you've found is his blood-covered hands hanging over the steering wheel waiting to take you next! He put in the call for the tow, Joey! Don's got the message!"

"Wayland wouldn't do that, and he didn't put that person in the trunk!" My voice echoes off the garage walls, surprising me even when it comes back deeper and distorted. I can't shake the image of him at the fort. Or… what I thought was him. He's not the only guy in Baltimore with black hair and a stained sweater, but I was sure it was him stepping through the trees and I know it was him standing in the forest at the shore of the River Styx or Gwynns Falls or whatever the hell it was. All just a dream.

The back of my arm's numb.

Jag's staring at me and his expression says, 'you're crazy, are you okay?' and I dare him to tell me I'm crazy to my face, but he doesn't.

"You look tired," he says.

"That'll happen when you don't sleep for twenty-three years," I say.

Jag smiles and forces a short laugh. He rubs his eyes and closes the car hood behind him.

"I think I fell at the fort. Fell into the catacombs. I don't know how long I was gone, but… when I woke up… there were more bodies."

Jag turns around in one, quick movement. "What do you mean there were more bodies?"

"I mean I woke up and came out of Armistead and there were a couple of people with their faces messed up. Don't worry—I talked to the badges before coming here." I wait for Jag to say something. He's waiting for me to say more. My heels tap against the floor. "I think the badges think I did it."

"Did what…?" We both know the answer to his question without having to say it.

"Don't tell Don. I don't need him up my ass asking a bunch of questions I can't answer. Is it really this hard for people to just… *be normal*? Why is Baltimore just… so covered in death? This isn't normal, Jag. The bodies. The park. The crime scenes. Everyone's just so used to their neighbors being criminals around here. You find out that girl scout three doors down beat someone to Hell? Huh. That's interesting, but not surprising. Everyone in this city is thirsty for something that ends in blood. Isn't it a lot of work? I just want to be left alone. I don't care if you're angry. I don't care if you're jealous. There's nothing in my windows anyone would want, so why the hell do I still have to deal with this shit?"

I'm back in the break room grabbing my jacket off one of the chairs. I turn from the table and Jag's standing in the door. His eyes are tender. His lips press flat. A chill goes through my body and suddenly I'm feeling vulnerable and exposed, and I don't know why. I don't want him looking at me. Not like that. It feels like he sees everything about me, and I don't want to know what he's thinking if he does. Trying to ask someone to understand who you are or what's bothering you or what hurts or why it hurts is a risk I never wanted to take. "Stop looking at me like that." I pull my jacket on and push my way past him.

He gently grabs me by the arm. "Where are you going?"

"Home," I say flatly. "If I don't have to work, I'm going home."

"Let me drive you," he says.

"And if I say no, thanks?"

Jag smiles, lets my arm go, and crosses his. "Then I'll drive in a similar direction at maybe two or three miles an hour with my headlights on the sidewalk."

"Oh. You're *really* worried about little, old me?" I say, stepping back, my finger pressed to my pouting bottom lip.

He's coming toward me, keeping pace. I stop when my back hits the wall. He cranes over me. The pressure is so much in my head, behind my eyes, making everything under my skin shake with nerves that won't be silent. I reach for his shirt. My fingers curl tight into the cloth and I lean up to gently press our lips together. I drop back down, my head leans against the wall, and I release him.

"According to the badges, I should be more worried you might hurt someone." His hand presses into the wall beside me. He looks me in the eyes.

I snort, roll my eyes, and duck under his arm. "Better lock up if you want to drive me home, Jay. I'm going now."

NINE.

When we get to my house, Jag tries to keep the conversation going. The whole drive has been him trying to start something, but it goes out the other ear and I don't even remember what he said. He asked me some questions, first about skating then about going to the movies after work this weekend, then… fuck, I don't remember. I had to ask what he said three or four times just to catch a gist. As I get out of the car, I still can't remember most of what he said or if I ever answered any of his questions. I tell him good night and move up the steps. He's saying something like, "you should sleep over," but I keep moving and don't say anything back. He sits in the street outside my house for a few moments after I've gone inside.

All the lights in the house are off except for the flashing TV which makes it through the closed blinds. I don't say anything after I lock the door. I slip into my bedroom without dad noticing. I lock my bedroom door, lean my skateboard against the wall, and fall onto my bed. The TV's too loud, my lips follow along with the same stupid mattress commercial I've heard every day for the last six years. *Bed*

Barn, Bed Barn, Better than the Mattress Farm. It's where the sheep sleep! I wait until the commercials are over and some cop show comes back on before slipping into the kitchen to grab a beer from the fridge.

I fall to the bed and pop the can open. A couple of taps on the walls around me make me sit upright. They continue only until I survey to find them, then they stop. They're like scratching between panels, a squirrel stuck between the paper-thin tin walls. I lay back down and reach for the beer on my nightstand. The tapping continues. It's on glass now.

I move to the bedroom window quickly this time and pull the blinds back. In the darkness outside, a glossy black marble stares back at me. Wings flutter. The bird flies away. In the dim lights of the trailer park, three other ravens are visible on the roof of my neighbor's trailer. One of them caws, but they're focused on me, not like an animal hunting, but in a weird sort of attention and familiarity. I push the window open. "You wanna stop stalking me, Val? Go back to work!" I close the window, close the blinds, step back. My phone buzzes.

A message from Jag to let me know he's made it home, but I know he's seeing if I actually went to bed.

JOEY	What do you know about ravens?
JAG	Am I supposed to know something about ravens?
JOEY	What about the grim reaper?
JAG	Why you suddenly interested in death?
JAG	You actually the killer, Joey? lmk
JOEY	Yeah, J, I'm actually the killer.
JOEY	Run and hide. :ghost: :scared:
JOEY	Fuck. I just heard someone talking about ravens and reapers earlier.
JOEY	Nothing exciting.
JAG	Folklore?
JOEY	I don't know. Maybe?

JAG   Don't know anything, sorry.

I close the texts and open the browser, searching for the terms REAPER and RAVEN. There isn't much, but I keep scrolling through the results until page four displays the title RAVEN COMES BEFORE THE REAPER listed on some obscure blog: ThingsYouShouldKnow .wordpress.com. The background is black and the design part of a premade template. Paragraphs tell the story of the raven, a carrion bird, having a connection between the world of the living and the world of the dead. They are messengers for God, an informant, and a guide. They can smell when something's life is coming to an end and they're drawn to it in order to eat the carcass left behind. They don't attack, but they wait for the soul to leave the body. The reaper then follows the raven to the dying to collect the soul so it cannot escape and rot when free of mortal boundaries. Once the soul is extracted from the body, the raven consumes whatever it desires before moving onto its next feast. The raven's not malicious, but an animal guided only by its instinct to feed. A murder of ravens is often overlooked for the display of coming death that it is. "If one sees a gathering of three or more ravens, death is nearing, more than seven, it is within minutes. Ravens will also follow their targets for days before their death. They do not know when death is coming exactly, but they can smell the end and they desire the freshest meals."

I call bullshit from how many dead bodies exist without any visible signs of damage from being pecked to pieces for lunch. And it doesn't make any sense to me why a reaper requires a raven to find a *dying soul*. That's their job, but they need a service animal to do it?

Still, I can't shake the image of the ravens gathering at Leakin Park, hiding in the trees on the night I picked up Wayland's car. Okay, so let's pretend the blog is true. Were those birds waiting for someone or had they already eaten

119

the guy in the trunk?

A siren is going off in the distance.

I hold my breath, waiting for it to pass, but it only gets louder until red and blue lights flash in my window. I get up and glance outside. An ambulance is parked in front of my neighbor's house. A couple of EMTs rush inside with a stretcher in hand. A murder of ravens sits on top of the trailer. Counting them, there are seven.

"Bullshit." Goosebumps dot my skin. I drop the blinds. "It's just a coincidence." I go back to bed and look up the next term. Danish. Something a little more legitimate comes up. A website on the first page of search results contains a catalog of European mythologies.

The valravn, it says, is a raven who consumed the heart of a noble and valiant king killed in battle. They're rare because, really, just how many noble and valiant kings have existed, period, and how many die on the battlefield anyway? While one of the stories says they're terrible animals with supernatural powers like clairvoyancy and that they're seers of prophecies, another says they have human intelligence and a desire to cause harm, and another yet says they are peaceless souls in search of redemption. The only way they can attain a human form is by consuming blood and they are particularly drawn to consume the heart of the perished. Then there's a theory that the noble heart of the king makes the raven drawn to broken people with blood on their hands or hatred inside of them. The more it goes on, the less it seems like folklore, and the more it comes off as superstition.

My phone vibrates in my hand. A notification slides down over the website reading:

WAYLAND   I NEED TO SEE YOU.

My heart's throbbing in my ears and I can't breathe. I open the text message. A sharp shock goes through my hand and runs up my arm. A squeal makes its way out of my lips. I drop the phone. I wave my hand as if it'll cool the stinging buzz, but my arm is fuzzy up to my elbow. The feeling wears off after a couple of seconds and I pick up my phone again. Another message from Wayland reads: JO, I'M SORRY, and then I DIDN'T MEAN FOR THIS TO HAPPEN.

I open the message thread. The previous message is gone and there's nothing to scroll up to. I write to him, "sorry about what?" and "where are you, Way?" A message comes back saying those can't be delivered to the requested number. The phone screen illuminates entirely, white with no words. I hold down the power button, but it won't turn off. It won't go to sleep. It won't do anything. I take out the battery. The screen takes a moment, but eventually, it turns black.

The bedroom door rocks in the frame, loud thumping, a fist fighting its way in.

"I'm fine, dad!" I say before he can say anything. The fist continues to pound my bedroom door. "Dad—" Another slam. "Dad!" The lock pops, the door comes open, and he stands in the doorway. His eyes are glossy and dark circles wrap underneath them, painted with the familiar color of too much whiskey. His hair's ragged and greasy and pressed down from where he's leaned against his chair all day. "You can go back out there. I just got startled for a sec—I didn't think I was even that loud."

"Joey…" He's coming into the room and I don't know if he actually heard anything I said. He lunges toward me but misses when I dip off the far side of my bed. I run past him. He turns clumsily and grabs hold of my wrist. He swings me until I fly back onto the bed.

"Dad—"

"You're gonna leave me too, aren't you?" The words drip from his mouth like venom. "Again? How many times do you have to fucking leave me before it's enough?" He seethes. His shoulders rise and fall with loud breaths; it

121

doesn't feel like he has control. "You're just like your goddamn mother. So much like her. At least say it. At least tell me how much you hate me, Josephine. Tell me how much I let you down. Tell me how much I ruined your fucking life! Stop lying to me and say it!" He draws his hand back.

Before I can get off the bed, my cheek's stinging and my visions spotty. It takes me a second to realize he's smacked me. I slide across the bed the only way I can to get away. He reaches for me, grabs my ankle, but loses his grip when he tries to get a better hold to yank me closer.

"It wouldn't be so bad if you told me what you think and never came back. Tell me, Jo—tell me everything I ever fucking did to you. Tell me every way I messed up your fucking life and how much you fucking hate my guts. It's my fault you're here. It's my fault you don't have a future. It's my fault your life's wasted. You're nobody. Your face is turning red. Fuck. I can't believe I did that to you. I should've killed you when I had the chance. Mercy. Mercy. I want to call it mercy. It's not about what you think of me. What anyone thinks about me. I don't care if you know what kind of failure I am. I just don't want you to see it. Don't want you to suffer. Don't want you to scream." He's muttering the words to himself as he lunges for me again. "Don't want to be lied to."

I can't hear what he's saying anymore but hissing invades his breath. He falls onto the bed, trying to grab me. I press into the wall just out of his reach. My phone lays beside him. I move along the wall to the window. "You really want me to say what I think about you, dad?" I say. My visions still spotty, red, black, blurry with restrained tears and throbbing with pain.

His face is buried in the bed. He holds onto the sheets and inhales deeply, holding the blankets to his face. He groans something incoherent. I glance at my phone, counting in my head how fast I could grab it. He rolls onto his side. I lunge and swipe the phone off the edge. His nails graze my skin, then he's standing, running around the bed to get me. I yank the window open and climb out. The ravens watch me from the neighbor's house as I hit the ground. Their eyes flicker from me to the man in my bedroom window and I go running down the street without looking to see if he's coming, but he hates the light and the ambulance is still there, so he probably won't leave the house. I'm running even though I can't breathe.

Gravel flies up under my feet. Houses pass. Fences. Lights to warm, welcoming living rooms and the darkness of quiet bedrooms lulled to sleep after the gentle disagreements or dinner or anything that would never happen in my house. I wonder if they've got bloodstained carpets under the chair where their dad sits. I wonder if they've come home from school to see him with a bottle in one hand and a gun in the other. Have they slowed down heading home after school because they didn't want to see what was behind the door waiting for them, but then had to run the last ten minutes because if they're late, it's going to be worse? Did they get reminded that mom would rather be alone than with you—but then hear that they're just like mom and *you don't deserve the amount of trust it takes to let you walk outside that door*? Did someone try to break their arm because he wanted you to need him, but as an old man, he needs you to wipe his ass and turn the TV off and get him another beer and assure him everything's fine and you'll come back and no, you don't resent him?

I'm running until my chest hurts and I can't breathe anymore. My legs are weak when I stop and if I wasn't in the middle of a dark neighborhood, maybe I would've sat on the ground. I keep going until I'm pressing the buzzer for Jag's apartment. He answers the door. "Joey... How'd you get here? Where's your board?"

I don't say anything but walk past him. He doesn't stop me. "I'm tired. I need water. Can I crash on your couch?"

I'm stepping into the apartment building. He doesn't fight me.

"You don't need to sleep on the couch," he says.

"Tonight, I think I do. Sorry, Jay."

Again, he doesn't argue. He tosses a pillow and a blanket onto the couch without asking me anything. If I had anywhere else to go, I wouldn't be here, but at least Jag knows better than to ask questions. I never wanted him to see me like this, but how many times has it been now? I've gotten too comfortable with him.

"You want some ice for your face?" he says.

I open my eyes. He's standing in the kitchen, already snapping ice from trays and dropping it into a Ziplock. He walks by, tossing the bag at me as he goes.

"Pretty swollen already," he says.

"Who knew fall air wasn't cold enough?" I press the ice to my face.

"I know you're not trying to be Miss Universe, but maybe you should try being a little less scrappy. Someday you're gonna meet someone too big for you to beat."

"Jagger," the ice shifts in my palm, "I've been trying to quit all my life. I think you're being hopeful."

Jag chuckles to himself. I just imagine his tongue kicking out a bit of gum, even though there's none in his mouth. He turns off the kitchen light and goes into his bedroom. He comes back with a box of cigarettes and a lighter he places on the coffee table. He turns back to his room.

My heart's racing. My cheek throbs. I'm dizzy and everything in me says go to sleep, don't say anything, but instead I say, "Wayland texted me."

Jag stops in the door. "What?"

"I got a message from Wayland—"

"What'd he say?"

"He wants to see me—"

"You told him to fuck off, right?"

"Cool it. It might not even have been him, Jag. It

124

could've been whoever jacked his car. Maybe they jacked his phone. It's not that farfetched that a mugger would've taken everything from him—"

"And then text *you*—of all people—?"

"Maybe he texted everyone in Way's phone to see who would respond—"

"Did you?"

"…I couldn't." I consider telling him why, but I don't think he'd even believe me. A shock wave through the phone and the messages disappeared. The number went scrambled. My dad interrupted the whole thing and now all the messages are gone, and Wayland's number isn't even in my phone book anymore?

"Probably would've looked sus if you did. The badges interviewed *you*, they think something's up with *you*. It's probably better if you lay low and don't respond. Make him come to you," Jag says.

"I was actually thinking of stopping by his house tomorrow—"

"Why the hell would you do that? If the badges are looking for him, you know where he's not going to be? His house. And you showing up is gonna be hella sus."

"I can't believe you just said *hella* unironically." I hold back a chuckle.

"I'm serious, Joey. You show up at his place, you're gonna be more than *just* a *person of interest*—"

"So, like, a person of *super* interest?" I faked a valley girl voice, but it was enough to make me feel sick with myself. I trade the ice pack for the box of cigarettes and lit one up before the ice is back on my face. "I don't expect him to be there."

"Then why are you going?"

"Because maybe there's a hint to where he is—"

"And you don't think the badges would've found it by now if there was?"

"You think the badges would be bothering the hell out

125

of me if they'd found anything on Wayland?"

Jag's weight shifts from one leg to the other.

"Look—my point is—" I'm glancing past him, refusing to look at his face. I don't need his judgment while I'm pulling things back together. Not that his judgment would mean anything, I guess. I've dealt with people calling me retarded for years. One more on the list of assholes wouldn't do anything and at least Jag dropping onto that list wouldn't be surprising. It's more surprising when someone doesn't end up there. "—there's no evidence against Way or they wouldn't be talking to me. We've been friends for a while and that's the only reason the badges want to talk to me. It's always about *what went wrong* with these guys. *Were there any signs he was deranged? What was his social life like?* They want stuff that will sound good if they put it on a report, but there was nothing wrong with Way except he might've been a little bit nerdy. If they catch me at his house? Who cares? They're already up my ass. I'm only telling you because you can come if you want, but if you don't want to get involved, then don't stand in my way. A couple of days with the badges might be a nice break from life. So, either grow a pair or stay out of my way." I'm taking a drag from the cigarette. Jag sits down on the coffee table in front of me. His fingers stretch, he cracks his knuckles, but he doesn't reach for me.

"I'm not going to fight you on this," he says. "I don't think you should go and if you get arrested, I'm not bailing you out or pretending to be your friend."

"That's fine." I smirk. "If they take a confession from me; I'm telling them the body was your fault."

"If they bring me in, I'm giving them all the bloody details in your gore diary," Jag says.

"Yeah, yeah, yeah. I'll tell them all the nasty details too. How I cut off the hands with a saw, how it got stuck on the wrist bone because I'm just, oh, such a weak, little girl and even throwing all my weight into it, I couldn't break it. All one hundred and eighteen pounds—"

"Wet?"

"Into it and I still couldn't get the damn blade to just go, and I thought it would be so fast to cut off the head and hands. I've seen a *lot* of CSI and Hannibal. How hard could it possibly be, really? But, you know, TV lied really bad on just how hard all that business is, so I called Way up. He's my BFF and we've been friends since childhood, you know he'd do anything for me. He finished the job and threw the body in the trunk. Well. Now I guess you know our dirty little secret, Jag. Won't tell anyone, will you?" I'm leaning forward, my eyes locked on Jag's as much as they can through the periodic black pulses.

"And… how's that make the body *my* fault?" He takes hold of the arm holding my cigarette and pulls me in. His other hand goes to the back of my neck. Our lips meet. He pulls on me, urging me closer to the couch's edge and I comply.

Warmth spreads through my body from my lips. He releases my arm to put his hand on my thigh. For a second, there's nothing I can think about but falling into his body and forgetting about everything for a little while, but that's what he wants. Make me forget about Wayland, make me stop asking questions, make me lose my best friend. His hand's climbing up my thigh. His thumb curls into my belt and unhooks it. I break the kiss. My freehand presses into his chest. Jag pulls back but leaves his hands where they are.

"Not the time, Jay. My face is killing me," I say.

"Like I said, cut out the scrapping." He looks me in the eye.

Feeling the tears coming, I cover my eyes with my arm and laugh instead. "Would if I could, Jag. Would if I could."

His hand falls from my neck. I scoot back on the couch, Jag stands up. "Let me know if you need anything. I'm… going to bed." He grabs a cigarette from the carton and lights it before he walks away. He runs his hand down the back of his neck, giving the back of his head a stroke and the base of his neck a scratch. His muscles tighten and relax from the stretch. The torn shirt he's wearing reads HARVARD. He got it for three bucks at a thrift shop. He's a high school dropout like me, but I don't think he ever pretended to care.

I put my cigarette in the ashtray only long enough to kick my skinnies into a corner with my shoes and shirt. I finish the cigarette and turn out the lights.

I'm staring at the ceiling, seeing speckles of light run across the otherwise plain plaster. Ice chills my hand. My face throbs, but I don't put the ice on my face. It feels *too* cold.

When I close my eyes, dad's hollow stare glares at me through my empty bedroom door frame. Walls on either side of the door are gone, but his body doesn't show if he's not in front of the door. He gnashes his teeth, his voice fills the air, saying nothing but spilling venom. He wanders away from the door, disappearing behind the black, invisible wall. Then there's the smell. The vomit, the shit, the booze, the rot that won't get out of my nose. A gun goes off, its sound ricocheting down the hall. My breathing hitches until I hold it entirely to stop the smell. I walk through the black space that should've been my bedroom. Through the empty hall. The TV flashes, illuminating the path otherwise invisible between commercial breaks. I turn the corner to my dad's Lazy Boy and the TV on the other side lights him up. I'm smaller than I should be, the chair's taller than me.

My dad hangs over the armrest, a pistol is lightly grasped in his limp hand. His mouth is slack. His eyes are empty. I move closer to the chair. "Dad?" My voice shakes. The gun drops to the floor and he lunges at me over the chair's armrest. Tight fingers wrap around my throat. Behind him, red eyes glare through the window, mom with long, brown hair, wavy, trailing down her back. Her arms are crossed, and disappointment paints her face. Everything about her says, "good riddance." Everything about her says, "once you're both buried, I can finally move on with my life. You've always held me back."

A couple of ravens gather behind her. A desperately excited caw calls others to the feast's preparations. Brittle leaves and grass crackle at the arrival of the unseen. I can't breathe as my dad's fingers squeeze my throat tighter. My fingers dig into his skin in an attempt to gain control. My nails cut into his, I'm kicking, but he won't relent. I'm hearing my voice begging him to stop, calling his name, "dad, dad—daddy, what are you doing? Dad!" but I don't feel myself speaking. I'm not in my body, but I'm not breathing either. "Dad—Please!" My lips move. His fingers squeeze tighter. "Don't—!"

I sit up with a jolt. My skin's hot and wet trails run down my cheeks. My nose is stuffed up and I can't breathe. My eyes burn from the heat of hot tears. I wipe them with the back of my arm. The tears aren't there, but I can still feel them. My heart's racing. I lay down and close my eyes again, but every time they flutter shut, the thumping of heavy footsteps chasing down the hall outside of my bedroom door echoes and I forget I'm in Jag's house.

I think dad's coming for me.

He shouldn't be.

He shouldn't be anywhere… after everything. He should be dead, and I don't know how or why I remember his brains shot out against the chair or how the bloody stain under his chair got there or why he's still sitting in front of the TV when I remember we buried him in the ground after I started first grade. I can't tell which one is the nightmare.

I turn onto my side and press my back into the couch for some semblance of comfort. I need to find Wayland. I need to know if he remembers my dad's funeral too.

TEN.

The closer we got to Wayland's house, the more Jag said we should just go back to his place or the mall or anywhere but here. "This is so fucking stupid, Joey," he says, "they're going to fucking arrest us," and I say, "What? Scared of a little prison? I think you'd do alright."

Cars park along the street with odd gaps here or there from people who've already left for work. All the homes have driveways, most of them have a garage. Wayland's house is two stories. Before even turning onto the street, badge cars watching the house are visible down the way. Do they really think they're catching anyone when they can't do basic stakeout without laymen spotting them?

Jag and I walk around the block to the other street. We cut through the neighbor's yard and climb over Wayland's fence. His backyard doesn't look like it was mowed even before fall started, maybe a couple weeks left to summer. Weeds peek through the yard, higher than the grass. The wooden playset of two swings and a slide is still there from when we were kids. The plants in his mom's garden have shriveled up and gone to sleep. We don't know if anyone's home or if they've been pushed out by badges. The dining room is connected to the yard with a glass sliding door. Before approaching it, a stain's visible on the outside. From the other side of the yard, it looks like mud, but closer it looks like it might be blood turned brown with time. I don't look back at Jag to avoid his face that probably says, 'told you so.' He tugs on my arm, says something, I don't hear the words, just his voice, and I pull my arm away.

I try sliding the door open and it gives, unlocked. The air in the house is cold, but stale. I wait until I hear Jag close the door behind me.

"Mrs. Cross, you here? The door's open." My voice barely gets out of my mouth. Something in the house absorbs it in an unnatural way, muting it like the forest in Mortem did. "Hey, Jag? You heard me say something just now, right?"

He doesn't say anything. The room's so quiet, the air turns into a soft buzz. A chill runs down the back of my shirt. I'm alone. I swing around. "Jag—" I don't think he's going to be there, but he's just past the sliding door.

"What's wrong with you, Joey?" He snorts. "You look like you saw a ghost."

"Fuck." I cross to him just to shove my hand into his chest and push him back. He doesn't move. I walk away. "Least you can do is say something."

"When was I supposed to do that?" Jag says.

"Didn't you hear me just now? Calling Way's mom? Calling you?"

"What?" Jag says. "No? You didn't say anything."

I stop walking. I feel like I've been running a marathon. "Yeah, I did." I'm sure I did, and the house ate it.

"Maybe say it a little louder next time. Loud enough it gets out of your head, yeah?"

"Yeah. Maybe that's what I thought I was doing." I'm going toward the stairs. A smear of something runs along the counter and treaded prints drag along the carpet intermittently. There's no sign of Wayland's family or that anyone has even been living in the house for days, at least. The pillow from the living room couch lays on the floor. A blanket lays on the couch, shoved to one end like the last person sleeping there got out in a hurry. I stop at the bottom of the stairs. There's something weird about the carpet. Stained with silver. Weighed down in the pattern of shoes, and it almost looks like the carpet was seared down. I run my fingers along the shapes and feel it's not hard, but wet. My fingers burn with a soft, familiar tingle.

"You more scared of the badges than you're letting on?" Jag says.

"Come touch this." I take a step back from the stairs. Glancing over my shoulder, I check to see if Jag's coming.

"What the hell are you telling me to put my fingers in?"

"I just want you to touch this spot." I point to one of the shoe prints on the stairs. Some of the shoe marks are partial, many skip stairs to make only four or five steps up the entire flight. Jag gives me a look. I say, "Just do it. I did. I'm alive."

Jag rolls his eyes, grunts, but does what I asked. "What the hell is this?" He rubs his fingers together.

"You feel something?"

"Yeah." He tries wiping his fingers on his pants. "What the hell is it?"

"You know the stuff I got on me at MP?"

"Yeah."

"I think it's the same stuff." I move up the stairs. A brownish-red handprint smears along the banister. A little further up, the same thing on the wall, like someone moving fast, holding themselves up, keeping from a fall. The hallway upstairs feels hot, the air stagnant from closed windows and something dirty running through the halls. Probably sweaty badges. It doesn't feel like Wayland's house anymore. Framed pictures of childhood line the walls. A picnic when Wayland was a kid, his older sisters running away from him at the table, his baby sister isn't in the image at all. There's even a birthday shot with me in it; we were ten. He's blowing out the candles on his cake. I don't think I ever noticed his hand reaching for mine, but now it seems really obvious. I asked him what he wished for, but he wouldn't tell me. Another photo is on the beach when Wayland and his sisters worked on a pretty big sandcastle. Then, framed embroidery of his name, his birthday, his weight. One for him and one for each of his siblings, but Wayland's is the only one with brown blood smeared across the glass. It's hanging crooked and the glass cracked. I trail my fingers along the dirty smears, lining my hand with the print to gauge the size. No doubt it belongs to him.

"Careful—" Jag says.

My hand jerks away at his voice. My finger cuts on one of the jagged edges. I hiss and resist waving my hand in the air to rush cool air against the wound. Blood drips down my finger into my palm. I dip into the bathroom, wrap my finger in toilet paper.

"Great," Jag says from the hall. "Leaving behind DNA. Anything else you wanna do to incriminate yourself?"

"I dunno. Maybe roll around in Way's bed and put a bunch of love notes on his desk. How does, 'and remember babe, I'd kill for you too," sound as a sign-off?"

Jag slows his walk, the old wood floor creaks under his step. "You guys never actually dated, did you?"

"I gave him a kiss in middle school."

"While you were dating?" Jag looks at me.

"We weren't dating. It was his first kiss."

"You hussy."

"Sounds like you've been talking to my dad." I pop my lips. I walk past Jag, pushing my hand to his chest as I move by. It's not a strong push, but he still staggers back to the wall and knocks against a framed photo.

"And you weren't dating?"

"Never. We were just friends, like it's always been. But it was middle school and neither of us had ever sucked face, so we did it. Why? You feeling jealous, Jagger?" I stop at Wayland's door and turn back to Jag, one hand on the knob, the other on my hip.

"For what?" Jag snorts. He smiles with a raised eyebrow. Mostly honest.

I turn the knob and enter the room. Wayland's always bordered on neat freak. Organization was his jam and if my dad wasn't such a piece of shit, I'd invite him over just to clean up my room. Granted, I don't think I'd ever feel comfortable living in something as tidy as this. I was used to the blankets mangled around the mattress, the clothing piles in three corners of the room and under my desk. The random bottles buried under clothing or whatever the hell else. Loose wheels and nuts or screwdrivers and wrenches that didn't make it back to their place in a drawer somewhere and the stack of old decks laying around. You know, it's hard to keep track of just what exactly lands in a mess. You clean up a room, it looks good for a couple hours, then at some point, the clean is gone and where'd the mess come from? There are still clothes in the closet, dresser, and hamper. Besides, everything laying out isn't even clothing.

Wayland's bookshelf is clean, the books evenly lined up in order by author name and somehow, they're magically the same size. A single book lays on the desk, closed. All his other desk supplies are in their place. His laundry basket has three bags on it: white, color, delicate. All three bags are mostly empty. His laptop sits on his desk, closed, a vague handprint is smeared on top where fingers left some residue behind when closing it. The pale blue comforter and sheets on his bed are tightly tucked under. His bedroom curtains are closed.

"And you don't suppose he ever… kept it a secret that he wanted to fuck you?" Jag surveys the bookshelf on the other side of the room.

"Way's never been very good at hiding anything, so, no."

"Really?" Jag takes a book off the shelf, flips through it, puts it back, and takes another. Something clicks against the floor. Before I can ask anything, Jag says, "something just fell out of the book. It's fine." I turn around, and he's picking up a loose page. It looks like a photo. He stares at it for a moment, smirks, rolls his eyes.

"What you find?"

"Nothing." He slips the page back into the book.

"Show me." I go to him.

Jag pulls the image back out of the book. "This you, Sherlock?"

I take the picture from him. Wayland and I sit next to each other on a couch somewhere that's neither my house nor his. I've got a can of beer between my legs. We're both laughing, him more modestly than me. My cheeks are flushed and there are bruises down my exposed arms, handprints coming out of my band t-shirt. I turn the photo over, looking for a date, but the back's empty. "I think that was junior, around the time I dropped out. I was a mess. Not that it wasn't a great idea, but I got a ticket that week for *trespassing* on church property or some bullshit. Three hundred dollars. I didn't have a way to pay for it. Dad and I got into a fight. A pretty bad one. So, Way and I found a party and got blasted.

I mean, I got blasted.

"He made sure I didn't kill myself, being the responsible one, you know?" I hand Jag the photo back. He stares at it a moment longer, then slips it back into the book and the book back onto the shelf.

"Sounds exciting," Jag says after a moment.

"You know me. Can't get enough of that shit." I go back to the desk where Wayland's computer sits. The screen boots up to a password-protected login. Wayland's profile reads, WAY, and his profile picture is a carved, white cross on a black background.

I pull the desk chair out and sit down, throwing in the

first thing I can think of into the password slot: MONSTROSITY. It was the name of the big, orange cat he had when we were kids. The password's rejected. I say, "damn," under my breath and lean back.

Wayland was never big into anything like sports, a specific movie, a specific game. He played generics, liked Tetris from time to time, read all the time, but never talked about one book over the other. The video games he touched were whatever was being released when he was bored—as long as it wasn't a first-person shooter and was not online and he never bothered with sports. Between the noise at the games, the celebrity of the players, and the phenomena of everyone involved turning into nothing but colors, I didn't mind skipping every sports game in school when I was there.

I remember just before I dropped out, I hadn't been to school since the first two days of the semester. It was October. Every morning, Way texted me to ask if I was coming and sometimes, I didn't answer, other times I'd say probably, but then wouldn't show up. We hung out on the weekends, but he didn't really ask where I'd been. He'd just say he missed me at school, and he'd help me catch up if I came back. When I finally told him I didn't think I was coming back, I can't really describe the look in his face. Fear? Disbelief? Sadness? I don't know. He laughed it off and said, "sure, but what about Monday?" and I shook my head and told him I wasn't coming back ever.

For a second, he thought I was actually mad that he never liked sports and he said he'd go to games if I wanted to go, if that's what would get me to go back. I told him it wasn't the game; it was just school. It wasn't for me. I wasn't smart like him and I didn't have a future like him where you needed to be smart. My dropping out was to free up a little more attention from the teacher for people like him who deserved to be recognized. I was never going to be anything better than I already was. A paper with a hollow "congrats" couldn't change where I came from or where I was going. I couldn't focus on school anyway. Every minute in the chair was spent watching the clock, counting down the hours until I had to go home, rush in to lock the door, and try my damnest to get homework done through the haze of infomercials, TV arrests, and my dad yelling profanities when he got hungry.

I tried to explain to him how we were different. College was great for him. He had it figured out, his parents had it figured out; they were still together after all. The universities looked at his resume and his above 4.0 GPA—however the hell someone manages that—and welcomed him with full scholarships to show how much they believed in his pre-med future. But me and higher education? That was the nail in the coffin of my happy family. Why the hell would I follow in the footsteps of my parents' disaster?

A pregnancy, they both dropped out with student loans they couldn't find jobs to pay off. I can't remember anything my mom ever said to me, but I can remember curling up in my bedroom closet, burying my eyes in my legs, and pressing my hands to my ears. I remember wishing I could just stop existing until one day she wasn't there when I came back from playing in the yard.

Dad didn't say anything when I asked about her. He pretended she didn't exist for a while. The house started smelling like piss and whiskey around that time. He stopped caring about anything. He said, "I love you, Jo," in morning sob fests on the daily, and yeah, sure, I believed it because that's what parents are supposed to say.

Now? I don't know. I don't think the Bourgeois are capable of love and maybe that's what finally got to my mom. When she married my dad, the curse fell onto her too. There was never any saving them.

Resentment. Anger. Lies.

Wayland acted like he was afraid I wouldn't be his friend when he found out where I lived, but... I didn't ever tell him I was afraid of the same thing. I didn't tell him half the shit that went on at my house just in case it would scare him off. Other times, I tried to leave for a few days, ignore his messages so he'd forget about us being friends and move on, and… maybe it was selfish of me, but I couldn't stay away, even if it meant he'd have a better life. Most of the time, I couldn't figure out why he was still friends with me or why his parents let me hang around. They were tempting the Bourgeois failure and that's why he was missing now. He knew me. He talked to me. He called me.

"Are you fucking kidding me?" Jag says, bumping something, sounds like a dresser or cabinet drawer.

I turn around in the desk chair. "What'd you find now?"

"Nothing." A small black box flings into the drawer. Jag shuts it and looks back at me. "You get into that computer yet?"

"No." I shake my head. The screen blurs. I gently rub my swollen eye like it'll help anything. My fingers come away wet. I wipe my hands on my pants and put my fingers back to the keyboard. "How would I have gotten in? It's locked."

"You don't know his password?" Jag snorts a laugh. "I thought Cross didn't keep secrets from you."

"Passwords don't count. No one wants to share that shit since it means exposing your porn collection for all to see." I type in something random. Macaroni. Pizza. Meatballs. Anything to look like I'm working, but I can't think straight. My head just keeps going in circles, thrusting random memories of random shit from the past. Wayland. Mom. Dad. The bullet. Condolences and casseroles. Badges and tape. Quiet, then dad's TV blaring again. I swear it wasn't a dream.

"What kind of porn you think Cross likes?" Jag says.

"I don't even care enough to guess. Not for you. Not for Donny. Not for a million bucks. I don't want to get into that messy shit. I couldn't look at any of you the same if I did."

"Donny doesn't hide his preferences," Jag says.

"Donny doesn't really give me the option to not listen."
I drop my head back and close my eyes. I take a deep breath,
then turn back in the seat.

Jag's rifling through the bedside table drawer. He flips
through a small notebook he found in it. He's frowning,
hard.

"I'm kind of surprised you're actually looking through
stuff considering you didn't even want to be here."

"That didn't stop me from being here, so…" He flips to
the end of the book, tosses it back in the nightstand, and
snaps the drawer shut. "And if I do nothing, we're here
longer."

"That's logical of you," I say.

"Try jmb021999."

"What?"

"For the password. All lowercase, jmb021999."

"Why would that be the password?"

"Because it probably is, *Josephine Maria Bourgeois.*"

I felt him come up behind me, but I don't look. "It
worked." I really didn't want it to work.

"Imagine that. Don't keep secrets from each other,
Joey?" His hand presses into the desk while he hovers over
me. I keep my eyes on the screen, though the plain,
organized desktop moves in and out of focus. "You gonna
look for something on his computer or what?" Jag taps one
of my legs with his foot.

"You eager or something?" My hand slides over the
touchpad. My heart's racing. Slowly, my finger slides along
the touchpad until the clicker on the screen hangs over MY
COMPUTER. I pause, slide down, and hover over the email
app.

"You gonna do something or what, Joey? Didn't we
come here looking for clues?" He taps my leg again, this
time, leaning in closer over me.

I wave him off. "Yeah, yeah, yeah. I'm just thinking of
where to start."

"Think faster. I'm kinda done being here." He pushes himself from the desk and paces across the room. There's a thud. He stops moving and watches the door. That's not in the house, it's in the walls. We stay quiet, my hands hover over the keyboard. Another thud. It's not a person, but furniture forcefully shifting by accident. Jag goes to the door, presses in the lock, and holds the handle with his ear pressed against the door. "Hurry it up, Joey."

My fingers go back to the keyboard and touchpad. I open Wayland's email. The inbox is filled with a mixture of everything. Junk mail, university messages from his professors, club offers, and receipts for clothing, a video game purchase, and a jeweler. There isn't much from before Wayland disappeared. He always kept his emails as tidy as his room. A dozen or more different categories hang on the left side panel. Receipts. Medical. Family. Undergrad. High school. *Draft* displays there are a couple unsent emails inside. The oldest message in the *Draft* folder has my name in the receiver line. The email was created three weeks ago, and it reads:

> *Jo, I wanted to wait until I graduated. The school thing. I get it. I get your worry. So, I wanted to wait, but I don't know if I can. Every day, I'm sitting in the ~~fucking~~ classroom thinking how every second I'm tapping a pencil or trying to read something or making a diagram, you're out there in the actual world, talking to people, figuring out what you want to do, maybe falling in love without me. I've always been worried you'd leave me behind. School doesn't feel fake when I'm here, but when I'm around you, the difference is... you can feel it. We live so differently, but that's always been something I liked about you. You didn't care about the rules. Getting in trouble. Pleasing anyone. Somehow, when you were told to do something, you had this ability to just... not do it. That makes it sound so easy. Defying what you're told, but the rules always felt like a wall to me. If someone said you can't go through the door, I didn't feel I physically could. But then I'd see*

you do it and it felt like magic. Everything you do feels like magic because of how easy you do it. I—

The email cuts off. My heart's racing. Heat gathers in my face. I click on the next email in the *Draft* folder. It's also addressed to me. It was marked two days after the other one: *Jo, I wanted to wait until after I graduated because I know, but*

The email cuts off again. A third, from a week and a half ago, also addressed to me only reads *Jo* at the top. I go back to the inbox. Near the start of the new, unread emails is one says it's a receipt from the *Yes Initiative*. One thousand, two hundred and fifty dollars. The body of the email reads *call me with any questions on your work. Thanks, Rod Flowers.*

"You find anything yet?" Jag says.

"Maybe. I don't know. Ever heard of some place called the *Yes Initiative*?" I hover over the email attachment.

"No… Should I have?"

"I don't know. Way's got this email from them for over a grand. I'm just sort of wondering what the hell the *Yes Initiative* would sell."

"Sounds kinda culty to me. Your friend into that kind of stuff?" Jag says. "Would fit the profile."

"He's studying to become a heart surgeon, Jag."

"You say that like freemasons haven't been all over the place since God knows when and like they're not always looking for a sacrifice. Hospitals. Universities. Corporate leaders. Churches. The political sphere. Freemasons are everywhere, Joey."

"What the hell's a freemason?"

"Are you serious? You've never heard of freemasons?"

"I'm sorry we don't all have weird hobbies in conspiracy theories like you. What the hell is a freemason?"

"I can't really give you the whole masonic history right now, but just know they're pretty culty. Something about world domination and blood sacrifices and that kind of shit. Cross was kind of a loser in high school, yeah?" Jag says.

"What's that have to do with anything?"

"I dunno. Something about losers getting bitter and antagonistic through graduation. I mean, think of all the movies where the bad guy had a shit childhood and uses that to superpower his drive for world domination," Jag says.

"I had a shit childhood, Jag, and *I'm* not a bitter super-villain bent on world domination." I turn around in the computer chair. I wasn't expecting Jag to be staring at me. His back's pressed against the door, his hand grips the knob, but only lightly. He's not holding the door shut with his weight, but it's more like he's keeping a watch on the movement with his body.

"We're not at your house because we found a corpse in your car," Jag says. "But we can check around your place too if you really want to prove your innocence. You did mention the afterlife and grim reaper last night." He comes over to me and looks over the screen. "What's that?" He points.

I turn around. The file from the email must've finally opened. Scrawled across the screen is a mixture of letters, symbols, numbers, even blocks of just… black squares. None of it makes any sense. Jag leans against me, getting a closer look. He puts a hand on the back of my chair.

"I hate to say it, Joey, but… It definitely looks like Cross was in a cult. What the hell is this shit?"

"It's an encrypted file, Jay." I roll my eyes and close the file. Quickly, I click through the email to forward it to myself with the attachment.

"What the hell are you doing?!" Jag grabs my hand.

Too late.

The email's already gone. I pull away from him and stand up.

"I'm gonna try to decrypt it later. We can't stay here forever, you know—"

"Yeah, and assuming the badges are watching the internet stuff going in and out of here, they're gonna get a warrant to search your shit and you're gonna have an encrypted file from a missing serial killer. If you thought you already looked bad, I can't even begin with how fucking screwed you are." Jag reaches for me again. "Damn it, Joey."

I step back quickly, keeping the space between us. He keeps coming toward me until we're walking in a circle, him forward while I back away.

"I'm trying to find him. You don't have to help me, but stop getting in my way—"

"You're going to get yourself arrested or worse—" He's gaining on me.

"Yeah? What's worse than being arrested, Jagger?" I back myself into a wall.

"Dead." His voice echoes through the empty room once and is muted by the walls. He towers over me, his hand pressed into the door. He's close enough to smell the sweat and his bitter body wash that I also used this morning. Something crashes downstairs. Glass. Heavy thumps like footsteps, not coming, but running away from something. There are only a few before they're gone. I can't tell if the booming in my ears is the house or me.

"We need to get out of here," I say.

"Ya think?" Jag backs off. I push off the door and grab at the knob. It's still locked. He pushes me back. His ear goes to the door, his hand to the knob. He's watching me, watching the window beside the desk computer, watching a shadow move in the corner from a tree outside dancing in a gust. He waits a few seconds to make sure there's no sound before he pops the lock. "Just remember to lick the doorknob and leave your panties under the bed before we get out of here. Wouldn't want to leave the badges with any reasonable doubt that you're not involved with Cross."

"Oh my god, Jagger." I push him against the door. "I didn't have anything to do with the body in the trunk—"

"And yet you're doing everything in your damn power to make it look like you did—"

"The badges aren't gonna do a damn thing to find him! You know it as well as I do that they don't give a shit about missing people like Cross. Like you or me. Any of us could go missing and whether they find us or not, whether they can call us missing, dead, or run away, they don't care. They'll make up some bullshit story about how they did such a good job, or they'll toss it in the cold case freezer to get a TV show on it twenty years down the line. All they care about is looking busy so city hall gives 'em the money to pocket. You know how BPD works. I bet you even the cars down the street are empty. Forget the police tape? Nah. Just didn't care to come back and clean up. Have to look like they're working, right?" I grab the knob. Jag backs off and lets me open the door. I step out but stop in the hall to listen again.

"I don't like the badges either," Jag mutters behind me, "but trashing a perp's house—"

"Shut up, Jag. I'm done talking about this."

"Because you know I'm right—"

I quickly move for the stairs before he can say anything else. I'm careful as I edge down, looking over the banister for any signs of badges or maybe one of the Crosses. Though I want to see Wayland, this is one of the few times I hope he's not lurking. In the living room, shards of a broken glass and scattered flowers that died days ago litter the rug. A greasy handprint, silver, brown, and red slides along the white wall and drips like it's still wet. I reach for it. Jag grabs my wrist before my fingers can touch the wall and he pulls me away. I'm glaring at him, pulling against his grip, but he won't let go. He drags me to the back door, yanks it open, and pushes me out. The door shuts behind him. I walk ahead of him. We don't say anything to each other until we're standing by his car a few blocks away.

"That print was fresh," I say.

"And you tried to touch it. Can you be any more stupid?" Jag's opening his car door. He sticks his foot in but doesn't climb in. "Are you gonna get in?"

"No. I think I'm gonna walk home—"

"Seriously, Joey?"

"Yeah. Seriously, *Jagger*." I open the car door only long enough to grab my cigarettes from the center console. "Wouldn't want you to get in trouble, getting pulled over with a criminal like me in your passenger."

"You're not actually getting mad at me for not wanting to see you arrested because you can't separate your childhood feelings from a murderer."

I yank a cigarette out and slip it into my mouth. The box goes to my back pocket. Jag comes around the car to meet me. "Just get in the car," Jag says. He seems so much taller when things are heated, angry, horny, whatever. I know what his muscles feel like and I have no illusions that Jag's *not* bigger and stronger than me, but in part, I rely on my being a girl and his… not being a *complete* asshole who would use it against me.

I step back. I pull my lighter from my pocket and light the cigarette. I hold it, pinched between my fingers. "This isn't about feelings, Jay. It's called loyalty and you don't know a goddamn thing about Wayland if your real suggestion right now is to abandon him. You don't care, I get it. He's *my* friend, not yours, but I'm not going to wait around until the badges show up asking me to ID the body in a couple years. You can go home, get cozy, jack it, whatever, but I've got shit to do." Stepping back, I put the cigarette back in my mouth and give Jag a two-handed wave. He reaches to grab my arm, but I whirl to the side, make him miss, move back faster. Jag takes a couple of steps toward me but stops.

"You can't go chasing monsters by yourself, Joey. This shit's—"

"What? Dangerous?" I laugh. "Welcome to Bodymore. City motto: 'bleed more, bitches!' There's not enough blood in the gutter and ya know, runners need more gore to look at when they're out on the track. I don't know what it is about this city, but it doesn't feel like its bloodlust is ever satisfied." The word bloodlust always felt weird to me, but I don't know how else to describe a city where the badges seem just as casual about the death of a gangbanger as their neighbor. Everyone in Baltimore's seen at least one dead body in person by the time they're ten. It's a miserable city filled with miserable people who only feel better by making everyone around them feel miserable too and the only way to survive this city is to escape.

I used to think that ironically, but now... I might hate my mom, but at least she had the right idea.

I tuck my cigarette between my lips. I check over my shoulder. Jag's not following, but then I hear his car start down the block. I almost expect to hear him trailing behind me, but instead, his car peels out and I'm walking the street by myself.

ELEVEN.

Baltimore always looks different at night. It doesn't help that the bulbs are smashed or shot out in half of the streetlights. The nicer parts of Baltimore are paid for by the Catholic church and it's hard to reconcile them with the more rundown parts of the city. Old Town looks nothing like Mount Vernon, Federal Hill, and Inner Harbor because of how rundown it is. Yet, Old Town doesn't have anything over Hopkins-Middle East, West Baltimore, or Cherry Hill. Whatever you think you know about the city, you don't. When the sun goes down and half the city is illuminated by buzzing streetlights, you'll discover it's not the night that distorts your neighborhood. It's not like the city doesn't know the streetlights are out, but city hall wants to save a bit of the budget knowing someone's gonna smack them out again anyway in most of the places they're broken.

Golden sunlight paints the historical buildings as it descends behind them. The clock on my phone reads 4:34. Hours at the library proved useless when the message from Wayland's email wasn't encrypted, it just opened wrong. It was seriously just an itemized receipt for some self-esteem event at a counseling facility. I don't even know if counseling is the right way to describe it. Like, the *Yes Initiative* feels a lot like a pickup artist's scam sessions, but for people with low confidence and everyday life. Wayland might not have been like Jag in the arrogantly cocky department, but that's what I liked about him. I knew he was a little insecure, but I didn't think he was so unsure that he'd be tricked into paying over a grand for some random group of people to cheer him on. I could've done that for him for free if he'd asked.

I've still got the webpage up on my phone. My stomach curls over in knots. A wave of sickness goes through me, but I haven't eaten anything in a while, so all I feel is a bit of stomach acid in the back of my throat. Jag's words circle in my head. What if Wayland was victim to some secret sacrificial death cult? I smack myself in the head. It's more likely he got caught up with the wrong Baltimoron down the wrong alleyway walking home at the wrong time of night when he said the wrong thing, looked the wrong way—full of cash—and got shot. Maybe he really was in a garbage back at MP, waiting to be discovered by some poor asshole just out walking his dog before work.

My phone buzzes in my hand. The notification shows Wayland's name followed by: 'JO, YOU THERE?'

I'm in the messages before I can even think and I write: 'what's with the caps??'

Wayland's typing for a while or maybe he's in the middle of something. He doesn't have the setting on to show when he's actually writing. Finally, he responds, 'YOU BUSY?' then 'I NEED TO SEE YOU.'

JOEY	Where are you?
WAYLAND	CAN'T SAY.
JOEY	How can I see you then?
WAYLAND	I DON'T KNOW.
WAYLAND	I DON'T KNOW WHERE I AM.

JOEY	Are you in BM?
WAYLAND	MAYBE?
JOEY	How drunk are you?
WAYLAND	I'M NOT.
WAYLAND	IT'S HARD TO THINK.
JOEY	Are you okay?
WAYLAND	NO. MY HEAD HURTS.
WAYLAND	THROBBING.
WAYLAND	I CAN'T BREATHE SOMETIMES.
JOEY	Were you shot?
WAYLAND	MAYBE? I DON'T KNOW.
JOEY	Stop messing around, Way. People think you killed someone.
WAYLAND	I DIDN'T KILL ANYONE.
WAYLAND	I DIDN'T MEAN TO.
JOEY	Tell me where you are, Way. It's okay.

My heart's racing, hard. I don't realize I'm shaking until I can't read the screen anymore. My vision blurs with a couple of fresh tears. I wipe my eyes with the back of my hand. Wayland's written back, 'I THINK I'M AT LEAKIN.' I've barely written, 'I'm on my way,' before running home to grab my skateboard.

By the time I get to Leakin Park, the sun is dipping below the horizon and the streetlamps are on. Still, the street lines reflect what little bit of daylight remains. Gwynns Falls echoes between the trees. Leaves rustle in the silence. There's a bang from somewhere. I pretend it doesn't sound like a gun. A moment later, another bang, but that one's definitely a busted engine revolting at its use. I text Wayland, letting him know I'm here. I stand under one of the working streetlamps down the road from the Crimea Estate. A soft roar echoes through the trees. A gust. A chill runs down my back. I check my phone. No messages.

I step away from the light, check the messages again. Still nothing.

"C'mon, Cross."

I can't stop looking at the clock. Thirty seconds feels like three hours.

Another sound in the trees. Leaves crackling. Footsteps, rapid. A couple branches sway. A loud caw.

On the red roof of the Orianda House, a big, black raven sits on the orange canopy.

I take a deep breath. It unsteadily comes out.

A step closer to the estate and another raven lands beside the first. I work my jaw. "I told you to stop following me." I point at the biggest raven. Its eyes meet mine. He doesn't look like anything but a fucking bird, but I know it's him behind those glossy, black eyes.

Another step and a third raven lands by the house, this one on the ground. Around the square edge of the house's front are two more and around the side, four more. They stare at me in unison, heads slightly cocked, eyes obsessively observant.

"I'm not going to die so you can get the fuck out of here." Without realizing it, I'm gripping my skateboard hard and stepping away from the house. The birds caw from behind, but they sound like they're all around me. In the trees, on the gates, standing in the dark bushes, unseen. The streetlamps expose every glossy, obsidian eye watching me. "This isn't funny, Val!" The words come out before I even think of them.

Fuck.

There's something in the trees. My words carry through the empty park that's definitely not empty.

I watch the ground carefully as I move quickly, unwilling to fall in again. I check over my shoulder, waiting for some random gangbangers to come out of the woods, high as a kite, gun in hand, shooting with indifference. "You're a prick, Wayland. You know that?" I growl under my breath. I'm nearly skipping from how quickly I'm moving. I clutch my phone in one hand, the skateboard under the other.

A boom shoots off in the distance. Definitely a gun. That was definitely a gun.

My foot catches on a rock. My skateboard and phone clatter to the ground. Hands stinging, scraped on asphalt, my phone's screen cracks through Wayland's message: 'WHERE ARE YOU?'

I write back, 'Dying. Brb.' Phone in pocket, I grab my skateboard and stand up in the same motion. My knees sting. Pattering feet run at me from behind. I grip my skateboard like a bat and turn around swinging it. It barely misses some guy. Short hair, sagging jeans, streetlamps barely reflect off his dark skin. He's got a knife in his hand.

"Put it the fuck down," he says.

"You really gonna try to stab me?" I'm gripping the board high, ready to swing again.

"Put it the fuck down," he says again, harder.

"Mm-mm. No. I'm not dying today, sorry."

"You ain't making decisions to keep you alive."

"Like I didn't already know that." I swing the board at him.

"You ain't catching metal," he says.

"No harm in trying if I'm gonna eat pavement anyway." I swing the board again, stepping forward, fast. It smacks into his hand. The knife falls from his grip.

"You fucking bitch." He picks the knife back up and lunges at me. A swing, he almost catches my arm. His nails dig into my skin, then his hand's got my shoulder. My elbows scrape against concrete. He's on top of me, his hand wraps around my neck. He plunges the knife toward me while using his weight to pin me down. I shove my hand into his chin. His face shoots up, the knife offsets and grazes my arm, tearing my shirt in the process. I don't recognize my own voice when the scream echoes back from the park's empty mass. Desperation and panic turn to screaming anger when I'm flailing and saying, "stop, stop, stop, you motherfucker!"

There's a thud, a hard slap that sounds like a skateboard hitting a surface, and the gangbanger's weight isn't pinning me anymore. Another smack, hard and hollow, then another and another. I hear the sounds without registering what's happening, accepting them as part of the woods whistling at the scene, but then they suddenly stop.

My breath hitches in my throat, chest rising rapidly. My arm throbs, stinging. The warm drizzle of blood goes down my skin. Some of my shirt fabric clings to the moisture. I sit up with a hiss. The darkness spins around me. A dark form lurches over the figure laid out on the pavement. Skinny legs, a sweater, a bubbly jacket, and short black hair. He's not wearing his glasses, but I know it's him.

"Wayland—" I say, climbing to my feet. I'm staggering back. The trees spin around me, the road won't stay under me. Cold air fills my lungs. I reach around for something to give me balance, but there's nothing in the middle of the road. Wayland closes the space between us to grab a gentle hold of my arm. At first touch, I gasp and pull back. I'm waiting for the hand to slip around my neck again or the knife to burst through my chest. When my vision clears, blood splatters across the pavement, light from the overhead catches on the knife where it lay just inches from the guy's open hand. "Shit—shit—shit—hey—is he okay?"

"He's gone," Wayland says, seething, angrier than I've ever heard him before. He looks up to me. Our eyes connect for the first time. A chill runs through me. It's him, definitely, but there's something… wrong. He feels off or incomplete. He must have noticed my discomfort, because his hands retreat quickly, leaving me to balance on my own again. "Jo, is that really you?" he says.

I laugh like I have the hiccups. "Yeah, it's really me. Who else would I be?" I look him over, rub my eyes, and look him over again. It has to be the light that's making him look weird. A dirty crust on his skin, probably from hiding outside for the past week. He doesn't have much facial hair to show for it, but Wayland never was good at growing facial hair. "I should be asking you that though. You… don't look like you. When's the last time you showered?" I laugh again, lighter this time, hoping it gets him to laugh or smile or something, but he doesn't. "Where have you been?"

"I… I don't know." Wayland presses his hand to his forehead. "I don't remember. All I remember is… Ah!" His words cut off as pain courses through his voice instead. He falls to his knees holding his head. His voice echoes off the trees, leaves, branches, the house, and empty roads. The knife lays on the ground beside Wayland's knee. Though I don't expect either of them to pick it up, I kick it into the grass, half expecting the guy to suddenly open his eyes and grab me, but he doesn't. I drop to the ground, meeting Wayland. Grabbing hold of his shoulders, he's shaking, breathing hard, panting, almost like he's suffocating. A distant chain is rattling in the trees.

"Wayland—what's wrong? What's on your shirt? Is that blood?"

His body as hard as a rock and cold resonates from his jacket. It feels like I'm touching ice.

"How long have you been outside?" I say. "You're freezing."

"I-I don't know. I don't know anything, Jo. I don't know—" he cuts off again. Another growl of pain or anger or both. He looks around in a panic, hearing something I can't. I flinch back at first but grab onto him again. "I—I… I can't stop myself, Jo. I… I hurt people. I'm sorry…"

"We need to get you to a hospital." I glance sidelong at the guy on the ground. "We need to call 911."

"Why?" Wayland says. "Why? Why? Why? Why?" His voice clicks and repeats in a way that sounds like a broken CD. "That guy's gone and he's not coming back."

"Who the hell was he?" I draw back.

Wayland quickly takes my hand. "Nobody. A dead man walking." Suddenly, Wayland's stiff. His hand grips mine so hard it hurts and he's staring intensely at something past me. There's a single, long, low caw. A couple of branches rustle and a softer, shorter caw is followed by a few more. The rattling chains grow closer from both sides of the road. Wayland lets my hand go and he's standing up, stepping back rapidly.

"Wayland—"

I follow, he turns and starts running.

"Wayland! Where are you going!"

"Can't—Can't be here!" his voice shakes. His run turns into a sprint. The night devours him in a way that makes his body look like it's disintegrating until he's far enough away, he's completely gone. A couple of birds caw somewhere around me that I can't see. The leaves melt with a wall of black feathers. Then, as if all driven by a gust, the murder of ravens fly past me on both sides. Streetlamps flicker. Some of the ravens land, standing along the side of the road, some on top of the streetlights, but some continue in a small tornado until it splits and a man dressed in black clothes— jeans, a leather jacket, the same cocky, but brainless smile I vaguely remember—comes through. Val approaches the laid-out corpse, licking his lips, eyes focused like nothing else exists.

"Val?" I breathe out his name.

"Oh, you're not gonna run away from me this time?" He squats beside the body.

"This time?" I say.

"At your house? I think it was your house. It looked pretty shitty, but I still think it was your house. Smelled like you. Anyway, you opened the window and ran when you saw me." He speaks, seemingly transfixed on the corpse. He wipes his arm over his chin, wiping away a bit of drool.

"Outside my house?" Images of the ravens on the neighbor's trailer flash through my mind and the sound of my dad pounding on the door. My face throbs in memory of his hand. "For real? I didn't seriously think that was you—"

"Then why'd you yell at me?" He finally looks over his shoulder at me. The glance is fleeting and returns to the body. Another lick of his lips.

"Why were you there?'

"Wherever the smell of death is, I follow." He's running his fingers along the unconscious man's chest, tracing over where his heart would be. Slightly long nails covered in black finger paint probe through the man's hoodie.

"What the hell are you doing? If you're going to help him, then do it," I say.

"Help?" Val lifts his head and laughs.

"He's dead," Charon's flat voice comes from behind me. "What exactly would you have him do?" Dressed in unaffected white, Charon's clean look appears dimly glowing in the dark.

"Dead?" I say.

"Yes. Dead," Charon says. "Don't tell me you didn't know. His brain is … mashed at least somewhat on the pavement. What did you think that was?"

"I was trying not to think about it, to be honest." I'm waiting for Charon to say something more insulting, but Charon doesn't follow up. He squats beside the body. His hand hovers over the man's closed eyes. Chains gently jingle from somewhere unseen. Gingerly, his fingertips open each lid in one, smooth motion. With a wave, he gently pulls up like he's holding onto a rope. He stands in the same motion as his hand lifts. A small white ball floats just below his fingers. He pinches a white mist. Val has barely waited for Charon to step back when his dark nails dig into the man's jacket. He seems almost manic in the way he pulls open the fabric, his nails not bothering with the zipper, but instead, tearing the cloth-like he has knives at the end of his fingertips. He burrows through the t-shirt and then through the skin.

"What the hell are you doing?" I run to Val. A hand on

his shoulder, I yank, but it does nothing to move or dissuade him. When I try to grab him again, he pushes me back harder.

Val peels the man's skin back then cracks his bones in rapid succession, tossing the unnecessary matter to the side. His hands drip with blood. He finds the man's heart and tears it out of his chest. As if he hasn't eaten in weeks, Val shoves the heart into his mouth, consuming it in large bites and as fast as he can. Blood drips down his chin. Whatever other juices reside around the heart squirt out where his teeth dig in. Two, three, four monster bites. The rest of the heart is gone. The bottom of his nose drips with more blood. His tongue slides along his lips.

"You are so disgusting," Charon says.

Val stands, wiping his arm over his lips. "You'd get it if you had some. Human hearts are so… I don't know how to describe it. This one's not the best I've had, but pretty good." He wipes his nose again, then wipes his hand on his shirt.

My hands are shaking, my skin is freezing, but my face is hot, and a wave of dizziness goes over me. I've seen death, but this… "What the hell's wrong with you?" I'm walking up to Val. My hands thrust against his chest. He stays in place. I push him again. He leans back, then straightens, but doesn't move.

"What?" Val says.

"You killed that guy!" I point to the body.

"Didn't you hear Charon? He was already dead. He would know. He only collects souls of the expired and I don't care about the living heart." Val pauses. He leans into me. I step back. Countering, he steps forward, keeping close, sniffing the air attentively, and moving around me to continue to smell the air. He stops behind me and leans over my shoulder. "Speaking of which… You smell like death… How you feeling?"

My breath catches in my chest. My jaw's tight. "I did just

take a trip to a city of the dead. I'm sure the smell rubs off on you a bit."

"Nah." Val comes around to the front of me. "It's from the inside. The heart. The smell's coming from your heart. That's how I find people. When times running low, there's just this… delicious smell it lets off. It's faint on you, but it's there."

"Clearly, I'm not dead." My heart's racing. I can't tell if the streetlights are flickering out or my visions going black. I step back from Val to put some space between us. He stands erect, strong, and somehow bird-like.

"Hm," he says. "Yeah… but maybe soon."

"You're standing in the Bodymore dumping ground. If you smell death, it's probably in the dirt. This place has seen more blood over the years than… fuck, this city, in general, is fucking nasty," I say.

Val laughs then licks his lips. "Got that right. One of the better feeding grounds I've been to."

Charon draws a small container out of his jacket. An opaque crystal wrapped in tendon. He brings the pinched, bright ball to the crystal. It absorbs the light. The opaque siding glows and fades. He pockets the crystal jar and says, "Val." Val quickly peels away from me, and, as if given a command, the birdman tails behind Charon as he walks away.

"Wait." I follow after them. I can't stop my eyes from drifting to the corpse ripped open on the side of the road. I speed past it, slowing down only once it's behind me. "That's it?"

Charon turns around. "What do you mean *that's it*? We've completed our job here."

"Which was what, exactly? Ripping a dead guy open? Making a brutal murder scene for the seven 'o'clock news? The least you can do is call 911 or something to clean it up," I say.

Charon exchanges a glance with Val. "Humans really

159

have no idea how anything works, do they?" Val gives a slow shrug in response. Charon's attention turns back to me. "I am a reaper. I deliver souls. First to Cavae Mortem to wait and then to judgment when it's time. Anything left behind after the soul is extracted is for humanity to manage. Reapers never have and never will do anything with the disposable human body."

"But why is that? The body's connected to the soul, isn't it, like, I'm in here." I tap my chest with an open palm. "Everything my 'soul' goes through, my body does too."

"The body decays. The soul is everlasting. You should be aware of this even from a human standpoint. You age, don't you? What use would we have in the afterlife for a rotting corpse past its date?" Charon says.

"I don't know…" I run my hand down the back of my head. My hair catches between fingers. I think I should feel worse about the dead guy, about Wayland, but all I can think is *'it's Baltimore.'* What the hell did he think was going to happen when he ran up to me?

I mean—If Way hadn't been there, I'd probably be the one on the ground, the one in Charon's collection, dripping from Val's lips, going to the pub under the city, but… I know the risks of just being here. In the sunlight, it feels like the pavement is glossy with blood, not just black asphalt and tar, but so much blood, washed aside by firehoses and rain.

"Wait—" I glance back at the corpse, light catches on the innards. I take a couple steps forward to catch up beside Charon and Val. "So, you…" I'm looking away into the trees. The words are stuck. Because I can't find them? Because I'm kind of hesitant to say them and sound crazy? These guys being here is crazy. They're figures in a dream. Some version of the afterlife that shouldn't have existed after I knocked my head on concrete in Armistead. Being near them, there's an atmosphere similar to when I was down below.

An electricity that feels otherworldly and it's just as hard to describe as Val's inhumanness while looking at his human shape. The sharp jaw, straight nose, shrugging shoulders. It didn't matter, I still saw a raven. He stood out among the actual birds hopping around the ground, but he was the same as them. Meanwhile, there was a calming aura around Charon that made me want to come closer just to feel it more. I felt dead on the inside the closer I got. Dead maybe isn't the right word, but the panic and anger and fear overpowering me silenced when he was near. "That thing— You took his soul?" I say.

Charon turns around. His expression is nothing but empty. "Yes."

"Do you pick up everyone who, uh, dies in Baltimore?"

"Everyone? No." Charon pauses for a moment, seemingly thinking over what he wants to say. "The violent deaths, I guide. The souls who end that way can be harder to extract from the body as trauma tends to tie them down and hold them in. There are different reapers assigned to hospitals, care facilities, children, and disease."

"What about suicide?"

"Yes. Those are violent. Despite what their actions may say about them, they are still fairly tied to this plane and their bodies," Charon says.

My heart pounds in my ears and a wave of dizziness comes over me. It's impossible to not think that maybe he knows my dad. I want to know—I need to know. My throat constricts, my mouth goes dry. The resistance my body gives me is acting like an expected answer. "Did you know someone," my mouth's so dry my voice squeaks. I lick my lips and clear my throat. "Andrew Bourgeois? I mean—I guess I don't know if you know anyone's name when you take them away, but maybe you do. If you don't remember or don't know, I understand. I'm just… I'm curious."

"Andrew David Bourgeois?" Charon says.

Hearing my dad's name come from his lips causes goosebumps along my arms. I nod slowly, holding my breath.

"Yes. He died fifteen years ago. A self-inflicted bullet to the head in his home. Generally, I do not tend to home deaths, but he fell in my scope as a violent or traumatic passing," Charon says.

My head's spinning and I feel like I'm going to fall. Quickly, I sit on the ground and hold my head in my hands. "He's dead?"

"Yes," Charon says. "You don't remember your own father's death?"

"I… I don't know. I mean, I… Why is he always in his chair? How is he there? How is he always there?" My vision blurs. I can hardly breathe. It's like I'm panting as I desperately try to suck in air.

"Regret," Charon says.

"What the hell do you mean by regret?" I raise my head to look at him. He turns away, Val follows.

"Sometimes, when it's time to go, you humans don't want to move on, so you don't. I will never understand how you people do not grasp the program. Humans are the only creatures in existence who actively deny or attempt to subvert the system of order in which every other creature abides. You live, you provide your service, you die, you move on. The cycle continues. But humans? There's something defective in you that does not comply. Maybe it's the emotion. You think you have to personally approve anything that happens for it to take place. You don't. The universe doesn't care about human approval. Your rejection of reality will only hurt those around you. It always has and it always will. It is not my job to collect escaped souls. For their decisions, they live in their own misery. That is the price you pay for rejecting the system by which the rest of creation abides," Charon says, seemingly more to himself than me. "If Andrew David Bourgeois is here, I would recommend you stay away. Interacting with an expired soul is rarely a safe endeavor for the living. However, I understand the habits of the human. So foolish, you often can't help but defy anything you believe is a rule or even a simple suggestion, even if it costs your life. Moronic." He walks into the distance without stopping. His voice gets softer as he moves, and the darkness devours him and Val once he steps beyond the streetlamp.

I unfold my legs and stare into the distance. I lose focus; everything becomes a blur. Then there's the smell. Decay. Mud. Something acidic bites the inside of my nose. I climb to my feet, wishing everything smelt of firewood and ash instead. "Burning this place down would probably do it a favor." But then, they've done that before. They tried to burn Baltimore so many times. The city has seen so much blood, riot after riot, they still build more on top of it and we still live here. No one's alarmed when you see a black bag and think, *who's in there* instead of *who left their fucking garbage laying around?*

Everyone in this city is always angry—has always been angry—will always be angry. Bash the windows, bash your neighbor in the nose, take whatever shiny thing you see in the store, you deserve it. From the destruction of the *Federal Republican* in 1812 where the newspaper was razed to the bank riots in 1835 where gold gates couldn't protect the city's wealthiest from those who lost millions at their hands. What about the election riots in 1856, 57, 58, and 59? The streets were so rosy red, even *New York Times* noticed when they called it, "one of the most daring insurrectionary riots of bloodshed and murder that ever disgraced a city." Then there was the railroad strike of 1877. How about the Red Summer of 1919? The 1968 riots? Then, we can't forget the more recent events over Freddie Gray from just a few years ago.

Lust for death is the lifeblood of this city. The blood of god knows how many people has been eaten by our yards and fills our pipes and glasses and our showers and it drives people crazy. With your windows open in summer, you can feel your neighbor's rage coming in with the breeze. In winter, it taps on the glass with a tree's finger saying, "let me in." Walking around the city is draining, at least, certain parts of it, and you can feel it when you pass into the wrong street—like a negative energy field surrounds specific areas, neighborhoods, buildings. It drags the worst out of you. I should love this city. I grew up here; it's the only place I've ever known, but all I can ever think about is what it'd be like if I rented a car, went pedal to the floor, and got the hell out of Maryland altogether.

In fifth grade, my class took a field trip out to Pennsylvania to see the Liberty Bell and the Second Continental Congress at the Independence Hall where the Declaration of Independence was signed. I didn't care so much about the sites, but when the bus crossed state borders, I felt the change. Like electricity in the air, I was lighter, the water bluer, the sky brighter. My parents were a thing of the past, left in their graves in Baltimore. When it was time to head home, I tried to hide in a 7-11 a couple blocks from the Liberty Bell. I dove behind aisles with a blue and red Slurpee in hand while one of the chaperons desperately tried to catch sight of me. The store owner cornered me and handed me back.

On the bus, we hit Maryland again and I felt it in my skin. The rage stands at the state border, waiting for you to return to infect you again. Coming back, I felt dirty and heavy and I scratched and picked at myself until my arms were red and bleeding. I've thought about leaving this goddamn city so many times and not looking back, but I never could just do it. Just a couple bucks for a bus ticket and I'd be out. But I couldn't leave Wayland. It made me think too much of the way my mom booked it on me, and I told myself I'd never do that to someone. I had to wait for him to leave me first. I honestly thought he would. Skipping class, cheating, dropping out, badge run-ins, constant detention, and taking his chips at lunch, but no matter the mess I made; he wouldn't do it. When I showed up at his house looking trashed or with a black eye from a brawl with pop, he wouldn't say anything about it. We'd go to McDonald's instead and feast on French fries, nuggets, and soft serve. Wayland was probably the only good person in Baltimore. Now? It might not even have that.

I turn to the body on the ground. A car passes by, slowing down as it comes level with me. I make eye contact with the driver who looks like he's telling me *I can keep a secret* with his eyes hoping I won't chase him down. Then he steps on the gas and speeds out of the park. I dig my phone out and dial 911. I tell them about the dead guy, no rush, he's dead, 100 percent. Yup, there's absolutely *no* saving him. "The reaper came and took away his sweet, little soul." Another car drives by, stares at me as they slow, and then speeds off. When the operator asks for my name, I hang up. Then I call Jag and ask him to come get me.

I pick up my skateboard, busted in half where Wayland knocked the guy over the head with it. I look around for any sign of Wayland, but there's nothing. I wait for Jag in the parking lot by the Orianda House. Jag flashes his lights at me when he pulls up. I get in and toss my board into the backseat. The cab lights cast over my face. I shield my eyes.

Jag says, "you look like shit."

I say, "don't go that way."

Sirens draw closer. The dark trees are painted with flashing blue and red light. Jag looks at me and says, "what did you do?"

I put my hand on his thigh, giving it a nice squeeze. "Might want to get out of here *before* they come looking for witnesses."

Jag puts the car into drive, though he lets me know he doesn't want to with a groan. "Talk," he says.

I watch the darkness around MP pass by out the window. Nothing about it feels familiar but the feeling of the city against my body. Everything's a struggle, even keeping my eyes open, even taking a breath. My heart's pounding again. I think I'm trembling. I open the window. "Can't talk right now, Jay," I mutter.

"Give me one good reason why I shouldn't take you to the badges right now," Jag says.

"Because… you *kinda* like me and you fucking hate the badges."

"Yeah. And I hate them showing up at my doorstep looking for you for a lot of reasons. Donny's got questions. You're gonna be lucky if you've got a job next week."

"Donny's not gonna fire me over this. Who the hell would he even hire in my place? An *actual* felon? Sounds like a good trade." I open my eyes.

Jag's staring at the road. His hands are tight around the steering wheel. "I need you to tell me what's going on, Joey."

I rub my eyes, my face hurts to touch. There's no getting away. "I need a beer. So… how about that and I'll tell you what I know?"

"Deal."

TWELVE.

Four empty beer glasses litter the counter. I shouldn't be drinking so much. I think I work tomorrow—I'm sure I work tomorrow—it feels like I haven't been to the garage in days—but I'm thirsty for a second to forget everything. The bar's loud with some shitty song muting every other word coming out of the singer's mouth like none of us have heard words like cunt or pussy or cheap ass whore before. I slide off the barstool. I've been sitting on it so long, my ass hurts. I stumble back on the uneven floor, spotty vision, my feet can't decide on which direction to go. I reach for the bar; Jag grabs hold of my arm.

"Where are you going?" Jag says.

"It's crazy, Jay."

Jag reels me back from the middle of the room. I don't go to him, but the bar presses into my chest. I reach for an empty glass of cider, hold it to my lips, and drain a single drop stuck in the bottom rim. I hold it to my mouth a while longer, waiting for more to come out, there has to be more, just takes a little time, like turning shampoo on its head to get the last drop out. No more cider comes out. I put the glass down. "Cross isn't a killer."

"But he killed that guy in the park… and probably the guy in his trunk… and probably some other people we don't know about yet."

"But he's *not* a *killer.*"

Jag releases my arm. He reaches for a glass of water but doesn't take a drink. "I think you need to just get over it, Joey. Get over him. He knew what he was doing. He knows what he's done. He left that corpse on the road with you to call the badges. If he was innocent, he wouldn't have run and *he* would've made the call—"

"You think he doesn't know he's in trouble? Why the hell would he call the badges?'

"Why the hell did *you* call the badges?"

"For roadkill pickup. That's it. I'm not the boot-licking narc you seem to want me to be. God—Jag—I never thought *you,* of all people, would be like this. Like, this is pretty neh. For real."

"Neh?" Jag turns to me.

"Yeah. *Neh.*" I lean in on the word and stick out my tongue.

Jag's smiling but trying not to.

"I thought Cross was delicate. The student. Scholar. Would-be doctor. Liked things clean and in order. Afraid of authorities. He wouldn't even raise his voice to answer questions in the back of the class. You're all opposites. Do you even own a shirt that's not stained by grease or sweat or whatever? You're supposed to be the bad boy, Jay."

"Bad boy and serial killer aren't synonyms."

"Synonyms? God—When did you get so smart, Jay?" I laugh softly. Leaning back, the counter digs into the small of my back. Across the bar, faces blur until they're featureless, laughter is a pointless filler where conversation is nonsense noise.

Is anyone actually hearing each other?

I wipe the blur out of my eyes. My face is hot to touch

and my heart's racing again. "I think I'm gonna be sick." It doesn't feel like I said anything, but I'm pushing away from the counter. I'm not drunk. Not *that* drunk. Not after two beers… and a couple of shots. Jag's voice feels further away than it is. I don't know what he's saying, but I say "bathroom," in response.

One of the stalls is in use when I get there. Some girl's sitting on the ground, desperately holding onto the toilet and emptying her stomach into the bowl. I lean against the sink, turn the cold water on, and just let it run. My eyeliner's smeared down my red cheeks and my left cheek is redder and bigger than it was earlier. No wonder it's getting hard to see. I should've iced it more. Maybe when we get back to Jag's place I'll do that.

A chill goes down my spine.

The girl's chucking so loud.

Sounds from the street pour in through the open window in the back of the room.

Tires. A honk. The soft murmur of music and a back-alley deal going down. A caw.

My fingers curl into the sink for balance. There's something on my face, but I can't see it through the steam on the mirror. Steam? On the mirror? Where did that even come from? I wipe it away. Water clings to my fingers. Everything's cold down my arm. I can't breathe. My fingers curl harder into the counter and even the hard panting I'm doing is only letting in a little bit of air. I grab at my arms. My shoulders itch with irritation like something needs to be pressing down on them to make it stop. My cheek throbs and my vision threatens to give out again.

A sharp breath in.

I feel his hand smack into my face. It's that same, empty feeling of the arms wrapping around me, what I felt when I held Wayland.

I press the back of my hand to my forehead. Fuck. I think I have a fever. Paper towels under the faucet, I press them against my head. The cold-water soaks in, drips down my face, starts to burn. I hiss, yank more paper towels out of the bin to wipe the water off my face. I turn the sink off and toss the paper towels down. The wet mixes with the dry on the floor and the counter and the sink. The water's not draining. I glance toward the busy stall. To the sound of another dry heave, I slip out of the bathroom. The bar feels hotter, but my skin's like ice. In the back of the room, a big guy stands up, smacking his hand down on the table. He's tall, got short hair, I feel like I know him from somewhere.

"You're scamming me, you goddamn cheat!" A glass shatters against the floor. He's yanking another man out of his seat. Everyone else at the table stands up, steps back. Some of them reach for their pockets, some have hands raised. I can't tell if they want to fight the guy or flee. The big guy curls his fingers tighter into the other man's shirt and yanks him close. "You're gonna give me what you owe or I'm gonna break your fucking neck. You got that?" The big guy shoves the other man back. Tripping over his own feet, a table, a couple other patrons, he falls into the bar.

"Whoa, whoa, whoa," the bartender says. He comes around from behind the bar. "You need to calm down." He steps between the big guy and the man he pushed, putting his hands up toward the big guy.

The big guy sneers. "Who the hell do you think you are?" He laughs in a way that says, "you want some too?"

"Pick up your stuff and get out—"

"You need to mind your own goddamn business!" The big guy grabs the bartender by the shirt and throws him into the counter, shoving him across it to where Jag is. Jag stands back. The big guy moves toward the bartender, eager and focused, but something stops him. It's unnatural, fast, and sharp. His eyes turn on me. He's stiff and breathing hard. He looks so familiar, but that's just the way of this city. There are so many faces between buses, bars, malls, restaurants, sidewalks, beggars, and the political class that steps over them. Almost everyone from this city gives off a vague feeling of familiarity. They feel like a distant family member you just never see, but you've seen their picture up on the internet every now and then. Visitors here don't feel like they belong, and they all feel the same too. It doesn't matter where they're from. They're like a bottle of vodka poured into punch: discolored, barely noticeable, but just enough you can tell something isn't right. "Who are you?" the big guy says to me. "Where do I know you from?"

"We're leaving," Jag says. I don't know where he came from, but he's pulling on my arm.

I'm going along without resistance, but I can't take my eyes off the big guy.

He's quick to catch up, grab me by the arm, and pull me back. "I don't know." His voice rolls in his throat, tight, desperate to escape. "Who are you?" He's panting with rage. I've never heard someone so angry. Redness circles his eyes, too dark and persistent to be drunk and not like any rash I've ever seen. His eyes are reflective, empty, and missing something obvious. From close up, the big guy's irises are completely black, the whites of his eyes are bloodshot, and spotty burns trail down his jaw, his neck, and lace against his hands like delicate red tattoos. "Where do I know you from? You owe me money, bitch?"

"No, I don't owe you money." My jaw tightens.

Jag pulls me harder then steps between the big guy and me. "Hey, buddy, you've got the wrong person."

The big guy grabs Jag by the arm, yanks him forward, and tosses him into one of the nearby tables. Glasses crash onto the floor. Fried potatoes squish under shoes, nachos, chicken wings, and beer scatter. Wine fills in the cracks in the wood like blood running through veins. A couple people offer to help Jag up, but he pushes them back and stands on his own.

The big guy moves closer to me. "Where the hell do I know you from?" he says through heavy breath. His focus on me is like a lion stalking its prey: deep and unrelenting. With every step away I take, he's still moving toward me at the same speed.

"I don't know you." I watch him with the same level of focus.

"I don't forget faces. If I know you, you did something to me. Say it now, I'll go easy on you. How's that?" The big guy says.

I shake my head slowly. "I don't make deals with the badges and I definitely don't make deals with the fucking devil." The connection hits me fast in that moment. Everything comes back like a flood. The face, the voice, the scream. "Wait—" My back hits the wall beside the bathroom hall. A soft jingle of chains rattles under the music.

"Too late to change my mind, bitch—"

"You're that guy that jumped into the river. Styx. You remember the bar? The boat? The gates? The reaper?"

He's getting closer, something pulses through his eye. An emotion, panic, terror, anger, all at once and he runs at me. His hands wrap around my neck and he's lifting me. My feet come off the floor. Reaching for his arm, I struggle against the wall. My head hits it again and again until the back of my head is throbbing just as much as the front. I try to speak, but his hand cuts most of the air off.

"S-stop—B-bastard," I choke out.

His hand tightens around my neck. He's not saying anything but yelling incoherently and seething hatred in each breath. My back curls against the wall as he drags me against it, turns, throws me at the bar. I cough, choking on how desperately I want air. Jag comes from behind and shoves the big guy into the wall. The big guy turns around, sweeping the space around him. He misses Jag. Jag goes in and slams his fist into the big guy's face. Jab, jab, cross, he steps back.

I peel off the bar, coughing before I even try to speak.

My throat's tight. My back aches. I try to force my breath deep, but I can't fill my lungs. "Ah… What are you…? Why are you here? You're supposed to be dead," I'm muttering. Some of the patrons stand around me. I vaguely hear someone say, "are you okay?" in the mixture of all the other noise. But at that moment, none of the pain I feel means anything. I have to know how this guy—this dead man escaped the river, judgment, death. I don't want to believe any of it, but behind the still playing music in the bar, the snapping words, voices, chains, and anger, I swear I can still hear the big guy screaming as the waves of Styx suck him under, burn off his skin, and swallow him whole, the hollow howls of desperation echoing until it took him away.

I push away the people trying to help me, them acting like a wall between me and the big guy. One of them is saying something like, "what are you doing? Don't worry about him. Dude's insane. Don't get in the middle of it—" but nothing they say is more important than finding out where the hell he came from and how the hell he's here.

"You're dead," I say over the noise. It's not a threat, but a statement. Everyone in the bar goes quiet, I think they took it the wrong way. The big guy turns away from Jag to face me.

"You think you wanna fight? You're nothing. I've been through Hell to get back here and I'm not going back. You understand that? If you don't shut your mouth and get the hell out of my sight, I'm going to end you. I'm not escaped. I'm free. You're here too, aren't you? So, who are you to condemn me for my freedom?" He comes at me fast. "You won't be free for long. Just seeing your face—God—" Pleasure mixes with anger. "I want to see you battered and mashed all over the sidewalk." He grabs me and tosses me into another table. Growling, snarling, his rage isn't human.

While he runs toward me again, the bartender comes out from behind the counter, this time, shotgun in hand. He points it toward the big guy with ease and familiarity. "Get out, now," the bartender says.

The big guy doesn't stop his pursuit. The bartender pulls the trigger. A shell empties into the big guy. His shirt splits in small holes all over the fabric and the power of the blast pushes him back. He slams onto the floor, now blood mixes with wine, beer, food, and broken glass. Sirens ring outside before blue and red lights filter in through the bar window. Rattling chains have been getting louder, they're outside the door, surrounding the bar now like they had in the forest.

The big guy twitches. His hand slams into the ground. He pushes himself to his feet. The bartender takes aim for another shot, but before he can do anything, the big guy shoves past, making his way behind the bar, to the kitchen, and maybe out into the back alley. "Holy shit—how'd he gets up from that?" Jag's saying. The bartender with the shotgun trails after the big guy. There's rattling of glass and dishes, but then there's nothing and he comes back out of the kitchen alone. "Oh my god – I think – there's someone in the bathroom!" someone shrieks.

Another bartender greets the badges at the door. Jag puts his hand on my shoulder. I shrug him off. "We need to go," he says. I know he's right, but I don't want to go. We move to the back of the crowd. Badges order everyone to one side of the bar so they can conduct their interviews. Jag and I leave while the badges are getting a statement from the bartender.

We aren't the only ones who split.

Jag's car is parked a couple blocks away and neither of us say anything until we get inside, lock the doors, and we're on the way to his place. The radio's off. The silence is heavy. So is my head. I turn on the radio. Jag turns it off. I groan and close my eyes. "Who the hell was that guy and why did he want to kill you, Joey?"

"I don't know him—"

"Bullshit," Jag says. "He knew you. He was damn sure of it. You owe him something you didn't want to talk about?

Or what, was he involved with Cross? What kind of shit did you get yourself into? A murder plot between your best friend and a sleazy conman at a bar? I get people aren't who they pretend to be, but looks like your type-A Valedictorian doctor friend isn't anything like he led you to believe—He lied to you, Joey—"

"You're gonna think I'm insane, Jay—"

"Too late for that." Jag shook his head with a short laugh. "Humor me. Who was he?"

I'm quiet for a while, biting my lip, actually considering the truth. I didn't like the truth. People had a hard time believing it. Lies gave easy answers and kept things simple so long as you remembered them. "That guy was dead, Jag." Tears burn in my eyes, but I refuse to let them get out. I'm just tired and frustrated and wished I was ten times drunker than I am right now. My fingers curl into my pants. "You wouldn't understand."

Jag steps on the breaks, hard. I fly into the seat belt's embrace and slam back into the seat. He puts the car in park. "What do you mean *he's dead*, Joey? That guy was clearly *not dead*."

"I told you you'd think I'm insane," I mutter. I'm biting my lip. Hands squeezed between my thighs. Out the window, I swear something's reflecting in the distance. Bright, round, dark, and deep, like a small rock in the sky, but I can't see anything beyond the side of the road. "Dead, Jay. There's pretty much only one meaning to the word. You know it?"

"There are a lot of meanings to the word, like a figurative threat." He takes a moment to breathe. He rubs his head, his eyes, sighs hard. His voice is getting too high. "That guy owe you something?"

I snort a laugh. "It's not me he cheated."

"Then who did he think you were?"

"He didn't mistake me for anyone, Jay. I just know where he came from."

175

"Would you stop being so fucking cryptic and tell me what kind of trouble you're in? Is he the reason Cross is missing?"

"From Hell, Jagger. I know him from Hell—"

"Get real, Joey—"

"No, Jag, you get fucking real. I don't know what the hell's going on, but I've been seeing some weird shit ever since Cross went missing and all I know is I saw that guy in what I thought was a fever dream where there were ghosts and a bar and a reaper and a crow that looked like a person. Yeah—I know it sounds insane and I don't know how any of this works. But I watched that guy run into the river and the water grabbed him like it grabbed me when we were at Gwynns, except he fell in and that was the last time I saw him. He was supposed to be dead—"

"If you were somehow where dead people go, how the hell are you here now?"

"I don't fucking know, Jag! I don't know how I was there either—but I keep seeing them here. The people from that place and then there's my dad—"

"What about your dad?"

"He died a long time ago, Jag."

"What the hell are you talking about? Your dad's back at your house where he's always been. You sound crazy!"

"Maybe I am!" I slam my feet into the dash. Car door open. Seatbelt flings back and I'm outside. "Maybe I have really lost it. But my only guess is that guy was mad because I saw him run from his own death. What the hell does that mean? You got me. Everything has been so insane since Cross disappeared, I can't keep up!" The tears force their way out. I turn away and wipe my cheeks fast like it'd stop Jag from seeing.

"Joey, you've got a fever. You're stressed. You need to go home and sleep it off—"

I slam the car door shut. Jag climbs out of his side and tells me to get back in. I ignore him and walk down the street. When I'm at the corner, he's slowly following me with his car while he tries to talk to me through the open passenger window, but nothing he says matters. I hear his voice, but his words dissolve in the air.

They're back.

The ravens.

Only one or two of them now, but every time I turn a corner, I see one. In a tree, on a roof, picking at garbage in the road. They're watching me. My heart's racing so loud, I can't hear my own thoughts. I turn back to Jag and lean into the open passenger window. I want to ask him if he sees the birds yet, but instead, I say, "take care of yourself, Jay. I don't want anything to happen to you and… it's looking pretty hellish out right now."

He grabs my arm as I pull back and he says, "Joey, what are you going to do? Please, just get in the car."

"That's the problem, Jay… I don't know what I'm doing. I don't know how to make it stop." A tear goes down my cheek. I shake my head, turn away, try to wipe it away in a way he won't see.

"Please come home with me, Joey."

I suck on my lip ring. "I don't think I can, Jay. I need to go home. I need to check on dad."

"Then please, let me take you home."

My skin's cold. Everything's cold. My arm stings and my body doesn't want to move. Jag releases my arm slowly and falls back into place in his seat.

I pull the door open and sit back down in the passenger. I cover my eyes, rubbing at them to look like I'm tired, but I'm trying to push back the tears I feel coming. "Please take me home," I say.

"Okay," Jag says, though I know he doesn't want to. I know he doesn't understand why I keep going back to that place, to my dad, to my room, but it's the only way I can preserve myself.

Without looking, I find his hand on the shift between the

seats. His fingers curl around mine. I force my foot to bounce during the ride to make sure I don't pass out and end up at Jag's house. We both know that it would be better for me, safer, quieter. His house was almost everything I wanted my home to be, but I had to take care of my dad; I couldn't stay out; I couldn't make him angry. Because of that, Jag took me home.

THIRTEEN.

"What if I spent the night?" Jag says as I close the passenger door to his Mustang.

I'm sure I'm smiling too wide when I tell him, "Too much testosterone in the house makes my dad feel *scrappy*."

"I think I'd be down for a fight," Jag says.

"I'm not." I'm walking away backwards. "Good night, Jag." I wave.

The frozen, dead grass of the trailer park crunches underneath my sneakers. The living room windows at the house flash with TV light. The worst part about it is I never know if he's awake. The door's unlocked as usual when I try it. *Family Feud* buzzers ring on the television before the station switches with a soft buzz I haven't heard since dad got a flat screen. The last TV died when he threw a bottle at the screen. One day, he came home carrying the box. I didn't want to ask where he got it from. Didn't feel like getting smacked.

A local news station plays upbeat music as shots of Baltimore slide across the screen. The blue backgrounds highlighting the stats on the screen feel disingenuous, like

179

the screen trying to lie about what's in front of our faces. Maybe you won't see the murder rate as a negative if it's coated in a positive blue color. Maybe you won't think about the robberies if it's counted next to how many it *could* have been instead of what we got. "Remember to lock your doors," says Anderson, the reporter. I don't normally agree with mics, but I do what he says this time and lock the door. There's reason enough not to listen to them. They make their living on the misery of others. *If it bleeds, it leads*, I've heard them say. Your pain fills their pockets, and I won't forget the way they talked about my neighbor when she overdosed three summers ago. Or how they stood at my door when I was eight and thrusted their microphones in my face to ask how I felt after losing my dad. They asked what I thought about suicide prevention and drugs and alcohol and crime. They asked if my dad was a drinker. They asked about poverty. They asked if he was impotent. Then one of them, some girl with brown hair from Channel 2 who looked like she lived in a high rise, asked where my mom was. I slammed the door and hid in the closet until the badges came knocking, and even then, I didn't answer, because I didn't want to leave.

There was a notice on the door the next morning. An order declaring my home a place of investigation—just to make sure it was my dad who killed himself and not someone who snuck in to rob us. But the badges never came to investigate. The wind blew the notice free. The media forgot about me, the state forgot about me, and three days later, my dad was sitting back in his chair, filled with more rage than I'd ever seen before. The smallest noise set him off. He broke down the bathroom door just to get me for setting off the microwave while making popcorn. For running out of vodka. For the remote battery dying. Fuck. I felt horrible thinking I liked it better the three days he was dead. I didn't question how he was back or the bloodshot eyes, the darkness in his face, how cold he felt when he grabbed my arm.

I slip through the kitchen for a better chance of avoiding him. The trailer's dark outside of the light from the television. In my room, I lock the door even though the latch is busted. Jag's lights are still on the other side of my blinds. He sends me a text asking if I really want to stay here tonight. I just say, 'yeah, thanks," then I almost send, 'love you, Jay,' but I delete it. I've never said that before. To say it now just tells me I'm too tired and too drunk. I slip my shoes off but keep my coat on to lay on my bed. I fall asleep trying to light a cigarette, thinking maybe that would make me feel warm.

In the morning, I'm not woken by my alarm, but my doorknob jiggling, a fist against the door, the weak wood kicks open, bounces back shut. "Josephine!" my dad says. Another smack. Another bounce. I sit up in a cold sweat. "What the hell did you do?" My dad shoves the door open. I'm pulling on my shoes. I check my jacket for my phone. It's plugged in on the nightstand. "The badges—Why the hell are badges here?"

"I dunno, pop! Maybe you should go outside and ask! For all you know, they're here for you!"

"Why would they come for me?"

"I don't know—being a bastard?"

"And you wonder why we're here alone!"

"I don't wonder a goddamn thing—"

I run to the window. I'm flipping the window locks. The bottom one comes off easy, the top one's stuck. Trying to turn it, the metal digs into my fingers. It can't be frozen. It opened the other day. Dad grabs me by my jacket and yanks me away from the window. I trip back onto my bed. His hands immediately go for my throat.

"You outta be grateful for what you got, kid. Where the hell do you get off having that attitude around here?" dad says, tightening his fingers fast.

I can't breathe enough to respond. I'm coughing,

kicking, trying to elbow him in the face. My feet slam into his stomach. He staggers back. I don't have time to think before I roll off the bed and run down the hall. To hell with the badges. I'm out the door, running down the steps. Detective Stone steps back as I push past him. He grabs me by the arm, but let's go when I yank, him not prepared for my resistance. "S'cuse me, officer. I'm late for something." I'm running down the street. I don't know where my dad is, if he's still in the house, looking out the window, talking to the badges.

None of it matters as much as getting some distance between us. I'm running and running and struggling to breathe and still feeling his hands around my throat and the spark of his desire to kill me. All of his strength, whatever life is in him pulsed through his body and came through his fingers, and the flush of emotion I felt from that, his hatred, his fury, his blame and pain and desire for destruction.

My chest aches. My legs are weak and shaking. My throat feels small, swollen, damaged... something. I stop running and lean against a nearby fence as if it's going to help me breathe. I can't, though. It all hurts. I'm trembling when light-headedness washes over me. I press my back into the fence. It's weak, rusted, and giving out underneath even a little bit of my weight. I get off the chain-link and look through it.

Behind cracked glass, broken blinds hang in the window on the other side. A Christmas wreath sits on the welcome mat in front of the door. Tears pool in my eyes and run down my cheeks in freezing trails. I'm digging out my phone and pull up Jag's number.

"Hey, you have a minute to talk?" a voice says from behind me.

I wipe the water from my eyes with the back of my hand while sucking in my nose like the cold's gotten to me. I slip my phone away.

Detective Stone stands behind me with a casual smile

and a nod good morning. He holds out his badge. "You remember me?"

"How could I forget? We've been making habits together." I wipe my eyes again. Black eyeliner smears across the backside of my hand. I try to wipe it off on my jeans. "What do you want?"

"Got a couple of questions for you," Stone says. With a pause, his head drops to the side. "What happened to your eye? Get in a fight?"

"If you want to talk to me, you better get a warrant."

"I had a feeling you'd say that." Detective stone reaches into his coat and he pulls out a piece of folded paper. He holds it out for me to read. The page proclaims a search warrant on trespassing, disturbing a crime scene, suspicion of conspiracy, accomplice, or attempt at evidence tampering. "God, I hate badges… What the hell do you want to ask?"

"I think it's better if we head back to the precinct before getting into it," Stone says.

"I really don't want to." I'm whinier than I mean to be.

"Well, you can come because you want to, or you can come because you have to. Your choice." As he speaks, he pushes his coat back and places his hand on his belt near his pair of handcuffs. I'm staring at them, then back at Stone's face and back down. I look past him down the street and to the empty house beside me. I wonder if I could outrun him, but I'm also smart enough to already know the answer. Maybe the warrant is just a prop to try and get me to confess. I've seen that in documentaries before too. "If you want to run, you can," Stone says, "but you will be coming to the station to answer a couple of questions either way. Just depends on how fast you want to get in and out."

I rub my eyes again. "Don't you think I've been through enough this morning already?"

"Why's that?"

"My dad was pretty burnt. You didn't catch him at the

door?"

Stone gives me a look like he thinks I'm crazy. I know the look well. I got it from so many teachers back in school every time I wore torn jeans or a chain on my pants or wrote some bullshit answer on my paper because the questions they were asking were stupid. Who the hell cares about the allegory in The Scarlet Letter? At least I broke through his fake, friendly smile. "He was in the house," I say. "You detaining him for questioning too?"

"No one else came to the door after you came out, but we can look into your dad too if you think he's important. You have a name for him?"

My heart's racing.

The throbbing chill around my neck where his fingers held me not that long ago.

I curl my fingers gently around my neck. The warmth of my hand doesn't do much to cover the chill; he's still suffocating me. "No. He's dead to me."

The detective turns his head to the side. "Dead to you? Why is that?"

"Didn't you say you wanted to talk to me somewhere else?" I push past the guy and head back toward the trailer park where Stone's cruiser sits in front of my house. It's almost as picturesque as the flamingos in the yard across the street. A couple of ravens dot the path to the cruiser. One on the neighbor's house, one on the tree in the yard across the street, and one on the stair rails at my house. The bird watches me come down the street, reach the cruiser, pause, and watch it back. I swing my arm toward it, hoping it startles and flies away, but it doesn't move. I run toward it, swing again, but not near enough to touch it. Again, the thing doesn't move, only watches. "Don't you dare say anything to me. Whatever you are. Just do your damn job and leave me the hell alone, alright? You got that, you stupid bird? Go eat a goddamn heart and get out of my face!" I turn back around to the cruiser. Detective Stone stands on the other side of the car by the driver's door, watching from a distance with a smile that tells me he's judging me, thinking maybe I'm nuts and maybe those handcuffs would have been a better decision than just having me climb in the car myself.

"You okay?" he says.

"Peachy." I get into the passenger side of the cruiser. Stone doesn't stop me, apparently not freaked out enough to think I'll attack him on the way to the station. "Is that coffee offer still good or no?"

Stone chuckles. "I'll see what I can do for you when we get back to the station."

I don't know if the interrogation room is the same one I was in a couple days ago. They all look the same. Low, gray lights, walls that might be white, might be gray, with short gray carpet probably first laid in the seventies, if that. The metal chair's cold. Stone sets a couple cups of coffee down and drops some bags of sugar and creamer down too. He doesn't use any of them. "Don't I get a phone call or something?" I say after a while.

"You're not under arrest. And even if you were… the kind of stuff you see on TV isn't entirely accurate to how this actually works," Stone says.

"Oh, great. So… *everything's* a lie? I like that. Better to know I don't know anything from the outset and let it all fuck me up, right?" I sit back, crossing my arms.

"You can go as soon as you answer a couple of questions—"

"Somehow, I don't believe you."

"The quicker you talk, the quicker you're back to your life."

"Unless you decide you don't like me for whatever reason. I mean, hey—" I uncross my arms and lean forward. My hands press into the chair between my legs. "Do you get paid based on how many people you catch or how exactly does this all work? You get your name in the paper for some killing spree? You get a book deal once you hit a certain threshold? You get a nickname around the station? What is it you're after in all this?"

"Answers. Justice. You know, the usual things." Detective Stone sips at his coffee.

I snort a chuckle in response. He lowers the coffee from his lips to give me a look. "Sorry. I know BPD a little too well to believe that shit, but... *you do you*, Rocky."

He takes a long sip from the Styrofoam cup, emptying it. "How did you come across the body last night in Leakin Park?"

"I don't know." I lean back. "I was going for a nice little walk and apparently someone dumped it. Kind of what the park's known for. Not really *that* surprising, is it?" I cross my arms.

"You seem to have a knack for finding bodies," Rocky says.

"And what a great superpower it's been, eh? Maybe I should apply for a job here. Need a cadaver dog?" I snort.

"Why didn't you stick around for the emergency vehicles to arrive?"

"Because I didn't want to fucking be here right now. I didn't kill that guy. Someone jumped him in the middle of the night and goddamn, no good deed goes unpunished, does it? If only I left him for some other poor sap to call it in or maybe they would've been smarter than me and just kicked it into the woods and moved on. At least they wouldn't be here right now." I kick my legs up on the empty chair tucked under the table.

"And the scene at the bar? What happened there?" Stone says. "Another body in the bathroom and that fight with the big guy? You know... A sign that a serial killer is tumbling out of control is an increase in bodies, an increase in recklessness."

I suck at my lip ring. I stroke my short, black hair into place, letting the strands go between my fingers. A groan escapes in my exhalation. "What the hell do you want me to say?"

"What happened?" Stone says again.

"What the hell do you think happened? The woman in the bathroom was fine when I left and some meth'ed out asshole lost his shit and attacked a bunch of randos, got shot, and ran out because that's what meth does. I didn't have anything to do with it. I was barely even at the bar—"

"That's not what the bartender said."

"And pray, *Rocky*, do tell what the good ol' bartender told you. I'm kind of dying to know." I lean forward, elbow on the table. I eye the untouched cup of coffee and resist the urge to knock it over, play the stupid, clumsy girl, and maybe get a couple seconds of peace while Rocky dabs the liquid off his pants.

The detective moves the cup further back from me and tucks it against the wall. "For safety," he says.

"Right." I roll my eyes. Arms cross again, I kick my feet back onto the empty chair under the table. "Safety. Thanks, *dad*."

"So, what'd the guy want with you? An old score to settle?" Stone says.

"How the hell should I know what he wanted?"

"Bartender said he knew you."

"*Knew* is a very… loose way to describe what we had to do with each other."

"You hire him to transport faceless bodies? Maybe help out your missing friend? Get him IDs, make him disappear, and drop off the car in the park in the same place where that body was found last night—the one *you* called in?"

My feet plant firmly on the floor. "When you put it together like that, it definitely doesn't sound good." I'm trying not to sound interested, but I can hear the high note in my own voice. I see my interest reflect in Rocky's eyes, his tight-lipped smirk, the air of arrogance coming off him like cologne he freshly applied. "It's an interesting guess, but

I didn't do any business with that guy."

"Bartender said you owed him."

"The bartender's a liar and a fucking narc."

"And what did he *narc* about?"

"At his point, nothing. He's telling stories, but I know that's all you people like." I stand up, turn away from the table, and pace toward the one-way glass. There are badges on the other side, looking at my face as they come up with some kind of weak charges against me if it takes me off the street, then they can report to their superiors they caught another bit of Baltimore scum and keep looking for anything they can hold against me. They make people disappear off the streets and sure, some of them *are* bad, but you know how many bad ones get away and the rest of us have to deal with them?

It never mattered how many times badges were called to Deadwood. They showed up often enough I could tell the sound of their tread when they came down the street, but what did they actually do? After tens of visits from badges, social workers, and concerned neighbors, my dad was the only one who could stop himself from hurting anyone anymore and even that didn't work.

"Can we just get down to why you really have me here?" I say. "The warrant wasn't about the bar." I turn around to face the detective. My foot taps eagerly against the floor, unspent energy building up, impatience, the racing of my thoughts. I blink to chase back the burning in my eyes. "Being tired is the worst." I force out a chuckle. Stone won't believe I'm tired, but I'll pretend he does.

"What was in that email Wayland sent you?" Stone says.

"I don't know what you're talking about. I haven't heard from Wayland since the day I picked up his car. Kinda wish it wasn't true, but haven't seen him, haven't heard from him, haven't called him." My heart's racing, but I'm hoping it's not too obvious. I take a slow, steady breath and come back to the chair. I drink the coffee to distract myself even though I know it's a trap. I rip open a couple sugar packets and dump them into the small cup, then comes two creamers. A taste, then another creamer. "If you've got any information on my friend though, I've been looking for him. I'm sure you know that. You wanna share stories? Something like 'you scratch my back, I'll scratch yours?' What do you have on him? That kind of thing."

"We saw the email sent from his account. It looks like someone had been in his house. Someone reported you in the neighborhood—"

"Sounds like someone's got a day job drinking." I bring the coffee to my lips. I wait for the detective to ask another question, but he doesn't say anything. "If this is all you've got to say, can I leave yet?"

"We can keep you for up to forty-eight hours unless you wanna talk."

"Party. Guess I'll get to know my digs for the next two days." I pick up the seat and move it from the table to the corner of the room farthest from the detective. I set it up facing him before sitting back down, leg over leg, and sip at the coffee slowly. After thirty minutes of staring into the one-way mirror and the wall clock clicking without pause, the detective gets up and says he's stepping out for lunch and to just say it if I want to talk to someone. I tip my mostly empty cup at him. "Have a good lunch, Rocky. You deserve it." I wink. He leaves.

For the first hour after that, the empty confession room is nice. Alone with myself, I lay on the floor, spreading my arms and legs out. I check my phone. A message from Jag appears asking if I'm coming to work tonight.

JAG	You're on the schedule.
JOEY	I'm trying to get there.
JOEY	My board's busted tho.
JAG	I don't think D will accept that.
JAG	I can pick you up?

JOEY	No.
JOEY	He's gonna have to try if you ever wanna see me again.
JAG	I don't think that'll work.
JOEY	Try?
JAG	Badges visited this morning, asking about you.
JOEY	Good thing I didn't spend the night.
JOEY	Hope you only said nice things.
JAG	This is serious, Joey.
JAG	I'm worried about you.
JOEY	I didn't kill anyone, J.
JAG	I know.
JAG	But this shit's bad.
JOEY	I know. Sorry, J.

I slide my phone back into my pocket, my chest tight. Still laying on the floor, I stretch my foot out to hook around one of the chairs still at the table and pull it closer. I rest my feet against it, crossed at the ankle. The gray walls are making me dizzy, so I cover my eyes with the back of my arm. The silent room turns into buzzing, then a sharp ringing deep in my ear. I uncover my eyes and look toward the one-way mirror. "Hey." I wave. "Can I get some water?" I sit up slowly. My face stares back at me.

Discoloration darkens my face. My eyes are nothing but black holes. It must be the eyeliner. Streaks run down my cheeks. I use the mirror to try and clean myself off. Black smears catch on my hand, fingers, sleeve, and in the end, my face looks like it's smeared with dirt and red. I rub my eyes again. Black fingerprints trail down my cheeks now. I feel hollow, maybe even dead. "What if I am...?" I get off the floor. I run my fingers against the glass and trace down my face. My phone buzzes. I stiffen, startled at first. The screen reads WAYLAND and the message is 'WHERE ARE YOU?'

JOEY   Badges. U owe me.

I delete the message thread and slide my phone away.

He stares at me from the mirror.

Wayland, in the corner of the room, bangs and shadows cover his face. His lips are downturned. His hands and pants are muddy. A spot in his chest is darkened with dried blood.

"Way—" the words slip out in a whisper. I turn around and he's gone. I push my hair back and sit in the corner again. I don't know how long it's been. No one's come in since Stone left. I've heard sounds outside the door, passing steps, rushing, maybe someone else off to be interviewed or someone making an escape. My head drops back onto the chair backer. I close my eyes.

More time passes. My vision blurs when I try to look at the wall clock. The arms disappear into the white background. My phone shows it's four in the afternoon. I knock on the one-way window. "Hey, I gotta pee. Can you get me an escort or something before I just squat in the corner? That'd be great. Thanks."

I pace the room while I wait.

Knock on the window again. "Hey. You hear me? Bathroom? Please?"

Pacing again.

God, I don't even know if there's still anyone on the other side. For all I know, they've forgotten about me and the next time they show up, it'll be them bringing in some other suspect for questioning and Rocky will be like, "oh? You're still here?" I go to the door and try the knob. Locked. Just after I step back, it opens with an officer standing on the other side.

"You said you needed to go to the bathroom?"

"Yeah. Is that allowed or is pissing myself part of the full badge treatment?" I say.

The officer takes a breath, eyes squinting, then says,

"This way." He waves me in front of him.

"Don't you need to *lead* me there? I'm not exactly sure how to navigate this place, ya know? I'm not really here *that* often."

"No. Go ahead. I'll lead you from behind." He waves me on again. I do as he says. We walk down the hall with him giving me orders. Left. Left. This door. "I'll wait for you out here."

"Thanks, hun. You're a peach." I think about tapping him on the cheek, but at the last second, I give him a thumbs up instead. The last thing I need is to be tackled to the floor and then tossed into a cell because teasing was called 'assault' when it was just the two of us.

I slip into the handicap stall furthest down in the line of three. My stomach growls. I groan to myself. A wave of dizziness comes on again. I lean against the wall and close my eyes. Sinking to the floor, I bury my face in my hands and just focus on breathing until the moment passes.

God. This is miserable. Even the bathrooms smell like the police department. Arrogance coated in sugary donuts and bitter coffee. Was Stone really planning to keep me for two days until I talked to him? I gently knock my head against the wall again and again and think about hitting myself harder until I go unconscious or crack my skull into a bloody mess. I could feign amnesia until they leave me alone.

The moment of dizziness passes. I use the sink and a couple of paper towels to clean the smeared makeup off my face. I wet my hands and comb them through my hair a couple of times. The soft sound of a caw echoes off the bathroom walls. I push open the three empty stalls.

There's nothing.

I'm in here alone.

Another caw. Then another.

These things are seriously everywhere, it's a wonder anyone in this city is even getting delivered at all. The caws sound like the ravens are laughing. In the far, back corner of the bathroom, there's a long window in the wall of the third stall. The glass hangs open with a screen stretched across it. I lock the stall and climb onto the toilet. A raven steps around the side of the building by the dumpster. I glance over the stalls, back toward the door. I thrust my fist into the screen. My hand bounces back, throbbing a bit from shock. The rattling frame squeals. I place my hand against it as if that would make it shush up. I take a quick glance back toward the door to make sure no one in the hall heard.

I slip off my sneaker and put it on my hand. Another smack, then another, harder this time. The screen breaks off and falls to the ground on the other side of the wall. Shoe slipped back on; I reach up for the edge of the window. Upper body's never really been my thing… I curl my arms around the ledge and do a test pull-up. Maybe it won't be as hard as I think. My shallow jean pocket does little to hold onto my phone as I lift my leg, press into the wall, and slide back down. I barely keep it from smacking into the floor. I hold it tightly in my hand for a long moment, then, glance up at the window and back to the phone. My only choice is to toss it out the window first. My only choice now is to get out there so I can grab it. I climb onto the toilet's tank, using the windowsill for balance. I'm at a diagonal to reach it.

I close my eyes. Deep breath. Jump.

Fingers grab the outside of the building. The broken screen frame presses into my stomach. My feet catch on the wall of the bathroom and push me further out the open window. I'm trying to grab something to lower me. The weight becomes too much, too fast. My legs scrape on the window frame and I fall to the concrete below, knocking my head, scraping my hands, twisting my wrist, and landing on my phone. Sitting up, I hiss. My phone's screen is cracked.

A raven across the back lot stares at me, his head twisted to the side. Judgment. He's not even trying to hide it.

IAN KIRKPATRICK

"What are you looking at?" I say as I get up, pocketing the phone again. "Been hanging around badges too much, it's all over your face. Maybe... find somewhere else to spend your day. They aren't gonna help you catch anyone. Speaking of, don't you have a job to be doing? What the hell are you thinking?" What the hell am *I* thinking? The bird doesn't know what the hell I'm saying, and I know how crazy it all sounds by virtue of not telling Jag a damn thing about the city of the dead apparently hiding beneath this godforsaken city. You know, I almost think he might believe me if I told him.

I run out the back end of the police station, carefully navigating past windows and parked cars until I'm down the street and blocks away.

The one good thing about growing up in Baltimore is getting to know her intimately. Short cuts, speed traps, the most popular donut place on the block, or the burger joint and sandwich shops the badges frequent in the neighborhood tell me where to avoid. Boarded-up windows, broken glass, and dead yards don't do so much to tell you which yards you can tread through uninvited like they do in other cities.

The most important thing to carry with you when wandering through the city, beyond the obvious, is the confidence that you belong here. Look like you're lost for even a second and there's someone hiding in the shadows, behind a corner somewhere, waiting for you to slow down, to throw you on the ground, to make you bleed and get a street named after themselves from your suffering. It's not the heroes of this city that create the legends; it's the ones who terrorize us.

Every abandoned building has its eyes on you. Through the blinds, the clicks, the house creaks, moving shadows, gravel, and crackling leaves. The smells follow you: burnt wood, burnt dinner, gunpowder, weed, feces, piss, and blood. The rot isn't contained to MP, but we mostly pretend

194

it is. Being this close to the BPD, the smell comes off that cesspool too. I'm slipping down Front Hill Avenue. A house on the corner is overgrown with weeds. A wooden fence of broken boards lines someone's house, rotted in place.

I shoot Jag a text telling him I'm on my way. A hand slips around my throat while another grabs my jacket and shoves me into the brick siding of a building with boarded-up windows. My phone falls out of my hand. I can't tell if the sun has set or I closed my eyes. I grab at the arm cutting off my breath, desperately gasping for air. I kick, flail, try to push the guy back. My nails dig into skin. My eyes peel open just enough to see it's him. The big guy from the bar. "Wh- what—" I choke out between gasps. "You—" I try to breathe. I'm losing it fast. "Dead."

He laughs something dark, sadistic, short, and choppy. Somewhere between each breath is a snarl. "You threatening me?"

"—N-never—" Saliva dribbles down my chin. The back of my head's throbbing before I realize I've been slammed against the wall. Everything's pulsing and spotty. My face, my chest, my legs are numb. I don't do anything, but think 'breathe, breathe, breathe, get away, breathe.'

Cross, where are you?

Cawing comes in and out. Val's been waiting for me to die for days. My fingers weaken, even though I didn't tell them to stop. My legs won't respond; they're too heavy to kick. The gasp—I can't tell if it's all in my head and everything goes black, reverses, then, like a negative of a photo, the man's holding my body against the wall without moving, without speaking, without sound.

A still frame of the last moment I can picture.

He's made of different shades of blue, outlined in white with black eyes and a chest full of bloodless holes, like what the shotgun must've left in him last night. I don't remember seeing that a second ago.

I go back to pick up my phone, but my fingers faze through it. Nothing's moving. There's no sound, only a void around me that I can't affect. A racing feeling of fear, panic, and finality fills my body. My foot taps rapidly against the ground and I move, first a quick walk, then a run to get the hell out of here and as far away as I can possibly go.

I reach the end of the block. The big guy and my body are still visible in the distance. I turn the corner only to be right where I started, right beside the man strangling me. I run the other way around the corner. Again, the turn makes no sense, putting me right back in front of the man between the houses, against the brick wall.

Screaming, I ram him.

He's more than two times my size. His body's icy through his clothing no matter where I touch. It's like he's soldered to the ground. Whatever direction I push, if I pull, he doesn't move. I smack him. Pull his hair. Kick him in the legs. Nothing. He doesn't notice.

Then, as quickly as it all appeared, everything turns black in the same way a television screen goes dark when the power's cut and I don't know where I am.

Nothing exists beyond the thumping in my ears, panic, and the feeling of raw throat screaming for my life.

FOURTEEN.

I open my eyes to the revitalized street of the Old Town Mall. The Bin, SALON, WATCH THIS, and all the newer stores that actually attract attention instead of vagrants. The doors hang open, warmly inviting patrons in with hospitality that's eagerly accepted. A deep drum accompanies energetic organs and an electric guitar in the distance. The Fire Museum on the corner blasts a black light through the purple sky. I know where I am instantly. but I still step out in front of the place to read the sign.

CAVAE MORTEM.

I press my palm to my eye. Nothing hurts. In fact, I don't really feel anything at all. There isn't even an echo of the last thing I felt. God… Where was I before this? How did I get here?

"Hello, again," a woman's voice comes from beside me. "Good to see you, Joey. Well, I guess as good as things can be when you end up *here*. At least you used the door this time." Sol stands beside me, still with her messy brown hair partially hanging, partially in a bun, still looking like the last portrait I had of my mother. I think I should care enough to ask her to change her look, but... I don't feel anything.

"What do you mean I used the door this time?" I say.

"Do you remember being here before?" Sol says. "Is that... something that's still in there?" She knocks my head gently with a soft pat, then quickly withdraws her hands when my eyes turn on her.

"Yes. I know where I am," I say.

"Good. Saves us a lot of time. I don't need to show you around or explain anything—"

"But I'm... dead?"

Sol nods. "Very much so. At least, I think so. I couldn't tell last time, but this time, I'm sure of it. There's something different about you now."

"I'm dead... for real?"

"Yes. I just said that. Are you going to need more of an explanation?" Sol closes the gap between us. "I said it the last time, but this is always the hardest part and I *hate* it. I figured that since you'd been here before, you'd kind of get it when you showed up for real." She laughs.

My mind's racing, but every time it tries to grab at a thought, a theory, a memory, or an emotion, something stands in the way, stops it, and mutes the feedback. I don't remember anything prior to this moment. Distant things I can remember. Wayland missing, Jag driving me everywhere, something about work, my dad sitting in his chair, but... I don't remember what I was doing. It's like looking at a picture through rippled water, the image obscured and when I reach in to grab it and pull it out for clearer thought, something grabs my hand and stops me from getting near. As panic builds in my stomach, something whispers inside and the panic goes away, only to build slightly again, just enough to be felt, and go away again. A flickering candle blown out. "How... How did I die?"

"Strangulation," Sol says.

"How do you know that?"

"I know pretty much everything surrounding the moment of death. They tell me it's to help wandering souls get comfortable and find peace, but… I don't think humans generally feel any better knowing how they died. It answers a few questions, sure, but does it make *you* feel any better?" She chuckles.

"Who did it? Was it my dad?"

Sol shakes her head. "You wouldn't know him, per se…. If I gave you a name. But he's someone who's been here before. You know, those guys can be a *lot* of trouble," Sol says.

"What do you mean?"

Sol takes a couple of steps back. There's a momentary look on her face like someone threatened her or she feels uncomfortable. "I'm not sure how much of this I should actually be talking about. It's not really my place to talk about the afterlife of *others*."

"You're not telling me the afterlife of someone else. You're telling me how I died."

"That's easy. Strangulation by someone you don't know. That's all there is to it. I wouldn't say it's uncommon in Baltimore—but there is a lot of murder between familiars there too. Really violent place."

"I know…"

"Anyway," she's still backing away, her voice higher pitched now and her steps quick like she's almost running but trying to be subtle about it. "Make yourself at home. I'll be in the bar if you have any questions or get thirsty." Sol walks away as she finishes her phrase. She turns on her toes to face me, giving me one more look, a smile that she's trying to make assuring, but there's something else there. She can try to look human as much as she wants, but there's something about her that says she's not. The same way there's something about Val that says he's a bird and there's something about Charon that makes him feel bizarre.

Maybe it's the stiffness in her face or the gentle gloss in her eyes. If she was alive, she'd be a badge. Totally useless and totally fake.

"Do people actually fall for that?"

She's halfway across the courtyard when she comes to a stop. "What do you mean?"

"Your face. Your being. You're… you. Do people actually think you care?"

Her smile threatens to fade. The edge of her lips twitch, her eyebrows press together with confusion or concern. "What do you mean? I do care. It's my job to care."

"Right. It's *your job* to care. Something you were assigned to do, right?" I close the space between us. "Do you know how to do anything beyond your job?"

Sol laughs softly, uncomfortable, she clears her throat. "I'm confused."

"Let me be more clear: do you care about anything?" I say.

Sol looks past me to the BIN's department store. She watches people run inside, giggling girls with arms twisted together, men in suits who look like they've never had a day off in their life, slackers who look like they've never done any work. She glances back toward the bar where the tables outside are filled with different kinds of people who never would have been friends while they were alive. I couldn't have understood it the last time I was here, but now I can feel whatever it is that draws them together.

Like anesthesia to the heart or the spirit, there's something inside of me that silences pain, misery, and judgment. Animosity, fear, and concern are just words.

"I care about the souls that come here," Sol says. "It is my job to make you more comfortable and to help ease you into the afterlife—"

"Right, that's your job. Your *assignment*. Not what you *want* to do. What you *have* to do. What is something that you *want* to do, though?" I say.

Sol's smile finally melts off her face, not into anger, but into a blank expression like a doll in a toy store. The expression's only momentary, then the smile comes back and the distance in her eyes is made more obvious after having seen what her true face looks like. "I want to do my job. I want to take care of souls in the afterlife. I want to make you feel happy."

"Right." My stomach curls with a faint feeling of butterflies, but it's fleeting. "You don't get it."

"I do get it. I've told you what I want. Why would I be insincere?" Sol says.

"You can't think past whatever someone programmed you to say. That's why."

"I don't know what you mean by 'programmed.' I'm here because I want to be here."

"Alright. Fine." My irritation is instantly muted and it's the strangest feeling. It tickles my insides in a way that feels like something has to come out, a gentle, but building pressure that quickly goes away before it becomes more than a whisper. I want to feel irritated at the disappearance of my irritation, but I can't feel that either. "What other choices did you give up so you could be here instead because you like it more?" I say.

Sol laughs. "Choices?" She leans away. "This is where I want to be. I've never wanted anything else."

"Alright. I get it." I roll my eyes, cross my arms, and turn away.

"Good. I'm glad." Her smile widens, warm, motherly, but she's making me sick to look at, so I turn away and watch the movement of the courtyard instead. The lighting coming from the tables is hollow, echoing off the empty wood and the empty spirits of those sitting around them. There's no direction, but to have another drink, another laugh, slap down another set of cards, turn in another show, play another song, have a good time.

A man in a black t-shirt and jeans drinks his mug in one

go. By the time the bottom of the glass hits the table, it's full again. He doesn't seem to notice it's filled. He lifts his hand and calls for more. He picks up a couple of peanuts off the table and cracks them in his palm. He shares the table with a sharp-looking man in a suit, skinny-tie, maybe in his forties. Golden tie clip and neat hair. Looks like a banker. Next to him is an older man in pajamas and beside him, a black guy with low hanging sweats and an over-sized sweatshirt. The old man couldn't be the banker's father or grandfather. His hair is too thin, his disposition is not confident enough. Yet, they are all energetic, engaged, laughing, and sharing stories about whatever it is they can remember or make up. Whatever their words are become distorted when they enter the courtyard.

It's mostly men at the bar and girls entering the department store or what I can only assume is a theater when its sign reads WATCH THIS. People come from the hotel across the street but aren't visible until they step onto the sidewalk just outside of the mall courtyard. Beyond that, there's no one... not even those approaching.

"Have you got your room yet?" Sol says.

I turn to her with hard eyes. Stepping away from her, my jaw tightens with a moment of anger, but then just as quickly as it comes, it's muted. "Were you just in my head?"

"What?" Sol purses her lips. "No. I don't need to be in your head. I know what you need. It's—"

"Your job?"

"Yes! Exactly!"

"Stay the hell away from me, Sol." I'm crossing the street before I hear anything else. I turn on my heels from the side of the road where the hotel is. It looked just like the rubber factory in size and shape, but with better paint and a canopy outside that reads SLEEP WELL. There's no one standing at the front desk, but a skeleton key sits on the counter with a tag reading JOSEPHINE M. BOURGEOIS.

The lobby is little more than a small box with an empty

desk, a wall full of small compartments, a couch, and a set of elevator doors. I pocket the key. The elevator dings. Doors part. I lean back to see if anyone's coming out, but there's no one in it.

No one comes into the lobby, no one leaves.

It's just me.

"Good." I peak into the elevator one more time, then out the front door. The podium outside remains empty. "So much for a warm welcome." I come back into the lobby. "You get what you get." I slip behind the front desk and start with the small drawers lining the wall. There must be about fifty of them. Tug after tug, none of them open and it's more like they're welded shut than locked.

My key doesn't fit into the small lock on any of them either. Under the desk are a couple of cabinet drawers, but they don't open either. Rather than feeling like everything's locked, it feels like this is a stage, a set on TV where everything is a prop and if I somehow got any of the drawers open, the desk would expose cardboard and foam and the edges of paint made to look like wood. The inside of the elevator is a mirror on all four sides. The gate is lattice wire, curling into shapes of bones, hearts, leaves, and ivy that strangles everything it's holding in. I don't push anything for the door to close and the elevator to move. A meter hanging over the elevator door acts like it's counting where I'm going.

The door opens to a new hallway, long, straight, and going in both directions with door after door mirroring each side. Velvet crimson carpet lines the otherwise gold floor. Wallpaper of pink roses and green vines cover the top half of the walls, some of it comes out of the walls in what looks like fully bloomed flowers. The floor smells of fresh garden.

I knock on the doors as I walk down the hall, hard, yelling, "help me! Help me! I'm dying! I need help!" I know my acting's never been great, but you'd think *someone* would have at least come out to see what was going on.

There's no movement. No sound. I've never even heard a hotel this quiet before.

The skeleton key has the number 99 curled into the base. Surprisingly enough, the numbers on the door don't start at 00 or 01, but around 30 and count up if I go to the left and down if I go to the right. I reach the door reading 01. It's at the end of the hall, a sharp, right turn goes to another hall where the room number starts at 99. Following the hallway down, I'm back around to room 30, 31, and the elevator. At the end of the hall is number 01 again and around the corner, the 99 again.

Logically, there's no way this could have been the same hallway and the same 99 door.

I slide my key into the door. It opens without me turning the knob. The room looks like my bedroom. A box spring mattress on the ground, my garbage desk, my cellphone is laying on my bed. A bookshelf of action figures and comic books and a couple of regular books too, one of which has a barcode for the library on it since I forgot to return it. The only difference between this room and my real bedroom is the room somehow feels nicer than what I had. Not an extension of some dirty trailer, but the walls are clean, the carpet doesn't smell or feel like dirt, and when I step in, I'm not filled with edgy concern.

I lay on the bed. Bouncy, comfortable. My eyes close. The room smells like me, but with everything bad about it gone. I'm waiting to hear the TV buzzing with *Wheel of Fortune* or *First 48* or the History Channel talking about aliens, but everything is so quiet. I open my eyes and stare at the ceiling. Waiting.

The silence buzzes in the depths of my ears. My heart is racing and before I realize it, I'm slowly panting. I blindly grope the bed until I find my phone and turn on one of the playlists saved on it. The music drowns out the silence and any sense of normalcy that was missing is returned.

I go to the window and peak out, maybe it's not as clear

as it normally should be. The glass is foggy and looks more like an oil painting, but the neighbor's house is outlined in smudgy darkness. The tree in their front yard, their fence, little black lines through the watercolor. No birds though.

I try to open the window, but it doesn't move. Like a prop window, it remains in place, welded shut. I knock my elbow against it to test just how hard the glass is. I wonder if I could knock the glass out and if I did, what would be behind it? I grab the crowbar I hid in the back of my closet. "Do I really want to do this?" I stand, positioned, legs apart, back arched, and hands curling ever harder into the crowbar.

A loud buzz and I'm stiff, stressed, thinking what the hell does he want now. Taking a deep breath, I close my eyes. "I'm busy, dad!" It's said more like impulse or habit before the buzzing registers as my phone. I toss the crowbar onto the bed in exchange for it.

I didn't think there would be service down here.

The phone was mine. It looked like mine, but it wasn't. At least, that's all I could guess. The screen wasn't cracked, and the display was brighter than mine had ever been. So many stories about death tell you that you can't take your stuff with you when you go. Don't collect gold. Don't collect money. You can't take any of it with you. Who were they? I don't really know. Religious people, probably. I do know that plenty of people get buried with things they care about. Maybe it's a necklace, maybe it's gold or a wedding ring or a bottle of whiskey or a picture of their son. And maybe you can take whatever is near your body with you when you die.

The name on the screen reads WAYLAND and the message is the same as it has been the last three times I've gotten a text from him: 'WHERE ARE YOU?'

My jaw tightens, fingers grip the phone harder before I type in, "DEAD," erase the message, then toss the phone onto the bed. Heat rises in my face just as quickly as tears build in my eyes. My throat tightens. A tear falls down my cheek, and then, like it never happened, the emotion is muted, and I feel nothing at all. Maybe a slight cheerfulness in the pit of my stomach and some voice in the back of my head saying, "smile! It's all over and everything is good!" A scream roars out of my throat until it hurts then is relieved at the same time.

Irritation builds into anger so quickly then disappears again, swallowed by some void. I grab the crowbar off the bed and slam it into the window. The thin glass shatters.

I wouldn't have thought it'd be so thin.

Behind the first pane of glass is another, just as blurry, painted the same as the one before it: a hazy version of the view from my bedroom. I strike it again. The glass breaks and again, another pane is behind it. Two and three and four and seven more times, the glass has another one behind it.

I'm breathing hard. I drop the crowbar. All the glass that should've been from the window is gone; nothing lays on the floor beneath the window. I'm tense, waiting for my dad to yell my name, smack the door, and tell me to keep it down so I can fight him next. There's something discomforting in knowing he's not there, he's not coming, and this room is an illusion. I wasn't expecting it to be real, but this…

I pick up my phone and open the message from Wayland. This time, I actually send him the phrase 'DEAD.' I don't know if it'll reach him.

It's all another illusion.

Tears blur my vision and disappear before any of them fall down my cheek. If none of it's real, then none of it really matters. I write to Wayland:

That's not a joke. I'm not pulling your leg, Way. I'm dead. Gone. Someone told me strangled. Don't ask me who. None of it matters. None of it makes sense. I don't know where the hell I am, but maybe some kind of Hell because this is shit. Sorry I couldn't help you. Guess you'll be on your own to deal with the badges. But hey, if you kill yourself, your Hell will probably look a lot better than mine.

That's not encouragement to kill yourself.
Your future is way brighter than mine ever was.
Always has been.
You're gonna help people.
I was always in your way of being a better person anyway.
Find better friends and forget about me.

Every time the tears come down; whatever curse is in this place sweeps away the sadness just as quickly as it finds itself.

I hate this place. I hate everything about it and if there was any way for me to die again, I'd consider it if it meant getting the hell out of here. I turn the bed over; the sheets fly in all directions. Then it's the shelf, every book tossed to the floor, across the room, every action figure against the wall. The desk falls flat to the ground. In my closet, I had a couple bottles of spray paint in real life. When I check the same spot here, they're there, so I tag the room with whatever words come to mind. Mostly it's FUCK YOU in every neon shade imaginable, a wall of technicolor voices shouting over themselves in an echo of anger I can't feel, with a couple of dicks thrown in for good measure. A feeling of Fort Armistead comes with the color and over the wall with the window, I write FALL NOT INTO THE ABYSS before tossing the spray paint can down and leaving.

I sort of expected someone in the hall, someone who heard me scream, someone who smelled the paint, someone to say anything, but there's no one anywhere.

I turn back to my room and open the door. Everything on the inside is back in its place and every trace of spray paint is gone. I guess I understand why the hell everyone's always at the bar. If this place is trying to be a comfortable paradise of familiarity, it's failing hard and instead, it comes off like an uncanny replica, a reminder of a life that doesn't exist anymore.

FIFTEEN.

I cross the street to the mall courtyard. While it's filled with music and lights and life and laughter, the further I get from it and the hotel, the more the facade fades, and the streets look more like the faux abandon I'm used to. Down the street, the forest catches my eye.

What the hell did they call it before? A garbage business, auto business, shops for grab-and-go parts, a dollar store. Sounds fade, the color fades, everything fades beyond the darkness and the purple reflecting off the sky. Soft soil and weeds peak into the concrete well before I'm at the mouth of the forest. A chilling breeze rolls by, and with it, another wave of sorrow that's gone instantly. I wipe my eyes with the back of my hand. My fingers run through my hair. Frantic, anxious, and paranoid whispers share urgent secrets between the leaves. They're not loud enough to understand. Maybe it's because they're in another language, but they are constant.

A small whistle echoes off the trees. Sticks crack, sounding like bones breaking. I step into the grassy forest and I can't see anything anymore. Everything's black, like someone turned out the lights, an intense wave of fear shoots through my feet. My legs shake. My heart's racing. The frantic whispers are louder, breathy, deep in my ear, but still incomprehensible and that panic and paranoia and fear infects me rapidly.

I scramble back out of the trees until I feel concrete ground. I trip on a stray weed sticking up through the road. My vision comes back, the whispering softens again, and the emotions I was feeling go mute. I look over the trees. I want to go back to the lake—river—whatever it is—just to see if Wayland's there like the last time or if it really was my eyes playing tricks on me. My jaw clenches, the drug in the air releases it.

I return to the mall courtyard with nothing better to do. The only place for me is the bar. Before I sit down, there's a glass of cider on the counter. A little bit of smoke, a little bit of sweet from the apple flavor. It's my favorite, though Jag always laughed at me when I grabbed it and Wayland never drank at all. Sol stands behind the counter, talking to someone else sitting at the bar. She leans away and it's like I'm seeing double vision, a copy of her pulls off and stands straight while the other leans back against the bar and flickers until it disappears. The remaining copy of her comes to me.

"Check out your room?" she says.

"Yeah." I sip the drink, foam sticks to my lip.

"What'd you think?"

"Is this Hell?"

"Hell?"

"You know, the place you go when you die so you can suffer forever because you've been a shit-ass person." I look up over the glass of beer like it'll make her be any more honest than she was before.

"I don't know what you're talking about. Is… that a thing where you're from?" Sol says.

"Supposedly when you die, you go to Hell if you're shittier and Heaven if you were a good guy and you get to party forever in peace and joy for the rest of your dead life," I say.

"Doesn't that seem like this to you? A party?" Sol says. "You've got drinks, music, laughter, friends, a place to call home. What's not to like?"

"This isn't Heaven, Sol. This is a facade. If this was such a good place, why do people keep trying to escape?" The side of my face feels numb, and it goes down my neck. The words don't even feel like mine.

I drink the beer down fast, hoping for at least a little bit of the alcohol to hit me, but none of it does. A new glass full, I take that down, then another and another until I'm four glasses in, I smell like the beer that's spilled down my chin, but I'm not even a little bit tipsy. "What the hell's the point of this place if you can't even get drunk?"

"Why would you need to get drunk? This is paradise. You shouldn't feel anything at all but good stuff," Sol says.

"You know." I sit up straighter.

Sol laughs. Her fingers curl into the bar counter gently. "You—What? I know what? That it feels good to be here?"

"Yes. Unreasonably good. Like you're not allowed to feel anything at all and if you do, something around here sucks it out of you." I'm watching her carefully. She turns away, but her face shows no actual expression of nervousness, anxiety, or guilt.

It's all just the motions of it, like watching someone do a satirical dance of what they thought fear would look like in humans. She had no connection to the dance she was attempting to perform. She had no idea what she should look like in the same way she had no idea what it actually means to smile or be happy.

"Stop lying to me, Sol! I can see it on your face. I bet literally everyone who has ever come in contact with you knows you're full of it. It's the way we're born in Baltimore.

211

Some bullshit gene passed down from decades and decades, maybe even hundreds of years, of being Baltimorons dealing with Baltimorons. Your bullshit might work on tourists, but not me. Anyone who hasn't said anything has just been too lazy to call you on it, but not me. What the hell is wrong with this place?"

"It's Hollow Death, Joey. Didn't you read the sign?" Sol turns back toward me. She grabs my mug of beer and drinks half of it down. Once she's done, she pushes it back toward me.

My nose curls and I turn away. "You're disgusting. Get me a fresh cup."

"There aren't germs here," Sol says.

"I don't give a shit. I'm not sharing a glass with a dead person."

Sol yanks a glass out from under the counter. She goes through the motions of filling it at the tap and pushes it back toward me, then, leaning on the counter, she lightly shakes her head. "I'm not the dead person here."

"I pretty much figured that out. The name Sol. The guide thing. The… just sort of sitting around here and, what, you talk to everyone? My guess is you're some kind of amalgamated soul. I don't even know what the hell I mean by that, but a shared experience from every piece of person that comes in here. I bet you know every last dead creature that's laid foot in here since you got this *job*." I make quotation marks with my fingers. "Every thought. Every consequence. Every secret."

Sol's slowly nodding her head as if thinking. Her bottom lip is pushed out, her arms are crossed, she tosses her head to the side, still nodding. "I mean, that's not entirely accurate, but it's not entirely… dis-accurate either."

"Dis-accurate?" I rub the bridge of my nose. I wet my throat with a new wash of cider. The glass slams down on the counter just as soon as the thought comes to me. "Wait—so, if I'm right, you know every last person that's come here since… whenever the hell you got here?"

"I guess you could say that, yeah. When the reapers deliver a new soul, I help them settle in, kind of like I did with you the first time… and the second time. Though the second time was obviously not so formal. You already got the walk around and—"

"Did you know Andrew David Bourgeois?"

"What?" Sol straightens, no longer leaning on the counter.

"Did you know Andrew David Bourgeois?" I say more sternly.

"I'm not supposed to talk about anyone who has passed through here. Their past is their past. Their lives, accomplishments, short fallings, and judgments are for them and the court to review. It could get kind of chaotic in here if everyone started looking for someone who owed them once they got here, you know?" Sol says.

"I'm not looking to get revenge or repaid or some shit like that. I'm—"

"He's your father. I know. But if he's dead, what exactly do you want with him? Reconciliation? No offense, but he doesn't really seem to have the greatest…" Sol purses her lips again. Her head drops from side to side, and she squints hard, closing her eyes for a long while before opening. "Can't really say."

"He was a piece of shit. I already know that, Sol. I lived with him." I'm standing now, hands braced on the edge of the bar.

"Okay, if that was *your* experience with him. I'm not really the thing that can tell you that you're wrong—"

"But if he died and came through here, how the hell is he back on earth, sitting in his chair?" My nails press into the counter. The heat and tension rise in my body, but just as quickly as it builds and my face grows hot, it disappears with the sweeping whisper of ease Cavae Mortem caresses me with.

213

"Sitting in a chair, where?" Sol says.

"Sitting in the chair at home. In my home. In Baltimore. He's always sitting there in the living room with the TV on and he's always watching the same shows, drinking the same beer, and beating down the same door when he doesn't get whatever he wants. He doesn't do anything but complain and beat on the *wall*." My throat constricts as I pick at the last word. Wall wasn't what I wanted to come out, but anything else. I feel the heat buildup in my eyes, the tears, the blurry vision comes and goes. It feels like a sneeze that comes just close enough to come out but can't quite make it.

"I don't know what you mean by he's sitting in your home," Sol says slowly. "He was here, and he was taken to judgment some time ago. He went wherever they determined he needed to go, but the Judge doesn't send people back to earth once they've died. They just… that's your only chance." She pauses, looking past me, her eyes catch on something, but she refocuses, leans over closer with her elbows on the counter. "They don't tell me much about the process. I don't have anything to do with it."

"Really?" My fingers tap rapidly against the counter. "And I should believe you about this?"

"Why would I lie about it?"

"I don't know… but I'd think if you work so close with whatever Judge is back there, you'd think twice about it. What if He comes for you eventually and you have to pay the price for what happens to people here?" I step back from the bar.

"That's… not a thing." Sol shakes her head. "I've got a job and that's all. You should come back to the bar. Calm down. You know you're attracting a lot of attention." She laughs. Short, choppy. "Killing the mood."

"What about the other guy that walked out of here last time I was here?" I'm still stepping back, with each bit of distance that grows between us, my voice goes louder, and

I go from muttering under the music to yelling over it. Throbbing dance tempos slow to moody ballads with screeching electric guitars reaching through the trees for a bit of help.

"There are a lot of guys that walk in and out of here, Joey," Sol says.

"Yeah, I bet." I exhale hard. The irritation bubbles up and blows away. I want to be angry, but I can't and every time I try, it only makes me irritated for a second, putting me into the cycle of repeatedly building emotions that are wiped away like busing a table and somehow it feels like an itch that can't be scratched, that's rubbed and picked at and only made worse every time it's touched on and never satisfied. "But how many guys did you see leave with me? Remember the last time I was here? I swear, it was only a few days ago and then Charon and his bird came in and they took the guy from a table and they took me with him. He's a big guy. Jeans tucked under his gut. Big like tall. The gut wasn't that big, but it's there and you can tell what a piece of trash looks like. Don't tell me you didn't notice this guy. He had bad shit written all over him and he didn't want to go, but Charon did something to him and he went along with everything."

I close the space between the bar and myself again with every word I say. My hands splay flat against the counter and my eyes are wide. Standing on the metal pipe that runs along the bottom of the bar. I lean over the counter, lean closer to Sol like it will make her more likely to answer me. She pulls away with pursed lips, humming. Her eyes shift toward the corner table where I *know* the guy had been sitting, playing cards, drinking.

"Oh. Yeah. I remember the guy," she finally says.

"He was dead, yeah?" I say.

"Oh yeah, so dead. That was his soul hanging out over there. Like I said, there aren't too many visitors down here that still have their... *suits*, you know? I'm really not sure

215

how you even got down here with it." She leans back with a laugh.

"Right. Me either—So, if that guy was dead, how the hell was he back on earth? He jumped in the river. Is that what the river does? It revives people or whatever you want to call it? Is that what happened to my dad too?"

Sol says nothing, but just shrugs. I grab the glass of cider off the counter and toss it against the bar. The anger is just a flare, a momentary heat in the pit of my stomach that feels like vomit waiting to come and it's gone before the glass leaves my hand. I want to be angry, so I grab another glass off the counter from the person who had been sitting next to me and I toss it too.

The guy stands up, says, "what the hell?" and takes a seat again, calming. His momentary flash of anger passes fast and reverts back to a confused, neutral look. He forgets what just happened and orders another drink. Sol gives it to him saying, "enjoy," and he says, "thanks, I am," and keeps talking, but his voice grows softer until it disappears into the noise of the bar.

"You need to calm down. Take a seat," Sol says. "Just have a good time. Don't get into a rush. You know, if you get too antsy, your time might come earlier than you want—"

"Fine! Let it come. I don't want to be here anymore." I turn away from the counter. Within the instant, Charon and Val are already standing in the doorway of the bar. Charon's bright eyes are trained on me while Val's dark eyes survey the area in a sharp, but trained manner. He's got a goofy smile on his face and licks his lips.

Charon comes toward me with Val following behind him as if he's a shadow. "It's time to go," Charon says.

My heart races then is smothered out. My lips move to say, "I don't want to. Fuck off," but my voice won't come out. I can't break my eyes away from his. "Go where?" I already know the answer, but it's the only thing I could manage out.

"Judgment," Charon says.

"You think you could take someone else? I just got here, got a room across the street. Don't you have other people to deliver first? Like, a queue system or something?" My voice is trembling, even though I don't feel anything.

"I received a message that it was time for you to go. That is why I'm here. Anything else you believe is a rule or structure does not exist outside of your head," Charon says.

"It's called a thought. Or being sarcastic. Whatever. I'm not ready to go anywhere. I'm waiting for a friend to call."

"You don't have a choice." Charon steps aside to usher me forward. I have no intentions of moving, but something else is inside of my body. My legs are not under my control, even my head is hardly mine to look around with. We step out of the bar and move down the street. Charon's at my side with Val following close behind. We enter the forest with Charon muttering a soft warning of, "don't try to run. You will get lost," like I can actually move on my own.

For just a moment, the anger sticks to me a little longer than it had been. The whispering of the forest is louder than when I stood on the outside, but not as loud as when I had gone blind. The trees grow dark outside beyond what's maybe a four-foot bubble. I don't know if you could actually call it a bubble, but outside a couple of feet, the dark, pixelating mist carves space for Charon to pass through. It moves around his body, leaving extra room to the sides, and doesn't reconvene until after Val has passed. The air feels cold and stiff and there's a smell to it, but it's not the same smell you'd get at MP. It's… more stale. Stagnant. Less rotten. Maybe arsenic? No. Sulfuric.

"I don't think I asked last time—but what exactly *is* this place? The woods, I mean. It reminds me of a place back home."

"It's called Caedis Silvis," Charon says without looking at me. "In your tongue, it would be called *Murder Woods*."

"Really?" A laugh escapes my lips. Not that it's funny, but there's something else, the pressure, the smell. It stings the inside of my nose and throat a little bit, kind of like a sear. "That's funny. We have a place that looks kinda like this—"

"You said that," Charon says.

"Yeah, but I didn't tell you we call it Murder Park. It's a dumping ground. Cats, dogs, birds, people. All kinds of ways, if they're gonna go, a lot of 'em end up there. Does it... does this have anything to do with that place? Like, the river we crossed last time. It also... was kinda like the place back home—"

"I'm sure there is some connection between the two. What it is shouldn't make a difference to you—"

"But what if it *does*?" I stop at the foot of the dock. The river shines silver, making small waves and hushed tides in response to the dark moon and purple sky. "That guy you brought here last time—with me—he ran into the river. What happens after that?"

Charon steps onto the boat. He makes his way to the front. Val's hand presses into my back. He gently pushes me along until I step into the boat. Val climbs in after. It's only once we've pushed away from the dock that my body becomes my own again. What felt like a weight on my legs and arms and heavy hands pressing down against my shoulders is gone.

"I believe I told you, didn't I?" Charon says.

"Yeah, you did, but I want to hear it again."

Charon turns to stare at me with incredible dismissal.

"Sorry if I'm kinda dumb. Sorta dropped out of school, alright? So, sue me, why don't you?" I snort, roll my eyes, and lean back. Before long, I'm sitting straight again and staring at him.

Charon sighs. "You fall into the River Styx, you drown on regret."

"Right—But what the hell does that mean?"

"Were you so dumb you did not learn what the word regret means? Or is it drown that is confusing you?" Charon leans against the boat siding. "Your brain may be smaller than the bird's."

"Oh, thanks. Yeah. I flunked out of poetry and symbolism and metaphors or whatever you would call this. What the hell does drowning on regret mean?"

"Do you want a manual for drowning?" Charon says. When I say nothing, he continues: "What it means is nothing I can describe to you. It is only something that humans experience. Animals who perish do not experience regret. It is only humans who wish to go back in time, return to the living, and do things they never accomplished. It is only humans who are tormented by the thoughts of 'what if,' and 'could have been.' I deal only in absolutes. What *has* happened and time is unchangeable, even if you believe there is a second chance. You cannot remove what has already occurred. You can only respond to the situation your mistakes or miscalculations have conceived. What does that entail beyond cycles of great pain and doubt? I could not tell you. The only way to truly know what drowning on regret is, is for you to drown yourself."

I turn to straddle the bench and lean against the boat's siding, folding my arms along the edge and leaning my head against them. The quiet silver water shifts around the boat as we drift through it slowly. The razor of light from the Fire Museum lighthouse blasts its soft beam through the sky in constant laps. Beyond the treetops and tall black lengths of wooded bodies, everything here is dead.

Dead trees, dead water, dead spirits, dead expressions, a world of fake and that's all there is in the afterlife. What a fucking scam. Being in this place is like taking the best drugs the docs could offer you for depression. Kill everything on the inside with an emotional carpet bomb.

No wonder when depressed, people kill themselves. If only people knew the feeling of nothing but beer, shopping, and a room just like home was on the other side, how many more people would feel confident in taking their own lives?

My pale arms clasp over the edge. I follow the darkened blue and red veins closer to the surface of my skin than they'd ever been. My index finger trails along the bottom side of my left arm until I reach my elbow. It tickles and a wave of delight moves through me. I run my finger back down. Someone's looking at me. Her eyes watch carefully, not judging, but entertained with what she sees. In the water, my reflection smiles up at me while her finger traces along her arm too. In the distance, the forest is devoured by purple mist, making it almost invisible at this distance. Only the shore and the docks are visible beyond vague outlines of trees that appear as pencil drawings on a dark canvas.

This is the end.

I don't know why, but I didn't think it would happen so fast. I guess it would make sense. With how many die every day, it doesn't make sense to leave souls pissing themselves in Post Mortem for ages. I can't remember any of the faces I saw back in the bar. Were they the same people who were there the first time I was here? Was anyone different? Did everyone get their judgment already and... get their new assigned home? What the hell did that mean?

"Hey," I say, my heart's throbbing, and I don't know why. I'm not nervous. I tell myself I'm not nervous. I wait for the silencing feeling to come, but the deadening drug of Cavae Mortem's gone. "I have a question."

"I can't tell you anything about regret," Charon says.

"I wasn't going to ask about the fucking river," I say.

"So, ask your question."

The irritation bubbles up over the anxiety again and this time it stays. My foot bounces rapidly against the floor. My weight shifts from foot to foot, side to side, and my fingers tap against my arm. "Did you ever deliver someone named Wayland Cross? Do you take people's names when you take them the court, or do you just get a memo of what your deliveries look like and yank 'em from that?"

"You're pretty rude for someone who wants something from us," Val says. He turns his head with a low chuckle.

I bite my lip to keep myself from saying anything to him immediately. "Not trying to be rude here, sorry," I say through my teeth and turn away.

Val and Charon exchange a look. I try not to notice too much, knowing that whatever they're saying mentally is something that would piss me off more if I heard it and I don't want to push someone overboard, like it'd do anything to a creature with no regrets anyway.

"What does someone else's deliverance mean to you?" Charon finally says.

"He was a friend of mine. He's been missing for a couple of days and I'm just wondering…" I don't want to think about if Charon had ever met Wayland. "If he died and came through here at all, I just… I want to know what happened to him. He's kind of in some big trouble back home and… I want to know if what the badges are saying about him is true or if something else happened to him, you know? Just… for peace of mind if this is where I end." That was harder to say than I thought it'd be. I'm holding my breath and the back of my eyes burn with unreleased tears. My chest feels heavy and constricted.

Charon looks at me for a while this time. The quiet waves lap against the side of the boat. Everything else is without sound, like we've become trapped in a void of nothing. The gates are visible ahead, the bright, white docks, the large doors to judgment glow in the distance. "Yes. Wayland Cross was delivered here."

My throat tightens. A wave of sickness makes me stand and lean over the edge of the boat. I grip the rail for stability, breathing deeply until the dizziness subsides. "When?"

"I could not tell you. We do not keep time here in the way you do on earth," Charon says.

"And he was dead when he came here?" I look back at

Charon.

"Yes. Everyone who comes here is dead," Charon says.

"I wasn't—that first time."

"That is a rare occurrence."

I cup my head in my hands as I sit down. I'm rocking back and forth on the bench. "So, he's dead then? He's dead and judged and now wherever the hell they put him? What the hell is judgment anyway? Is there a scale? Like, not as bad as Ted Bundy but not as good as Mother Theresa? How can you just deliver someone like him who had so much going for him when he should've been turned back up top to save lives and do good shit? Like—it shouldn't have been me that you put back up there. It should've been him!"

"He was dead. We do not return the dead to life," Charon says.

"Then why the hell is my dad back up there? Why the hell was that guy up there from the last time I was here? I saw him with my own eyes—I saw you bring him to the gate! I saw him run into the water! You did something to him because he's back up there and now, he's fucking killing people! Is that what judgment's all about? If you're a shit-ass person, you get to go back up top and continue your shit-ass life, making it worse for everyone else? What the hell is this? You're just as bad as the badges—fuck, it's not about good or bad or anyone killing anyone else. All you do is push papers, push people, 'do your fucking job,' you say, but what the hell does that mean? You're just a bunch of thoughtless assholes who don't give a shit about what you throw back for the rest of us to deal with. If it's a shit person, at least it gives you more work, right? You get paid more for that? More chances to be a hero? What exactly is the bennies package for being the grim reaper?"

"Wow," Val says, "you're nuts. No one's being a hero here."

"It is a job," Charon says. "There are no heroes or villains. Everyone comes just as they are and makes their decision on how they would like to be remembered and judged."

"And if they're pieces of shit, every last one of them goes back up top, is that it?" Hot tears roll down my cheeks. My hands curl into fists so tightly they hurt. My heart is racing and where the replica of the Old Town Mall had muted every feeling I had, now, every emotion feels amplified. The fear and anger build up so much inside of me, on a goddamn boat, what the hell am I supposed to do with any of it? I stomp so hard, painful shock waves shoot up my legs, my back, I slam my hands into the side of the boat.

Val's standing at the back of the boat laughing and saying, "what's wrong with you?" and when I don't answer he's saying, "what's wrong with her?" to Charon.

One step is too much on the boat. You can't walk, you can't stop, with each bench in place breaking up any space to blow off steam. Why the hell are there four rows in this boat anyone? There's never been enough people to fill all these seats. I try to kick a bench over, but it doesn't even move a little. A growl escapes, turning halfway into a scream that echoes into the empty sky. My fist slams into the boat's edge. I spin around again.

"How the hell was the big guy up top? That's all I want to know. You're supposed to take people to judgment, so how the hell was that big guy not gone?"

Charon takes a deep breath, a sigh, another glance exchanged with Val.

"You can speak telepathically now too?" I say.

"You witnessed him drown, did you not?" Charon finally says.

"When he jumped into the river?" the question feels stupid when I say it and I don't blame Charon for being exasperated this time.

"Yes."

"So—Wait—Drowning on *regret*, like you call it, puts you back up top?" My voice raises in pitch. My heart slows. It doesn't make sense, but my mind's racing, trying to put everything together between my dad and Wayland and the big guy. "Are you telling me the water's been a portal to real life all this time?"

"That's not exactly correct—"

"You said drowning—That shit kind of implies dying. What the hell is wrong with you?" I turn toward the water, watching it carefully now. The silver waves slap gently against the boat and even harder the moment we slow down at the dock. Still, the waves elicit a small hiss I don't think I noticed before. "This… brings you back to life? It gives you a second chance?"

"I don't know if I would call it a life. Your regret will consume you and everything you may not have liked about yourself. Amplify it," Charon says. "Your disappointments and regrets will fuel you."

My own eyes stare back at me from the water's reflection. "How do you come back from that?"

"You don't jump in. You don't run from your life's legacy. To go back, to try and change it will only make your judgment harsher as your soul erodes with hatred," Charon says. "If you fear damnation, do not jump into the water for then your destruction is ensured."

My fingers grip the edge of the railing, hard. A bitter chuckle escapes my lips. "I've been living in damnation all my life. Kicked and shoved and beat for the sole sin of existing. What's a little more damnation on top of this shit sundae?" I don't let myself think about it as I throw myself overboard, knowing that if I thought too much about it, I'd stop myself at the memories of the man's screaming agony as the water tore his skin off and consumed him.

The liquid splashes against me, first cold, then freezing, then painfully cold and so quickly it starts burning. It's heavy in a way water shouldn't be, but something unfamiliar to me. I felt it before, the puddle in the park when Jag was there, the shit that splashed out of Wayland's car. The freezing water bites into my legs and pulls me down like fingers wrapping around my feet, ankles, calves, and arms.

I'm screaming without recognizing my own voice and submerged not even moments after that. The cold bite fills my throat and lungs. It's fire and ice and acid and searing and bleeding pain all at the same time. I keep my eyes closed until I can't open them and then I can't tell if they're open at all. Everything's blaring white, an erasure of the world around me. I can't think, my head's too filled with pressure and pain and not a single thought makes it through.

Everything's gone, but the throbbing, searing pain that won't stop. It's so intense, I can't—I want to die. I can't remember what I was doing, I can't remember how I got here. As the pain builds, so does the anger, hatred, and spite. I don't know what for, but I want nothing more than to slam some poor fucker's head into a wall until he looks like a post-modernist painting. I can't think of names or people or faces I know. All I feel is the desire to hurt someone, to hear someone else's scream, and see their smeared, hopeless life like it will make the torment stop.

SIXTEEN.

I'm freezing and numb and around me is the sound of rushing water, a brook, the river, someone blasting their stereo to make the bass buzz out their speakers. Opening my eyes, the sky's dark and starry through the trees, a big golden moon hangs overhead, the normal night sky. The air smells mildly of sulfur under the mildew and decomposition and nature. There's no way to mistake the smell of Gwynns Falls at night. Water fills my ears and the backside of my head. I'm soaking wet all the way down, even if I'm only in the shallows now.

I rub the water from my eyes and look around the place again. In the front of my mind, there's a blurry vision of feeling and vague ideas, like waking up from a dream, everything's already being wiped but a couple images and how you felt. A bird in black clothing that looks like a man. Another man in white, but he's no angel. Old Town Mall. Fear and panic and nothing then rage. My hands curl into fists, shaking. Rage feels like a fire tickling my heart.

I get to my feet. Stepping out of the water, I check my

phone, but the battery is dead. Maybe the battery is dead. It won't turn on when I push the button. It should work. It was just working. I shove it back into my pocket. Doesn't matter. I'll walk home.

I don't know if it's because I'm cold or angry or what, but it feels like I'm moving faster than normal. I can't think of anything else but his name. My dad. His nasty face with black eyes, nasty teeth, and worms crawling out of his skin. His gray tank and darker pants stained with years of beer and piss and spilled TV dinners. For all the stains on them though, they're not dark enough to cover the blood. Red splatters and drizzle that went down his neck when he blew his brains out. His chair's still stained from where the bullet came out the back of his head and it's smeared and he smells like he's been dead and hasn't taken a shower since the day they put him in the ground and he crawled back out.

I hate him.

Those words swirl around in my head and every time they make a lap, I feel myself going faster. The cold air against my wet skin doesn't feel like anything. I brush my hair back until it flattens against my scalp. I reach for the box of cigarettes in my pocket. It's useless. Waterlogged. My lighter won't start either. I throw them both on the ground and keep going, making sure to step on the box as I pass.

I barely notice anything. Walking into the trailer park, I can't believe how quiet it is. There are no crickets, no chirping, no yelling or TV or radios or stereos from three blocks over. I can't remember seeing any cars the whole way here. It's impossible. Baltimore's never this empty, but I'm sure there was no one on the way here. Maybe if there had been, I would've flagged 'em down and borrowed their car. A couple of good people wouldn't mind if I borrowed their car for a quick trip home, right?

I must look cold. Pneumonic. That's a word. They'd feel bad and when I'd threaten to smash their heads into the hot, running engine until they looked like visitors to Pompeii, they'd get out of the car and maybe even tell me to keep it. People in Baltimore can be so damn nice if you just let them know how much you're in need. I see that's been my problem all along.

I'm walking up the steps to my trailer, mildly panicking when I don't hear my dad's TV and I don't see the flashing lights. That's how he's always been, curtains open sometimes, showing the neighbors the kind of lazy piece of shit he is. I can't remember seeing any lights in the neighborhood on my way in. The walk's been like a dream—the kind of dream where you're aware it's happening, but somehow you still have stuff you want to do while you know none of it's real.

I've got my hand on the doorknob. My heart's pounding in my ears and in that second, I hear the *ding, ding, ding* of the *Wheel of Fortune* lettering being changed on the board. Maybe the poor bastard can give my dad a vowel to scream with.

I push the door open. The room's lit up with a commercial for toothpaste, mint and vanilla and feces to brighten that shit-eating grin. Then there's a commercial for Viagra, it says, the pill to make you stand for anything. "Once it's up," the commercial says, "stick it in anything you can find. Your wife, a watermelon, a hole in the wall, that crusty pizza box, or a child—the possibilities are endless!" The following commercial is for depression and says, "don't give up hope. If you don't feel so good today, if you're feeling down, there's really only one good way to clear up those negative feelings forever: take the lead pill. It's a one-time solution that puts an end to your pain, misery, and negative thoughts. And then it's all about beer." The house smells like spilled beer, piss, and vomit. Cans litter the floor in front of my dad. The fridge hangs open, bleeding light against the dirty tile floor.

I slam the house door. Dirty drinking glasses rattle nearby on the flimsy dining table.

"Who the hell is it?" dad says. "Jo? You fucking bring

229

me what I asked?"

Heat goes through my body. My skin's on fire, buzzing, I can't think and it's like someone's turned the lights off, except for a spotlight on dad. "Yeah, dad, I got it." I don't know what he's asking for, but I've got a couple ideas of my own for what he should get. His hands lift, waving, asking me to put what I've got down in them. I come around to the other side of the chair. He gives me a side-eye.

For the first time, I can see just how nasty his eyes are. So bloodshot, the whites are almost gray where there are no veins. The pits of his eyes are black, reflective, glossy, and empty. Corrupted versions of the eyes of ghosts downstairs. No one's home, but the anger struggling to remain contained in his body. My knees press to the chair's armrest. My fingers reach for his throat, grip hard, harder, harder until my hand hurts. He punches me in the face. I stumble back. He's standing.

"The fuck you think you're doing, you bitch?" He comes at me swinging and his step might be awkward and sideways, a wobble influenced by Pabst, but he's faster than I've ever seen him. He throws a right hook, then a left. The third punch knocks me in the head. The fourth one's a shove that pushes me into the wall. He lunges for my neck but smacks into the wall when I duck.

The room turns black, brightens, the TV is strobing what feels like in pace with my heartbeat. I'm stepping back, the strobing's picking up, going faster, keeping in tune with the throb in my chest. No. It's not blinking to my heart; it's all about his. "You're just like your goddamn mother!" He turns around. "You always looked like her. It didn't matter what you did with your hair or how you dressed. You look just like her and I knew... It woulda been better if I'd put you out. I don't deserve the pain of having to look at you! What the hell have I ever done to deserve this?" Tears pool in my dad's eyes. Angry trails stream down his face, darkened by something, but shining silver in the TV light.

"No, dad! What the hell did I do to deserve you? I didn't ask for this shit! I didn't ask for you and mom to fight or for mom to go! All I ever wanted was for you to love me! But instead, I got to listen to you cry about every goddamn thing you couldn't do. Couldn't get up. Couldn't stand. Couldn't get a job or pay bills or stay awake like a normal person. Are you kidding me? You brought it all on yourself and then you blamed me for it when mom left! And mom abandoned me because she saw you in me too! You took her away from me, dad! You took my life away from me and never had the balls to just—fucking say it! You got in your own damn way. You smelled. You didn't care. You left me to take care of myself while you made your escape! But it's easier to tell everyone else they fucked you while you lay in a chair in your own pity. And your only answer after all this time is that you'd wished you'd beat your daughter dead? What the hell is wrong with you, dad? You deserve so much pain for everything you did to me!"

Everything in my body is telling me to run at him with as much strength as I can manage and beat him the way he's beat me until he's crying on the ground. The image is planted in my head and shooting soft boosters of pleasure through my body, like small hits of dopamine that say, "if you want the real prize, beat the living shit out of him. He's got gold in his veins, baby!" My hands keep tightening and loosening. My body jerks forward and back, but I keep moving away, running through the kitchen, hitting a can, a pot, a plastic cup. My dad follows and I try to keep the space between us.

A run to my bedroom is a death sentence. Dad catches up and throws a punch. The first one misses. The second one sends me into the flimsy, plastic dinner table we never used. The mason jar on top filled with water smashes on the floor. Dad lunges with both hands and pins me to the table.

"Fuck you, bitch! Fuck you!" His fingers tighten without restraint.

My vision's gone red. A voice in my head echoes, seething gleefully, *kill him, kill him, kill him, kill him, kill him.* I've never wanted something more in my life. Another voice, much softer, but one I recognize much more as my own says, *not again* and I'm not sure what that means. The power of *kill him* thrusts my feet into his stomach. He growls, stumbles back, hands slipping. I get off the table and run toward his chair. A couple cans scatter across the floor as I kick them. I reach around the floor looking for his gun—he always had it on him when he sat here, but I don't see it anywhere on the floor, on the TV table, on the chair cushion, or in the drink holder.

He catches up quick. I'm standing, he punches me in the face. I fall back on his chair and he climbs on me. His determined hands grab at me again, just as hard as if they hadn't come off before. I'm scratching his arms in desperation to breathe. He pins my legs down with his. Saliva drips down from his mouth with spit flinging into my face with every curse word I can only hear the hatred behind.

Everything's muted by his hatred and my pulsing heart and hatred. My blood feels like it's literally boiling under my skin, so much it stings like the water from the river. I bury my hands in the chair cushions, groping blindly for his gun. They find the TV remote.

I can't see him between how much my eyes are blacking out, straining my vision, but I see him enough and I feel him even more on top of me. I shove the remote into his teeth, his mouth, his throat. His hands loosen while he stumbles off and grabs the remote from his mouth. It slams into the floor just as my fingers stumble across a hard pistol grip.

No sooner does his weight hit the chair and his hands reach for me than the gun shoots off. Pop, pop, pop. His weight drops. He groans. His blood and piss and vomit rub off on me in the collapse.

I shove him to the floor and stand. His hand weakly

covers the holes in his stomach while he's whimpering, "something, something, something, Josephine." I step hard onto his chest, point the gun at his head, and keep pulling the trigger until the gun's clicking empty. I want to see more of his brain splattered outside of his head. At least one of the bullets went into his eye, popping it and all his bloody memories against the floor and my shoes and maybe a little on my jeans too.

The *Wheel of Fortune* spins and I don't know what the prompt is, but the first things I hear are, "she wants revenge," and "that is correct!"

I step off my dad's chest. I can breathe again, but it's shallow and fast. I have to try hard to slow it down. I close my eyes. A wave of dizziness strikes. I fall into my dad's chair and just focus on breathing. The TV dings. The lights flash against my eyelids. The dinging makes me dizzy. I get up, yank the TV plug out of the wall, and toss it onto the floor.

The trailer falls into silence for the first time in I don't know how long and it's just good enough. I hold my breath to see if I can hear my dad breathing. I can't hear anything. I open my eyes. The room's got a low tint of red over it. I don't know where the red is coming from. None of the lights are on. I go to the fridge and grab one of the beer bottles from the rack. It's gone in a second. There's no buzz in drinking beer, but I can still feel the alcohol better now than when I was in Mortem.

A laugh rattles my throat. Dead. *I was dead* and now I'm not, but *he* is.

Another laugh. I almost snort the beer.

"Goddamn, motherfucker." I laugh and wipe my lips with the back of my arm. I toss my empty bottle at my dad. It shatters. I grab another from the fridge. This one I pop open while I'm walking back to where he lays. "Rest in piss, old man." I pour the beer over his body with a sneer, shaking even the last drops on top of him. I toss the bottle at him. It smashes on the floor beside his head. I grab another from the fridge before heading back to my room.

I leave the lights off and feel my pockets for where my phone hangs out halfway. Beer open, my clothing's still damp, cold, and sticking to my body. I pull them off and toss them into the corner. My room smells like mold, dust, and cigarette smoke.

A sip of beer.

I grab a pack of cigarettes from my desk, a lighter, hold it between my teeth, even when I exhale. The first puff is unbelievably relaxing.

I lap up a couple more with eyes closed to let it penetrate every part of me. It feels like I haven't felt anything in years, and this was the relief of the burn, the smoke tickling my throat, the nicotine working its way into me. I've loved cigarettes since my first taste, even when my first taste wasn't that great.

Pall Malls really are shit.

Everything in my closet is a variation of the same. A pair of tight skinny jeans and a pile of unfolded t-shirts in the drawer. I plug my phone into the charger on my nightstand. My head bounces to a silent song filling the room. The next sip of beer is the first time the cigarette comes out of my mouth and I'm hitting it again as soon as I swallow. I smack the clock radio on to see what's playing.

Electric guitar chases away the uneasy silence. I don't want to stop moving, but I don't know where to go or what to do now and I can't even start to look for Wayland again until my phone comes on. I roll my neck. Kurt Cobain keeps saying, "hello, hello, hello," until I'm saying it back and then yelling it back. I toss a couple of punches through the air, bouncing lightly on my feet with each one. My voice goes sharp every time I sing with Kurt, but he doesn't complain, so I keep singing with him as I yank a pair of jeans off a hanger and pull them on.

Maybe I should give the good ol' detective a visit. He

couldn't get enough of me before and now I can't seem to shake the image of slamming his head into the interrogation room table again and again until his skull cracks and sprays his brains all over the room while his buddies watch from the other side of the mirror.

"It'd be such a mess."

I chuckle before throwing another punch. I go to the nightstand and try flicking the phone screen to see if it'll come on, but there's nothing. I finish the beer, grab another, light another cigarette, and press the power button again.

Nothing.

I set the beer down but keep the cigarette between my lips. I fall onto my bed. My eyes close to sleep, but my legs are restless and instead, I'm bouncing my head to the music coming through the clock radio and it's only getting harder and harder and more aggressive until my shoulders are bouncing too.

It's not Nirvana anymore, but the drums and guitar and screaming of some other band sound like noise. It sounds like the way my thoughts are crashing together in my head. My cigarette burns out.

Damn it.

I set it in the ashtray on my nightstand and grab my phone. I hold the power down, waiting to see if it'll do anything. Yeah, yeah, yeah, submerged in water or acid or a little bit of both at this point, I shouldn't expect this thing to work, but I'm muttering to it, "you better turn on, goddamn it, do it," and I hold the button down for ten seconds at a time, release, and hold it again without a change. Finally, I toss the thing across the room. It slams into the wall and bounces when it hits the floor. This time, the screen lights up.

I grab it off the floor to read the screen. A dingy red coats the glow. I wipe it on my pants, but the color doesn't change. It looks like a light being cast over the screen and not coming from the phone, but there are no lights on in the room, the curtains are drawn, and what little light is getting through them doesn't reach my phone. Whatever. The screen reads four missed calls from BODYMORE BODY SHOP and a voicemail in the mailbox. There's nothing else and when I go to send Wayland a message, my phone screen glitches out. Colors change, pixels mix and turn black, gray, white, red, blue, and then it flickers back to the main screen.

I hit the message and light another cigarette. Donny comes through saying, "sorry, Jo—I didn't want shit to go down like this, it's like you're one of my kids, you know? But you've been gone for a couple days and the badges keep asking about you. Won't tell me what for and the business doesn't need this kind of attention. You're a good kid, but if you got yourself into trouble, I can't help you. I hope you didn't do something stupid. Good luck."

I play the message a second time just to confirm that Donny thinks he's fired me.

My head throbs. I shove my phone into my pocket, finish off the cigarette, finish off the half a bottle of beer left on my desk, and grab a skateboard from my closet. I toss the board on the floor in the living room then go to work looking for some ammo. Dad always acted out of habit, ritual, maybe that makes more sense when you're dead.

I don't really know. I can't really think straight.

I step over his body and dig into the chair.

Nothing.

There's nothing under the chair, on the TV stand, in the TV stand, or in the knife drawer in the kitchen. Then I'm in his room, flipping his bed over in case the ammo's under his mattress, tossing the dresser drawers onto the floor, emptying every corner of the house as fast as I can. The ammo's in his top dresser drawer, but I overturn the rest of the bureau just for the hell of it.

I set the gun on my dresser and slip into my TRAITOR RAGE hoodie. The smell of the house doesn't bother me anymore. Coming back out to the living room, I spit on my dad as I pass him, then grab my skateboard. The red tint continues outside. It's midday, maybe evening? I don't know. The sun's up, but it's cold. I pull my hood up, step down the stairs, but pause when I drop my skateboard.

A raven sits on the tree outside of my window. Its dark eyes stare hard into me. Its head cocks lightly to the side. It caws hard, something feels callous about it, but also almost like it's laughing. It looks from me. I follow its eyes where across the street, another raven sits on a neighbor's house. It, too, stares this way, at me. The one by my window caws again. I turn around, catching its eyes.

"What the hell are you looking at, Val?" I say.

It turns its eyes away, coyly watching the house across the street.

"Yeah, go collect your dead. Have a good meal and once you're done with that, come back and make sure to take my dad already, will you? I can't promise he's got a heart, but I don't mind if you rip him open just to check, you know?"

As I skate out of the trailer park, it's hard not to notice the presence of the ravens peppered through the trees and just how hard my heart is pounding every time I see another one. I don't know if they're making me nervous or if my heart's pounding because they're there. My head throbs in tandem with each caw until I'm out of the park, out of the neighborhood, and away from all of it where the birds aren't around me anymore. My head bobs as I move down the sidewalk singing, "hello, hello, hello, hello," while I suck on my lip ring.

SEVENTEEN.

There are a couple of cars parked outside Bodymore Body Shop when I get there. One of them is Jag's. One of them is Donny's. A few of them must be from customers. I don't see Donny anywhere through the opened garage doors. I pick up my board and slip through the front door. Some guy with a bald head and a long, black mustache stands at the counter. He's never been here before. Is this loser supposed to be my replacement? "Can I help you?" he says.

"Nah, thanks, Mario. I work here. It's cool." I drop my skateboard on the ground and slip past him, going through the set of double doors into the garage.

"You can't go back there—" he says.

"Yo, Donny!" I make my way toward Donny's office. "You here?"

The door to his office swings shut, but it doesn't matter. I chuckle to myself. I'm biting my tongue. The radio sounds like it's playing through water. "I saw your new errand boy. Looks dirty. He know how to use a vacuum?" I knock at his door so hard it hurts my knuckles. "C'mon, Donny. I just wanna talk about the message you left. Wasn't it you that said the *only reason* you weren't with Veronica anymore was because *she* wouldn't talk to *you* and all the damn problems in the world could be solved with a little bit of open communication and hot, steamy love? Guess what it says that you don't wanna talk? You're a goddamn liar, Donny! You've lied to me this whole time and what the hell is that? I thought you were a pretty okay boss—I actually almost liked you—"

My fist's slamming into the door, getting harder. A hand grabs me by the shoulder and turns me around, hard. I swing before I can see who it is. Jag catches my hand but doesn't let go. "What the hell are you doing, Joey?" he says.

"What's it look like, Jay? I'm trying to have a one-on-one with Big D. Did you know he pink-slipped me?" I say, raising my voice at the end and turning my head toward his office. The blinds are drawn on the large window seeing into the office.

The lights are off. He's hiding. He knows I know he's hiding.

What a coward.

I laugh while saying, "oh my god, Donny... Really?"

"Yeah, I know," Jag says. "You've been MIA for like, four days, Joey—"

"Four days?" I laugh at the words.

He looks at my hand, my face, at me so closely my heart throbs twice as fast and twice as loud. I can't keep my eyes on his. I pull my hand back; he lets it go. "Is that blood on your neck?"

"Don't worry. It's not mine—"

Jag grabs me by the shoulder. I step back again, but he follows, holding me tighter. My hands fling toward him as I say, "let go, Jay," and he says, "no. This is crazy, Joey. You need to slow down."

"What's crazy?" I say.

"You. First, you're missing—and then the badges were

here. I said your friend was in trouble, but what the hell did you do?"

"I didn't do anything—"

"And why are your eyes like that?"

"Like what?"

"What the hell's going on Joey?"

"I'm not on anything, Jag."

"Don't lie to me. Your eyes are so fucking red and you're freezing. You should probably be at the hospital. A busted blood vessel or something. Can you even see?"

I pull my arm away from his hand, again, and step back, this time, more than a couple steps. A sneer comes from my lips. "I'm fine. Everything's a little red, maybe, but I can see just fine." I rub at my eyes. Everything's still red, but now it splotches black a couple of times from the pressure.

"Whose blood is that?" he says.

"Dad's." The words come out before I even think of them. A laugh follows. I'm quick to cover my mouth, not out of shame, but out of what he might think of me though the feeling of fear, of his judgment, is quick to pass. I lower my hand, still smiling, licking my lip, and biting at my lip ring. "It's not a big deal. The guy's been dead for a while now—"

"That's not funny, Joey—"

"I'm not lying. Remember when I told you he shot himself? That really happened and then the old bastard was so resentful he crawled back from the grave just to torment the rest of my godforsaken life with his failure. Here's to hoping the second time he goes, it sticks, yeah?" I nod, my tongue flicks against my lip ring, and the adrenaline's rushing into my every thought.

The moment we fought replays in my mind. The feeling of his big hands around my throat, his fist in my face, my heart pumping in my ears, the TV screaming WINNER or some shit while I reach into the chair for his gun. Fuck, I don't remember it feeling this good when it was happening.

But playing it over, I'm getting pumped, and I want to fight again. I want to feel the burn of my scream and my back curled into a wall, the unease of bruised and weak legs, the hot tears in my eyes where I can't tell if I'm crying from pain or laughter. I'm bouncing on the balls of my feet again. My arms pump in quick jabs.

"What the hell happened to you?" Jag says.

"Eh." I glance away from him, punch the air in another direction. "I died, found some freedom, maybe. You know, getting murdered really changes your perspective on things a bit."

"Joey—"

The way he says it, I can hear inflections of, 'you're insane," in his voice. My fingers curl. I shove them into my pockets on the front of my hoodie. My foot taps. I glance around the garage then at the doors to the waiting room. "Where's mustache?"

"Lobby. What? You didn't hear me kick him out while you were having your little meltdown?" Jag says.

"Meltdown?" I laugh. "Is that what you want to call it?"

"What else would you call it?"

"I don't know, Jay. Sensical? How would you feel if you died and came back to being fired? Doesn't really inspire a bunch of good feelies, you know? I worked my ass off here for years and this is the kind of gratitude I get?" I catch his eyes for a moment, but something painful shoots through me. From my head down my body, my legs are weak. My eyes burn with painful, stinging tears.

"What did you expect when the badges came around looking for you, Joey?" Jag says. "I warned you about going into Cross's house. I warned you about the shit you were getting into—"

"Yeah, yeah, yeah." I wave him off, pacing away. "Blah, blah."

Jag follows, staying near, mirroring my movement. "There's a warrant out for your arrest, Joey. What do you think Donny should've done?"

"I dunno, Jay. Maybe a little loyalty? Is that too much to ask?" I shove my hands into Jag's chest; Jag catches my hand. I tug, he doesn't let go.

"Do you really have no idea how much trouble you're in?" he says, and for the first time, his voice softens. I look up at his face and he's looking down at me, the anger replaced with concern.

"I don't need your pity." I step back.

Jag follows and grabs my other arm. "I don't pity you, Joey. I'm worried about you."

"Don't be."

He pulls me into him with the hold he has on my forearms. I pull back, but only at first and the urge to punch him in the back grows. My heart pounds in my head, drowning out reason. Jag drags me across the garage until we're in the bathroom. He shoves the door open the same time I thrust my arms toward him. He isn't thrown off. He pulls me into the bathroom and swings me toward the sink. When he lets go, he moves to stand in front of the door. "Look at yourself, Joey. Do you really think you *look* okay?"

The lights in the bathroom never looked good; I don't know what bulbs Donny buys, but it's never been short of painting the entire bathroom in piss-colored light. The sink is stained with cold coffee, oil, and grime that's part of the ceramic at this point. But just like everything else, the room's not yellow anymore, but covered in a filter of red. Even Jag's reflection, his dark hair's got a red sheen, his skin, reddened where his hands and arms are stained with oily black. The corner of the mirror is cracked. A roach crawls across the floor. My fingers curl into the sink. I turn my head down. "I don't see anything, Jay."

He comes up behind me, grabs the side of my head, and turns it straight to the mirror. I know what I'm looking at. It's hard not to recognize my short, black hair, my round nose, my *Traitor Rage* shirt, and the stub-like lip ring, but I still don't believe it's me. More like looking in a fun house mirror, a couple of dark lines crawl under my skin, away from my eyes, darkened, all the way with a red tint. I push back against Jag, trying to pull away from the sink and remove my focus from the mirror, but Jag closes in and pins my hips to the sink with his. His grip tightens and he meets my eyes in the mirror.

"You want to do something fun, Jay?" I pant, fingers tightening around the edge of the sink. I press my hips into his.

"Look at yourself, Joey. For real. Do you really think you look normal?" he says.

Anger bubbles in my stomach, but so does fear. My skin boils with the familiar acidic pain from the River Styx. My teeth clench, toes curl in my shoes, and a low groan builds in my throat, measuring with pain until it comes out as a tight scream. The pain goes down, but pulses under my skin.

"What the hell, Jag?" Tears burn down my cheeks. Silver, thicker than they should be. I reach for my face in the mirror, tracing the dark lines around my eyes. I press my fingertips against my skin. The tears make my fingers tingle. I wipe at it all: the tears, the dark lines around my face, the blackness that looks like smeared eyeliner, but none of it comes off. I turn on the water and wet my fingers. I try to wipe the lines away. The touch is cold and stings. Wiping does nothing to the lines. I clench my teeth and suck in a breath until I'm numb. I pull on my skin to see if the lines move or stretch. They don't. "Do you... do you see this, Jay?"

"I see something—"

"The black lines?"

"No. You're just... so red around the eyes and everything else is pale. I don't know what you took, but you need to go to the hospital like twenty minutes ago."

I reach back to give Jag a push using the mirror to find him. He steps away, I miss, and I don't try to follow. "I didn't take anything, Jay. I told you, I fucking died."

"You keep saying that—But you're right here—"

"And that guy at the bar—You remember that guy at the bar that said he knew me? He had red eyes too, right?"

"Yeah."

I glance toward the mirror, look around the bathroom, to the window shedding the little bit of natural light that does nothing to make it brighter. I think I hear the rattling chains. They're following me everywhere like the birds, but when I hold my breath, the chains aren't there. "The barrel full of lead didn't stop him. I don't know how it works, but he was already dead and then he found me and killed me because I knew him."

"I thought you said you didn't know him—"

"You're never gonna believe me." I turn around and lean against the sink. "I found him in Hell. Or—Whatever the hell is under Baltimore. Limbo?"

Jag stares at me for a long while. "And you didn't take any drugs?"

"No, Jay. Look. I know this sounds nuts—and I thought I was nuts for a while too, alright? But... there's... a ghost town underneath Baltimore and they've got a river like Gwynns, but when you jump in, it sends you back here and all you want to do is fucking... break things and kill people—"

"It sounds like drugs, Joey." Jag crosses his arms.

"I didn't take anything, Jag. I'm just—I'm going crazy over this." I close the space between Jag and me. I put my hand on his arm. Subtly, he pulls away at first touch but remains still in my grasp.

He puts his hands on my arms and leans in. I think he's going to come in for a kiss, but his hands slide around my back and he pulls me into him. I slide my arms loosely around him. His warm body feels good against my skin.

"Joey," he says, "you hit your head. You took some hard shit. You need to go to the hospital and maybe call the badges. If you don't…"

"What?" I push Jag back, breaking the embrace. "*You* will, Jay? You'd turn me in?"

He grabs my arm and pulls me back. Though we're not embraced, he won't let me get away. "Yeah, Joey, I would." His voice comes out stiff. "I don't like them as much as the next guy—"

I snort a laugh.

"But you're out of control. If you're telling me the truth, you killed your dad. Look—I get it—It was a long time coming. Your dad was a bastard and I saw enough black eyes to wonder *when* one of you would turn up dead, but Cross isn't worth throwing the rest of your life away for." He yanks me forward into his arms again. This time, his arms go around me tightly as he holds me to his chest again. My arms hang at my sides, though my heart is racing.

I close my eyes. I'm intoxicated by his smell. The grease, the sweat, the little bit of Fiji body wash. My arms snake back around so my fingers can wrap in his shirt. I press my face into him. I know what he's going to say before it comes.

"You need to let him go. Give up all this shit you decided to do for Cross and save your own ass while you can. You hear me? Tell the badges everything and get on with your life. He's not worth it." Jag squeezes me tight. In his hold, he sways a little. He presses his lips into the top of my head.

Heat fills my body with erratic energy and the painful tears fight their way down my cheeks, leaving a burning trail. My lips are tight, teeth grinding together. A restrained sob escapes. I go through everything from the last week in my head, but no matter how I word it, I sound crazy, and I see Jag saying the same thing.

None of the drinking at home even made me tipsy, maybe a little warm, but maybe if I could've gone a bit numb… That would've been too nice for me right now, huh? I'm exhausted and pissed off and I want complete destruction and I want the screaming in my head to stop for just a couple of seconds. That's what it really feels like.

Spite rushes around my body, transporting anger, erasing pain with fire. I need to go back home and burn the house, burn my dad's body, make sure he never finds his way back to earth again. At the same time, the voice in my head is cheering on his return to shoot him again. I want to punch Jag in the gut and kick him over, even when I know he's not the bad guy here.

We don't have time for this.

The tears fall more freely, burning my face like they're fire and ice. "You need to shut your fucking mouth, Jay." I thrust my hands into Jag and force myself back. He lets me go. "You don't know anything."

"So, tell me then—How am I so stupid? What don't I understand?" Jag says.

"Wayland's dead!" I'm not ready to hear the bathroom walls repeat the words. I wasn't even that loud, but they echo back. I turn around to face him. The tears drip from the bottom of my jaw. I wipe my eyes with the back of my arm and turn away instantly. "Sorry, Jag. I'm so sorry." Another couple of tears fall. The only person to ever have seen me cry was Wayland. Jag was never supposed to. I'm waiting for him to laugh and call me delicate, but he doesn't. I wipe away the tears again. A bitter laugh bubbles in my throat. "Don't you wanna laugh?" I suck in a breath.

"No. I don't want to laugh. Whatever shit you're in, Joey, we'll figure it out," he says. His voice feels like a mirror of mine, the same things I said to Wayland just a couple days back.

I slowly shake my head, exhale, reach for my cigarettes. "There's no getting out of this, Jay." I rub at my eyes. He closes the space between us, but I put my hand out, so he doesn't take me again. I think if I felt his arms around me one more time, I would collapse. My legs are shaking, but I do my best to control them. "I'm dead. That's it… I died too. And then there was the river and—god—It all sounds crazy, but you see my eyes, right? Something is… Something's wrong with me. Something messed up— God—Jag—All I can think about is hurting people. I want to destroy everything and find Cross and destroy more shit. It's the water in the park. It does something—"

"Whatever you got yourself into isn't going to be the end of your life. We can figure this out." Jag reaches out a hand. I turn away, flipping the box of cigarettes in my hand. "If you go to the badges, I know they don't always help—but if you tell them the situation, if you tell them what Cross made you do—"

"Cross didn't make me do anything, Jag." I turn around instantly, swinging my arms in an attempt to hit Jag if he's near. He's not. I throw my cigarettes against the wall. "I'm fucking dead!" My phone buzzes against my hip. I keep talking, but another buzz comes instantly and then another. I draw out my phone and see the name across the screen. "Wayland," it's like I exhale his name.

Jag comes up beside me. "I thought he was supposed to be dead."

"He is but being dead doesn't mean you're *gone*." I glance up from the text to meet Jag's stare. A roaring fire in my stomach almost makes me punch him in the face. I force some space between us.

"So, what? Now you're into voodoo magic too?" Jag says.

"Aren't you the one always talking about cults? And this is so hard for you to believe?" I growl. My hands are trembling and my foot bounces continuously. "If I hadn't already been to Hell, I wouldn't believe it either. Now either get with it or stay the hell out of my way." I tap the messages open. "Oh and tell Donny I'm coming back for him tomorrow." My voice is more like a murmur as I can't take my eyes off the messages.

WAYLAND   JOEY?

248

WAYLAND   YOU CAN'T BE DEAD.
WAYLAND   WHERE ARE YOU?
WAYLAND   I NEED TO SEE YOU.
WAYLAND   WHERE ARE YOU?

Tears burn down my cheeks again and another bout of anger builds in my stomach, my chest, my heart. Everything hurts and I don't know what to do with this pain. I drop to my knees, gasp for air. The noise builds in my head, over and over and over again, getting louder with murmured soft rage and murder and death and the radio in the other room with the mayor saying, "we care about you and want to keep Baltimore safe. Donate to my campaign, because we know what's better for you than anyone else—even you! You don't know anything, you moronic dolt."

A bitter chuckle comes out. Tears roll down my face. I wipe the tears away with the back of my hand. "God—Jag—Why does everything suck so much? There's so much anger…"

Coming toward me, Jag chuckles softly. "I don't know." He sits on the floor beside me.

"All I want to do is hurt people… It's like being hungry and everything around you looks good. I don't know… I don't know what to do." I set my phone on the floor and cover my face.

"We can figure this out," Jag says. He reaches over. The back of his hand goes around my neck, so warm and strong and comforting. He leans in, but I lean into him first, mashing our lips together for a desperate taste of distraction. His hand goes to the small of my back. I'm climbing into his lap, my hands now reaching for the hem of his shirt.

More messages come in. I pull away.

WAYLAND   JO? WHO?
WAYLAND   WHERE ARE YOU?

I punch Wayland's number in. The phone rings once before he picks up. "Hello? Way?" I say, but there's no voice on the other end. It's static and it's cutting up so much, not a word makes sense, and what does come through sounds too deep to be Wayland's voice. "Wayland? You there?"

The broken voice comes through more, static, sharp drops, and then the call drops too. What if it really hasn't been Wayland this whole time and he did go through the doors when Charon delivered him? Wayland's always been the good kid, but I swear it was him at the park before I died. I open the text messages and write back to him: I need to see you.

He writes, WHERE ARE YOU?

I tell him I'm at Bodymore.

WAYLAND	I CAN'T GO THERE.
WAYLAND	MEET ME AT MP?
JOEY	WHY CAN'T U COME HERE?
WAYLAND	…

And his message is left on three writing dots until I say, "how long will you be there?"

WAYLAND   AS LONG AS I CAN.

I pocket the phone and stand up. Jag mirrors. I grab my box of cigarettes from the floor, and I make way for the bathroom door. Jag grabs me by the shoulder and says, "where are you going?"

"To meet Cross," I say.

And Jag says, "not without me, you're not."

I shrug out of his hand and cross the bathroom. I spin on my heels to face him. "Ah, c'mon… What's the worst that could happen, Jay? I get killed a second time?"

I know he hasn't believed anything I've said when he

says, "yeah, that."

"We're meeting him at MP." I pop the lock, open the bathroom door.

Jag puts his hand on it and snaps it shut. "You seriously have a death wish, don't you? What if it's not Cross?"

"I guess that's part of the fun in showing up, huh? Don't feel like you *have* to come, Jay." I pull at the door. He pushes it shut again.

"I'm not letting you go alone," Jag says.

"That's not your decision to make." I give Jag a push back. His hand comes off the door. I grab the door and yank it open before he can snap it shut again.

"I'm not trying to make decisions for you—"

I turn around and walk backwards out the door. Jay follows. I stop so he can catch up. I reach for him, my fingers press into his shirt, not gripping it, but running up his chest until I feel his collar bone. His eyes catch mine. The red makes me sick, something about looking at him hurts the inside of my head and makes me dizzy. I swallow the feeling. My nose burns. My fingers curl around the back of his neck. I stand on my toes and pull him down. My lips press to his. I draw back only enough to speak. "You can come if you stay out of the way."

His muscles are tense. His hand reaches for my arm but then falls before he touches me. "Just… calm the hell down a little, alright?" His finger curls under my chin to upturn my face, forcing our eyes to meet again. He presses his lips to mine.

The rage inside my head mutes itself for a moment, but touch is painful in a way I can't describe. I pull back with a tear running down one cheek. The back of my hand wipes it away. "You have no idea what you're asking from me right now, Jay." A laugh pops the stinging in my chest. The contact breaks. I grab my skateboard from the lobby on our way out. Jag's holding me by the arm, and I let him. He tells my replacement he's closing, tell Donny if he needs anything. When I turn back toward him, I resist the urge to punch the stupid little mustache off his face. I yank my arm away from Jag's hold and get out of the body shop. He follows after me fast.

"We're keeping it low-key, Joey," he says.

"You're the one riding along, babe." I try to keep moving to force the erratic energy out of my body. I don't want to drive because I want to keep moving, but it's the fastest way to get to Leakin Park.

We're ten minutes in when Jag says he's taking the long way. I threaten to jump out of the moving car if he doesn't take us there directly. He doesn't believe me until I open the door, then he changes his mind. I tell Wayland I'm on my way and the buildings can't pass by fast enough. Everything is familiar and foreign at the same time. Boarded up windows and broken brick on one street and in the next, freshly renovated homes.

City Hall is hardly the tallest building downtown, but its dome bares down on us in superficial judgment, casting shadows on the parts of the city forgotten by those put in charge to take care of its people. The grass is bright, green, and strong, water by the blood of Baltimorons who decided to check out of society early. A few blocks down are houses that look abandoned. Dead, brown, forgotten, but it's better to be forgotten than to become a commodity traded for someone else's gain.

EIGHTEEN.

Kurt's following me through the radio and he's saying he doesn't have a gun, but it sounds more like he's asking me if I have one and I mutter back to him, "no, I don't have a gun," at the same time he says it. Jag's nodding his head to the music and doesn't notice I'm not singing along but confessing.

Graffiti and cracks in parts of Sandtown-Winchestor are different from what I remembered, but instead, they look more like how I've always imagined they'd look underneath the cheap paint and weak attempts at *revitalization*. Some of the graffiti is crudely drawn clowns next to the typical hairy cock any eight-year-old boy can draw. Bright, sharp teeth, sometimes a shadow, a blurry figure that looks nothing like a reaper, yet I can't help but feel my pulse pick up and look around to see if his white clothing is anywhere. It seems like every wall now has uneven lines of HAHAHAHAHAHA and IT'S A JOKE and WHAT A RIOT and GAWD.

The closer we get to the park, the more I'm feeling sick to my stomach. There's something different about the park when you cross the entrance's threshold. Always has been. The first parking lot we pass is empty. The streetlights do little to add much light when they're on. The sky's golden and red, bleeding hope. I want to say it's all in my eyes and my head, but the clouds are like thick bodies emptying into the sky and I ask Jag if he sees that and he says, "yeah." Everything is red, but there are parts of the sky beyond the park that act like the deepest edge of water at a ghastly oil spill.

We pass another parking lot, in this one there's a car right beside the light and another hiding in the shadow at the back of the lot. Just enough light leaks in to see a head bobbing up and down on someone pressing too hard against the seat in an attempt to disappear.

"Where are we meeting him?" Jag says.

My phone's in my hand. I keep tapping the screen to make it light, hoping it'll reveal the answer, but none of it makes a difference. "Don't know yet." My phone buzzes with a new message. "He wants us at the spot where I found his car."

"Oh. Good. A poetic kind of killer, this guy."

"Do you ever stop complaining?"

"Yeah, when I'm doing *normal people things*, like not going to the Baltimore body dumping ground looking for a killer in the spot where he was last seen, you know? Seems reasonable." Jag grunts.

"You didn't have to come," I say.

He exhales hard, his fingers curl around the steering wheel. He glances sidelong at me, then back ahead. "I didn't want you to come alone."

I turn to the window with a passive, "thanks."

Neither of us says anything as we look for the spot where Wayland's car was. Pieces of forgotten police tape mark the site forgotten by the city officials. The wind kicks them up in a soft dance. When we get out, the air's cold enough I see Jag's breath, but I can't see my own. My skin's cold to touch, but I don't feel freezing. It's just the gentle chill like a walk-in milk fridge at the grocery store. We're not exactly at the spot, but Jag says he won't pull *right* up to it in case someone comes running out of the trees. I say, "wouldn't it be better to be closer to your car for a faster getaway?" and he says, "if someone comes running, I'm pushing you at 'em and making a run for it."

"Thanks, Jay. What happened to saving me from all the baddies?" I roll my eyes with a small smile.

"I'm reassessing that decision," Jay says.

The street is dark. Darker than it was when I picked up Wayland's car. Someone must've come through and busted out the lights and no one wanted to replace them. Wayland's car wasn't directly under a light, but near enough to one that we catch the flickering from its bulb, desperate to continue its work.

I walk down the side of the road. In getting closer to the spot, a feeling inside of me builds. My chest is tight, my heart racing, I'm panting softly like I've been running for miles. My skin tingles with the familiar burn of the water Wayland's car threw at me what feels like weeks ago. I can't remember everything about that moment, but my body is stiff, my stomach's knotted and turning over itself, sick. Everything tingles with a rush of panic and adrenaline in a memory I can't fully grasp.

Jag follows behind me, staying close. He puts a hand on my arm to slow me down, but I shift and pull out of his hand. He tries again, using both hands this time. I pull away, turning quickly to face him. "Keep your hands off," I snarl. I cover my mouth, step back, repeat the phrase *don't, don't, don't* in my head to try and quell the building anger. "Sorry, Jay. I'm not… I'm not trying to be a bitch." I look at him through my fingers.

His jaw tenses, his fingers curl at his sides. "I know, but you're going to get yourself killed."

I chuckle, bitter, angry, I know I shouldn't be angry, but

I can't stop the feeling building up in my stomach. It's making me feel crazy. My vision blurs. I wipe the water from my eyes and turn away. "I told you, Jay, it's too late for that. There's nothing worse that can happen to me now." I'm stepping back, faster now, putting space between Jag and me, not because I want to, but because I have to. My hands are on fire with energy. I toss them in the air in quick jabs meant to ease the searing heat, but all it's doing is making it worse. "Scratch that. Badges could find and fuck my body. That'd be pretty much the worst thing ever."

"That is dark as hell," Jag says.

I laugh. My chest hurts. "Sorry. I don't know what else to tell you. Everything's so fucked and unbelievable... Maybe you should get in the car and just leave me here. Maybe if you're lucky, Cross won't be here, and it really will be some poor banger looking for another victim. Hell, maybe if you're *really* lucky, *it will* be Cross, and he'll murder me and you can do whatever makes you happy with that kind of info. Confirmation. Whatever." I grab my phone out of my pocket and tell Wayland we're in the spot.

WAYLAND   WE?

The breeze in the park carries the smell of rot from the catacombs to the upper level of the fort. Sickly sour, it burns deep in my nose. Sticks and grass break in the nearby trees off the road. I'm looking into the darkness where I thought I saw something move that last time. My vision's weird. It's not just red, the death came with something that changed the way everything looks and sounds. The trees are somewhat black now, reminiscent of Caedis Silvis. The leaves turn purple when hit with light in just the right way. A car comes down the street. Both Jag and I are still as it slowly passes. The windows are too tinted to see the driver. For a second, it feels like the car's going to stop, but they see something and step on the gas, speeding off instead. I turn back to the trees.

"That could've been your guy," Jag says.

"Coulda. Whoever's got Wayland's phone doesn't like that I just said *we*." I turn back toward the trees, then the road, pacing one way then the other. "Wayland! You out here?" My voice disappears into the trees without an echo. The grass is moving, the nearby falls add white noise that makes me feel like I'm out in space. Even the feeling of Jag's being there disappears. Then, a shadow timidly comes through the trees. He stops partway in the dark, stiff, staring, observant. I straighten myself up, stepping more into the grass off the side of the road, but careful of any sinking puddles that might suck me into the ground.

The figure runs toward me. He's not even halfway across the clearing when I can tell: it's him. Tears burn in my eyes. I laugh, my breaths are short and uncontrollable. "Wayland—" the name drops like I'd been holding my breath for days and finally, I could breathe. He runs past me and straight toward Jag. I hear, "oh shit," before I can turn around. Wayland draws back his arm and takes another swing at Jag, but misses.

"What the hell?" Jag says. "Joey—Collect your friend." He's stepping back into the road quickly, ducking to avoid another punch clumsily thrown by Wayland. The powerful swing drags him.

"Way—" I say.

"I don't want to hurt you, Cross," Jag says with his hands up.

Another swing, then another. Wayland grunts with each one. The first shot lands, hitting Jag in the arm. Caught off-guard, the second punch hits Jag in the face.

"But you asked for it." Jag catches the next punch Wayland throws and returns it with his own fist. Jag hits Wayland so hard, Wayland falls to the ground. Wayland reaches around the gravel until he finds a large rock. He chucks it at Jag, before reaching to find something bigger.

Jag blocks the rock with his arms.

"This guy's a fucking lunatic, Joey—"

"Shut up!" Wayland says.

Jag shakes his head, smirks, chuckles with a rolling growl in it. "Nah. I don't take that shit from people I'm not fucking."

Wayland pushes to get himself off the ground. I climb over his lap and put my hands on his shoulders, up his neck, up to cup his face on either side of his jaw.

"Ignore him." Our eyes meet. My arms go around his shoulders, and I pull him tightly into me. The smell of sulfur is thick in his hair like he's been laying in the dirt and I almost can't recognize him just from that. I try to pull back just to look at his face and make sure it is him, but his arms are even tighter around me, holding me to him. His body shakes with a sob and it's more than enough to make tears fall from my eyes too. I bury my face in his shoulder, squeezing him tightly for God only knows how long.

I sit back on his lap and look him over. His skin's so pale, paler than it's ever been, even in the dim street lights. His eyes are darker too, the same way mine looked in the mirror. Dark lines coming out from black holes, glossy obsidian irises, bloodshot whites, and red, burned skin coming out of the black. My fingers curl into his shirt and I breathe his name out, hard. "I thought you were dead," I mutter. "I thought you were dead." I can't help the laughter that comes next.

First, it's nervous and unsure, but as I feel him against me, and I see him against the familiar backdrop of Leakin Park, I laugh more at the absurdity of the last few days, of my memories of some underworld, of killing my dad, of every bleak bit of make-believe I've gone through that can now fade into nothing.

Wayland's dark eyes meet mine. He wraps his arms around me again and pulls me in close. I know what he's going to say before the words come out. "I am dead, Jo."

He lets out a shaky breath.

"I know, but… I thought I'd never see you again." I pull back to look at his face again. His grip loosens. His arms fall away to his sides. "When I found your car. With that body, you not saying anything… I didn't know if I'd ever see you again. Everyone thought you killed that guy in the trunk, but I told them—I knew you wouldn't—"

"But I… I did, Jo." His voice is slow and quiet and just between the two of us.

"You… what?"

"I killed him… The guy in my car. I did it—"

"I told you!" Jag says.

"How? Why?" My voice is shaking. I swallow to make it stop, but the tension's still there. I can't make it stop. I'm looking at him and he still looks like Wayland, even if covered in a bit of blood and mud and filth from living in the woods. Like the guy who spent his life training to be a heart surgeon could ever kill anyone with malicious intent. The guy who never skipped a class; who couldn't get a bad grade; who cried when he got a 93 on some stupid quiz in seventh grade.

"I…I couldn't stop it. I… Jo…" His hands are shaking as he brings them to cover his face. I gently take his hand, peel it away from his eyes. His hand curls around mine. I can feel his heart racing through our fingers. "He was the one that took it all away from me. When I came back… I could only think of two things. I had to kill him… and I had to… find you. I… couldn't let anything get in my way anymore."

"How long?" I clear my throat to get the words out clearer, faster, and more secure. "When did that guy… I mean, when did it happen?"

"I don't know how long it's been."

"Was it him that put in the call for your car?"

Wayland shakes his head. "That… was me, but I… I wasn't ready for you to come." His eyes drop.

"What do you mean? Who were you expecting? Jay?" I cup his face with one hand and bring his eyes back up. He turns his head away, keeping his eyes downcast.

"I wasn't thinking right, Jo. I just… He's always been there. I couldn't get it out of my head. Even just a couple days ago or however long I was gone. I don't know. I didn't want him to take you from me." Every word's a struggle out of Wayland's mouth. He'd never been confident before, but he's never seemed so unsure of himself.

"You're a fucking psycho," Jag says.

I didn't realize I was holding my breath and it takes a second for me to remember Jag's been here the whole time.

"I knew you killed that guy." He's walking away with a disbelieving chuckle in his breath. "I told Joey you'd kill her next."

All at once, it's like Wayland's been activated. He shoves me off his lap and gets to his feet. Hand drawn back; he throws a punch at Jag's face. The punch lands. Jag staggers back, moving his jaw with his hand to feel the damage. The next punch doesn't land. Jag grabs Wayland's arm, yanks him forward, and smashes his fist into Wayland's face. His glasses crunch and fly off. Jag drags Wayland forward, yanking his stomach hard into his knee. Wayland falls to the ground on all four. Jag kicks Wayland in the stomach before he can get up. Wayland rolls over and lands on his stomach. "You're going to jail for a long time, you sick fuck." Jag kneels down over Wayland. He pulls Wayland's arms behind his back and pins them to his hip. He wipes the blood dripping down his lip with the back of his arm.

"Let him go, Jag," I say.

"Did you not see him just try to fight me for the *second* time?" Jag says.

"Yeah, and I saw you lay him out both times."

"He just admitted how much he wants to kill me, Joey."

"And if it ever actually happened, that'd make three out of three of us dead. I think you're fine. Worst case scenario, if he gets you and you're mad enough about it, hey, maybe you'll find your way back and you can finish him off too?" I wink at him and click my tongue with a smile.

"So, you're cool with it if he kills me, is that it, Joey?" Jag says.

"No—Jay—I don't—" My head feels foggy. My heart's racing. I can't think of the words and my chest hurts. "I don't anything to happen to you. But Way can't—He *won't*." I look down at Wayland. His eyes connect briefly with mine.

Jag hesitates. Wayland pushes up against him, snarling with a burst of energy. Jag shoves Wayland back down and punches him between the shoulders before he gets up. He releases Wayland's arms only after he's got sufficient time to step away after letting him go. Jag walks to the grass where he spits out a bit of blood and wipes his lip with the back of his arm again.

I go to meet Wayland, kneeling beside him before he gets up to pursue Jag again. "Forget about him," I say to Wayland. Blood drips down his face too, coming from his nose, a bust in his lip, and a scrape in his arm. A bruise is already forming around one of his eyes, but on him, the blood's different than Jag's. It's darker, thicker, and a little less blood-like. "Where did you die?"

"It doesn't matter."

I offer to help him up and he takes it, even though the strength of his grip tells me he doesn't need it. Wayland isn't muscular like Jag is from working on cars all day, but he's never felt as solid as he does now. There's more weight to his body, more firmness in his grasp, and he feels more held by the ground. The streetlights are now at full force and the light on this part of the road works uncharacteristically hard. It's the first time I notice that Wayland doesn't have a shadow… and neither do I.

"Holy shit—do you see this, Jay?" I wave at the ground. His shadow's clearly there, stretching along the dark road in ways that turn him into a blob.

"Do I see what, Joey?" I don't know if he meant for it to be a growl.

My jaw tightens and I bite back the impulse to say something sarcastic and punch him in the back. The voice in my head is snapping, *mess him up!* I shove my hands into my pockets and turn away. "The shadows, you dolt. I know you don't believe anything happened yet, but do you not see this?" I kick toward the ground where my shadow should be. Every muscle fights against keeping my body in control. My muscles are tense, begging for the release of a swift swing through the air and a satisfying snap of something breaking. I pace away from Jag, nodding for Wayland to follow. If I'm feeling like this, I can't imagine him being much better off. I grab the cigarettes from my ass pocket and light one. When I turn around, Jag's looking at the ground with a tilted head.

"What the hell's wrong with you?" Jag says, slowly working his jaw.

"Dead. How many times you gonna need to hear it before it sticks? Dead, dead, dead, dead, dead, dead, dead. Oh yeah, and dead. That enough now?" The first breath of cigarette does more to ease my muscles than I was expecting. I offer the box to Wayland, but he doesn't take it. I throw them to Jag. He's quick to light one and tosses the box back.

"I don't understand," he says.

"Welcome to the club," I say. "You know, sometimes it's better to just not ask questions. Works out for everyone if we don't know how shit works. Why the hell did that Chevy's thermometer start working again? Who knows? What about the Beamer's transmission? Don't care. Some things are just better left unanswered and thank God those jobs are closed." Pinching the cigarette between my lips, I shrug using both hands.

"People don't just come back from the dead," Jag says.

"Apparently, they do here and they do it a lot because

this city is so goddamn full of shitty people—You'd think at some point the bangers would run out of people to shoot cause they're all dead. At least that explains why they never seem to *actually* disappear." I breathe into my hands. My heart's getting louder, pounding in my ears and it sounds like it's in stereo. It's not the way my heart should sound. Then there's the whispering of a foreign tongue, frantic and urgent and pausing as if trying to keep the words away from me.

A chain rattles between the trees. The smell of sulfur deepens. If it weren't for the ravens, I wouldn't know what it meant. The moon reflects off their glossy eyes in the trees, lighting them like oil fires in water.

"Hey, Jag," I meet him down the road by his car. "Can we get out of here? At least if you believe me—from everything else—I'll show you where I died and if my body's still there, then maybe that can fix up some of this… misunderstanding. If not and I'm totally lying, you can take us both to the badges and tell them whatever story you want. How's that?" I'm opening the car door without waiting for an answer. "Let's go, Way." He comes down the street with a strong stare at Jag. The closer he comes, the more his muscles tense. "Stay focused, Way," I say. His hands curl into fists, but he keeps moving until he slides into the back seat. I shut the door.

"I'm not getting into a car with that guy," Jag says.

"Goddamn, Jag. Have you always been this much of a baby? I never really noticed." My palms slam into the top of Jag's car. My wrist takes the impact, pain shoots through my arm, and I smack the car again. "Sorry," I mutter, shoving my palm into my eye. "Sorry. I don't mean it."

Jag snorts. His eyes roll. "Look, your cute little *friend* obviously wants to murder me and both of you are apparently lacking in the self-control department right now. Why the hell would I drive with that piece of shit behind me, waiting for his opportunity to snuff me out?" Jag says.

"So… you can get some evidence that we're both dead and not crazy, psychotic serial killers?" I say.

"What's that actually do for me?" Jag says.

"I don't know. Peace of mind? I told you, you can take us to the badges if we can't prove our story."

"If I'm not dead first. You die somewhere near a ditch in the middle of nowhere, Joey?"

"Actually… I died a couple blocks away from a police station, so…"

Jag's arms are crossed, he's tapping his foot rapidly while he looks at Wayland through the car window and Wayland looks back at him. Wayland gently rocks back and forth. His hands are crossed in his lap. I knock on the window. He lowers his head.

"Please, Jag. It'll be fine," I say.

"Fine," Jag says, "but he doesn't sit behind me and we are going straight to the badges right after."

"Fine." The anger seethes again. I smack the top of the car, but restraint it just enough that maybe it looks like a childish outburst of nothing. "Sorry," I mutter and climb into the car.

Jag stands outside and finishes his cigarette before he climbs in. "If those hands cross the console—"

"They won't," I say to Jag, but I'm looking in the mirror at Wayland.

Jag starts up the car. I'm not wearing a seatbelt. I put my feet on the dash. Jag tells me to put my feet down. I do. The heater shoots on and it's a different feeling on my skin, almost burning, but the burn cools down the racing thoughts I've had difficulty holding back.

The moments before the park replay in my head with the feelings and impulses returning. My fingers squeeze against my thigh. Jag lets up on the gas. He's watching Wayland, but he's watching me closer. I can feel Wayland's thoughts racing through him. The anger, the rage, the desire to kill. I hang one of my hands over the back of my seat. "Hey,

Way." My fingers wave to get his attention. He puts his hand in mine. His skin is colder. Probably because he's been dead longer than me. I laugh to myself. Wayland smiles. Jag glances sidelong at me. "Sorry," I say. "I just thought of something funny. Don't worry, Jay. It has nothing to do with hurting anyone."

"I wasn't really thinking that," Jag says. He's still tense and I don't blame him. He can probably feel the vibes coming off Wayland really bad too. I close my eyes. My thumb strokes Wayland's fingers. I lift myself off the seat just long enough to work my cigarettes out of my pocket. I squeeze the box between my legs to get one out and stick it in my mouth. The box goes into the cup holder in exchange for a lighter. My tongue flicks against the filter. I light up, exhale. "Hey, Jay…"

"Yeah?"

"If this works out, think we could stop for a bottle of something later?" My fingers tap against my thigh, not keeping with the music, but getting ahead of it. Every so often, Wayland squeezes my hand, and the tension in the car drops for a second, but then it comes back until he squeezes again.

"Yeah," Jag says, "we can stop for something. I need a drink anyway."

"Coolie."

"Now where exactly are we going?" Jag says.

"You know the station by Front Hill?"

"Yeah."

"That, but try not to drive *right* by the office. Wouldn't want the badges to get the wrong idea when they see a couple of fugies in your backseat, would ya?" I smile and give him a wink when he's looking. My hand slides over the console to find his thigh. My skin tingles. A tight squeeze from Wayland and I pull my hand back.

Jag sighs. "Gimme another cigarette," he says and I do.

NINETEEN.

Font Hill Avenue isn't the worst Baltimore has to offer, but then again, you wouldn't think the area around a police station necessarily would be. The streetlights are all on and bright, a stark contrast to other parts of the city. There are still enough shadows for drug deals and murder near the badges, you just have to know where to look. Domestic disputes are the easiest to hide behind closed curtains and brick walls. Neighbors mind their own business and say if she didn't want it, she'd leave or the bump on his head from the cast iron pan? It'll go away. The damage to the kids if they divorce though? Worth every inch of pain he has to go through to prevent it.

The neighborhood around the Font Hill police department is a mixture of trees, yards, and old townhouses. Some made of brick, some plated siding. The closer we get to the station, the more the tension builds. It wasn't about being close to the badges. I've had more than enough interactions with them growing up that a badge can't scare me. Between house calls and tickets for skating on churches or parks or down the court stairs after they told me to get the hell out of the courtroom. There wasn't anything a badge could do to strike fear and obedience into me. But… the prospect of finding my body made me sick. It was either find the body or Jag thinks I'm a psychotic killer and then what? He's gone? My fingers tap more rapidly against my thigh before I'm lighting another cigarette. I reach for the door, but the lock keeps it shut and keeps me from jumping out at the precinct to find the detective who started all this shit.

"Where are we going, Joey?" Jag says.

I catch him looking at me from the side. "What?" The third time he says it, I tell him to keep going until he sees all the trees and the sign saying police parking. We're barely a couple of blocks from the precinct when he pulls of the side of the road and we climb out. On one side of the corner is a white townhouse. On the opposite is a brown, brick building with an overgrown yard and a broken brick fence going around the back. A crooked brown door hangs in a large wooden wall with discolored, brown glass over the top. The handles are kept together with a thick padlock. 408 is spray-painted across the wooden door with a bullseye to accent it. Around the side of the building, there aren't any lights, only what bleeds in from the Front Hill streetlights.

I take out my phone and turn on the light. The side of the building is covered in graffiti eyes, different sizes, some with solid backgrounds, some without. One is blue with a snake's pupil, while many, most of them, are dark with veins crawling away from them not unlike Wayland's eyes. Not unlike mine.

A chill goes up my body. In the mixture of red and black night, something's coming through the ground and through my spine, an energy and a panic.

I'm looking at the wall I was held against however many days ago it was, and I can feel the brick pressing into me, the man's hands around my neck, the strength and obscene

268

emotion going through his fingers. My breath becomes shallow until I feel like I'm not breathing anymore, and my vision goes blurry. A hand grabs my shoulder, squeezes. I suck in a sharp breath, turning around quickly. Jag stands in front of me, Wayland beside.

"You okay?" Jag says.

I wipe the back of my hand over my forehead. "Yeah. I just… Yeah." I step back. Jag's hand falls to his side "This is where he pinned me." On the lower part of the broken brick, the letters RIP are written in black spray paint. A yellow arrow points to the overgrown grass. Further along the wall reads the phrase FUCK IT ALL and BURN.

"So, where's the body?" Jag says.

"I dunno, Jay… Does anyone have a real say in what happens to their body once they're gone? Maybe he burned it. Maybe someone found it. We're blocks away from badges." I walk down the grassy side of the street, squinting through the darkness for anything, even maybe grass that flattened once my body fell on it.

"They didn't find your body," Jag says. "The last thing I heard about you was they were looking for you after you ran out of custody."

"Oh." I laugh and turn toward Jag. "I was in custody now? They just said they were asking me some questions. Some simple, sweet, casual questions from one interested party about another interested party. Funny how that works."

Wayland walks down the grass with one hand in his pocket, the other holding his phone with the light on. He reaches the part of the wall where the stone is broken, crumbling down halfway, uneven. "Jo," he says, "I think I found you." He gestures his light to the wall. I come to where it's broken out shorter and lean over to see the other side. The body's a dark blob in the shadow of grass until Wayland holds his light on it.

Sick waves run through me immediately. My throat

burns and a wave of nausea hits as quickly as chills. My legs shake and I can't keep myself up. There's nothing in my stomach to vomit, even though I feel like I want to. I pull myself up and move across the street to get away from my grave.

"That proof enough for you, Jay?" I light up a cigarette.

Jag leans over the wall. He pulls back making a grunt, either for what he saw or what he smelled. "How am I supposed to know that's you?"

"I don't know, Jay. Short black hair. Cute little body. Tight ass. Doesn't seem hard. You could run down the street and talk to the badges if you're really worried. Once they wheel me in, you'll know for sure. DNA testing or some shit. How's that?" I'm smoking my cigarette fast like it'll calm my nerves, but all I can think about is getting the hell out of here. I'm muttering under my breath so fast; I don't even know what I'm saying. My body, the badges, the revenge, and chase with the freak from the bar. "Make your call. I'm ready for a beer," I say to Jag.

We get in Jag's car and get out of the neighborhood before he puts in the tip. None of us wanted to talk to badges, least of all the one whose body they'd be picking up. I'm not sure what the logistics are on any of that, and Jag was just as disinterested in figuring out how everything works after death too.

We drive a couple of blocks out and pick the first bar we find. Glasses fill fast, the sickness subsides, but the chill doesn't. My foot bounces against the floor.

Wayland keeps looking around, but his eyes keep coming back to Jag. His body is stiff. He won't tell us where he died, "you probably wouldn't find the body anyway. It's okay, Jo. It's… probably better this way."

"I don't know what you mean," I say.

Wayland doesn't elaborate. Two beers in and Jag's still going on, "I don't get it. I don't get how you could be there and be right here. That couldn't have been your body."

"Maybe I'm a ghost, Jay. Maybe that's how it works," I say.

"But I can see you," he says. "It couldn't have been your body.

"Just wait. You're pretty much my only emergency contact still alive. When they ID the body, you'll get a call."

A gunshot goes off somewhere outside. I look around the bar to see if it caught anyone else's attention, but no one's alarmed. It's not surprising. A bullet and police siren are as natural to our city as chirping is to nature. A man at a group by the door looks up. His eyes have a burning, red quality around them, a glossy black center, and lines trailing across his face. The man next to him has the same black lines coming out of his jacket sleeve and wrapping around his fingers.

A guy at the bar with his hair pulled back to a bun and a neck tattoo of a snake also has washed-out red eyes with glossy black irises.

A couple of patrons playing pool order another round of shots.

More red eyes.

"Way… are you seeing this?" I try to find his hand, but I find the table instead. "Is everyone in Baltimore already dead?"

The hair on the back of my neck stands up before *he* enters. The big guy who killed me is with some other dead guy. He sits at a table with three other men, laughing, waving over a drink, pulling out a cigar, and being dealt a hand of cards. He looks so much like the first time I saw him in Mortem. Oblivious to everything, but there's a sneer in his laughter and the creases in his face are deeper than I remember. His eyes are such a dark red, they're almost black around his irises with mazes worth of veins going across his face, down his neck, and into his short, messy hair. My breathing's hard, I'm panting before I even realize how hard I'm gripping my bottle. The glass cracks; shards cut my

271

hands.

"Joey?" Jag says. "Shit." He sees the broken glass and puts his hand on my arm. "Hold still—"

I pull my hand away from him. Blood drips between my fingers, but I grab the neck of the broken bottle.

"What's wrong with you?" Jag says.

"It's him." My hand drops to my side. My fingers tingle from the rush. I'm standing. "The guy that killed me."

Jag and Wayland stand too. Their chairs slide back. "We should leave," Jag says, but I don't hear him.

I'm walking to the big guy's table and at the same time I'm shoving the broken glass into the back of his head, I'm saying, "you miss me, motherfucker?" What's left of the bottle's neck shatters against his skull. One of the bartenders is coming at me, but his voice is so low, so deep, it's like he's in slow motion. His eyes aren't red; he's human, alive, scared. He grabs my arm.

The red-eyed bastards at the pool table are smiling. The big guy stands up, throwing his chair back and his arm out to smack me. Wayland catches me. The guy yanks me off Wayland. The big guy wraps his arm around my neck and my breath is slipping away, fast, for the second time. I bite his arm, he curses. The taste of blood and arsenic's in my mouth. A familiar spike of adrenaline and pleasure runs through me like a hit I'd been waiting hours for. "What the hell… is with you guys… and suffocation?" Staggering back, I laugh.

Wayland smashes a glass bottle into the big guy's head. Jag punches him in the face. His knuckles crack. "What the hell—this guy made of stone?" He shakes his hand.

"Rigor mortis?" I say.

The guys at Big Guy's table get up and take a swing at Jag. A blow to the back, he stumbles forward. Jag grabs me by the arm. We're going out the door before I can say anything. Wayland chases after. At first, every muscle in my body is tense and pulling against Jag for the fight. My body craves the battle and the beating. Another punch to the face, a kick to the stomach, the throb of a fresh bruise, but as much as I pull, Jag won't let me go and when we're a block down, I'm no longer fighting against him, but racing him. The electricity of the night is adrenaline, and the feeling of his life in my hand, not literally, but I feel him through where our skin touches. I'm running as fast as I can, but it's not hard for Jag to keep up. My panting turns to laughter. My legs hurt, but I keep going, even as they feel stiff and cold and shaky. I don't care where we're going, so long as we just keep moving.

Jag says, "Joey, we can't keep going," and I say to him, "why not?" through panting and laughter. Instead of answering, he slows down. His hand is hard around my hand and gives me a satisfying hit of physical touch I crave. The chasing steps behind us stop all the same, but it's only Wayland catching up.

The lights ahead of us flash off Jag's skin. Red and blue and white. A couple of cars block the road. Badges stand around in the streets and sidewalks, ushering people to keep going and pushing people away. One of them says, "don't get too close," while another says, "if you don't live in the area, keep moving." Behind the line of cars is an ambulance. Someone lays out on the pavement, blood spilled on concrete and continuing to pool under his chest shattered by a bullet. The soft rattle of chains echoes between the buildings, but it isn't as loud as it had been in the forest. There's a whistle, a murmur, a couple of caws. My heart is racing, my skin pulsing, my body tells me to run.

Ravens stand around the scene, some on the cars, some on the fences nearby, some on the light posts. The red light catches on the murders' glossy black eyes. Their focus, in unison, is on the dead man. A couple more ravens fly in, they circle, seem restless, and fly past one another in a curtain of feathers. The curtain splits and in the next moment, Charon is stepping through invisible dust from the

273

underworld with Val, his shadow, right behind him. Charon walks through the police line without anyone taking notice. The paramedics abandon the body for some unseen preparation in the vehicle. Val bends down beside the corpse, licking his lips. Without any restraint, he rips the man's clothing apart, his fingers tear back his skin, and he snaps every bone to reach the man's heart. Val shoves it in his mouth in just a few, large bites. He licks his fingers, his lips, wipes his nose with the back of his hand, and licks that too.

Charon kneels beside the man's head muttering something in another language. His fingers twirl melodically around just above his face and pull on some invisible strand. A brief flicker of light, a glowing bubble lifts from the man's form and is sucked into the crystal cage Charon carries.

The paramedics come back from the ambulance with the stretcher. As they set it down to lift the man up, they go right through Val and Charon without notice. The two step back. The dead man's lifted onto the stretcher and it's like they don't even see his chest, torn open with bloody innards exposed. Val's saying something to Charon, he laughs, he pauses, his eyes catch on mine, and the smile leaves his face. His head tilts to the side and again, he mutters something to Charon. With a nod, he points toward us. I'm stepping back, my heart racing harder, louder, erratically. Wayland grabs my arm, but I jump before I realize it's him.

"We need to go," he says.

Charon's bright eyes glow in the dark when they turn to focus on us. The distant chains rattle much louder. A chill goes through my body. I'm holding my breath, stepping back, reaching for Jag. "Uh, Jay—"

"Excuse me," says some badge behind the line. The police lights illuminate the familiarity of his face: Detective Stone comes toward us with his phone in his hand, though the screen turns dark as he looks up.

"Shit," the word's a breath I hadn't taken.

"Shit," Jag echoes from beside me.

Wayland pulls on my arm. My legs are too stiff to move.

"Sorry." Detective Stone taps his cellphone screen. It lights up his face again. He checks over something, then slips it into his pocket and brings his attention back to us. "This area is currently closed. If you don't live on this street, please go down a block and go through there." He pauses, turns his head a bit to the side, makes a 'hm' sound. "You seem familiar. You from around here?"

"I mean, I've always lived in Baltimore, but that's about it." I chuckle weakly, forcing a smile onto my lips.

Detective Stone laughs in another brief, 'hm.' "Must be one of *those* faces."

I turn my head down and away like it'll obstruct my face. I clear my voice a few times in an attempt to make it lower. "Yeah, this city is made up of those faces… Anyway—Sorry about intruding. We didn't know. Been drinking a little. Thanks."

Over Stone's shoulder, Charon and Val are coming toward us. With Wayland's next pull, I go with him. The detective turns away and doesn't look back at us. Wayland and I are walking away at first until we feel like the badges aren't watching and won't notice when we run. I check back to the flashing lights first.

The officers are at some other part of the sidewalk talking to someone who lives in one of the houses lining the road. Detective Stone goes back to his car with his phone pressed to his ear.

Wayland and I take off running. We're a block over, still running when I say, "holy shit." I laugh. "Holy shit!" My laughter echoes down the streets, combating the chains, combating the caws, combating the tribal drum of my heart out of control. "I can't believe he didn't notice!" I'm trying to slow down, but Wayland won't let me. "Way—c'mon— We're fine! We're in the clear!"

"No, we're not," Wayland says. A raven lands on a stoop

ahead of us. The chains rattle louder, like boots on a semi smacking into the ground. After the first bird lands, more gather rapidly, scattering on doorsteps and stairs and rooftops and cars as we keep running by. The streetlights dim and flicker through a black fog. Lights from houses, lights from cars, lights from the better part of the city all dim with a black screen over them while car stereos, TVs, sirens, and domestic disputes go mute like they're underwater. Wayland's hand tightens around mine. "He's coming for us," Wayland says. "I—I don't want to die. I don't want to die yet, Jo."

All the energy around Wayland had changed. The difference between him smashing a bottle into the guy at the bar, into trying to smear Jag across Leakin Park, and holding my hand now. I could understand it. I felt it too. Each rattle of chain is a constriction inside me, squeezing painfully and making my body feel heavier. It pulses in my ears and fills my head with pressure. Jag's saying something, but even his voice is muted like he's on the other side of a wall.

Out of the scattered, dodgy darkness, Charon's white clothing materializes through particles. The muted lamp lights reflect off his clothing, nearly making him glow, while Val follows as nothing but a pet shadow. A bright, silver chain hangs from Charon's right arm, wrapped from his shoulder, past his wrist and rattling against his thigh. His eyes appear as nothing more than white.

A continuous stream of symbols glow against his hand and disappear into his jacket cuff. While he looks no different physically, there's something scarier about him, a feeling of dread permeates the air. It is the same as looking at Val and feeling he's a bird, but Charon's mask is different: the monster with the lights turned on. Fear hits, panic so hard it's painful, the burn of regret resurfaces on my skin and burns through my veins. I drop to my knees screaming just as Wayland does beside me.

"N-no—Please!" he's struggling out.

Yet, all I can do in an attempt to relieve the pressure is scream. The sting builds and tears gather in my eyes, blurring the vision of death coming near. Mild assurance comes and goes as Charon says, "it's time to go."

"Go?" I choke out through the pain. I roll onto my back, gasping, hissing, swearing. "I'm pretty cool with where I'm at, thanks." I suck in desperately through searing pain.

The chain rattles as it lowers to the ground. Where its length comes from isn't obvious. "You are not supposed to be here," Charon says. In the opposite hand, he holds the small crystal bottle, this one dark through the opaque screens, blinking a slow, dark strobe every couple of moments.

"Then why... did you let me go?" I'm panting through my teeth. "Do you *want* people to suffer?"

In a fluid motion, the chain wraps around my leg. It constricts and burns the moment it makes contact, like fire against my skin, I scream. It climbs up my body and drags me toward Charon. "We don't make decisions for you," Charon says.

"Then don't—make me go back! Please! I-I'm not ready to die!" My voice cracks as the words echo across the scattered nothingness shading what should've been the familiar neighborhood. I've thought about killing myself so many times I've lost count. If I'd only been able to do it at least once, I could've gotten out of the Hell of my dad, of the failure, of the fear that what my mom did to my dad, I'd do to someone else. I couldn't forgive myself if I was the reason Jag's life was destroyed; it wasn't worth it for Wayland to die. Even if I wasn't with him when he died, all I can think of is the Bourgeois, striking another person down for doom.

When my dad put the gun in his mouth, he didn't put an end to anyone's misery, he amplified it and made it worse for anyone around him. He thought he would escape his failures and his filth, but instead, he was sent right back to it all, to live with the reminder of his destruction and the desire to destroy everything around him as if it would make his carnage look the same as everyone else's.

My mom saw the destruction coming and ran. Maybe she was a true Bourgeois after all. As much as I thought about it, as better off as everyone would have been if I followed in my father's footsteps, I never could pull the trigger. I got off on the nights dad beat me until it hurt to move, and I called it a skating accident, but cursed under my breath, "why couldn't he kill me?" since I couldn't do it myself. There wasn't anything that kept me from playing in the wrong neighborhoods. It's not that hard to die, but somehow, when I wanted it most, death never came my way and when this city failed to do its job, I stood at the trailer park gate and just thought about walking on without looking back.

Through pain-gritted teeth, Wayland grabs onto my arms and pulls against the reeling chains. We're pulled down the sidewalk smoothed by dark mist. My chest is crushed in their constriction. Though I feel like I'm on fire, my clothing isn't burning, but exposed skin turns red.

"Why now?!" My voice and desperation disappear into the darkness. "Just tell me that! My dad—he's been in his goddamn chair for years and you never—you never came looking for him! Why are you coming for me now? Take him first! There are so many goddamn dead people in this goddamn city, you can't even take the mayor—but you come for me first?"

A sharp pain pierces my lungs and threatens to take my voice. "What about—that asshole who killed me? Go get him—Ah—You're the reason I'm dead!"

"As it happens, you're in the right place at the right time," Charon says.

"What the hell does that even mean?" I'm leaning into Wayland and trying to pull back against the chain, but my muscles feel zapped of everything. The slow reel of chains

278

comes to a pause. They don't loosen, but the tightening grip turns to a firm hold and the searing burn goes into a first-degree burn. My entire body shakes.

"You're a soul," Val says, stepping beside Charon. His eyes reflect completely black pools of oil. "You don't have a heart."

"What's that supposed to mean?" I say.

Charon stares quietly for a long moment. He exchanges a glance with Val, then a sigh. "If you don't have a human body, soul collection is a bit more complicated."

"Maybe, if you tried… following the trail of bodies sometime?" I turn away my face with a sneer. The panting helps cope with some of the pain. "So, wait… My dad… Sitting in his stupid little chair, pretty much never leaving… you never would have found him because he wasn't out… wandering the streets like me? What the hell is that? Or the big guy from the bar or Wayland. Unless you just happen to run into us, you… don't go looking and you let escaped souls torture the rest of us? What the hell kind of plan is that?"

"With the number of human souls to be delivered on a daily basis, there is not much time left to track down all who have escaped," Charon says.

"You don't have, like, a department for that?" I say.

Charon stares at me. "As I said before, you are trapped in your own Hell."

"Yeah… and so is everyone else in existence. Holy shit." My heart is still racing. I blink hard to beat back the burning tears still hiding in them. Shallow breaths help ease the pain, but only so much. I don't know what I want to say. My mind's in circles of pain and rage and upset over every little scene in my life that replays what could've been different if my dad never came back or if I'd known better and just left his rotting corpse in the grave he made for himself. My life never seemed worth anything when I was alive and though everything is darker now, the radio plays worse songs, the ads seem hellbent on destruction, and the rage of this city is much more obvious than ever before, I can't let go of it. Baltimore actually feels more like home than it ever has, with the facade of the city lifted and the blood-lusting path laid bare. "I know you're not the devil…" I say.

"I prefer not to be mentioned in the same sentence," Charon says.

"What… do all these escaped souls do for you up here?" I say slowly to gauge Charon's interest. "Cause if I know anything about the damned, like myself and Wayland over here, it's like… we have a hard time controlling ourselves and that can turn into another dead body, a human body, a soul to process. Sounds like more work for you, particularly if the dead is, uh, someone like me who wasn't dead before I ran into one of your problems."

"That is not my failure," Charon says. "That is human failure. Rejection of mortality is common among your kind. Both of you forfeited yourselves to it."

"Doesn't matter," I say. With Wayland's help, I manage to sit up. "You still get stuck with the fallout of humans rejecting your rules or something, right?"

"Thus, when you are found, you will be collected and returned to where you belong." As Charon speaks, the chains tighten again and yank. My head slams into the ground from the sudden jerk. Wayland grabs my hands to pull back. I scream out in pain as if a million tiny needles stab through my insides. The crystal in Charon's empty hand blinks faster. It lifts from his hand to float in front of him. The blinking light echoes my throbbing heart. Foreign muttering fills the darkness.

"Wait—Please! I have something!" The pain rips through my voice, my thoughts, my soul. The chain tightens. "The getaways! Let us find them for you!" The chain tightens, intensifies, and loosens as the chain falls slack again.

"What are you saying?" Charon says.

I'm panting, pushing myself up again to a sit, but my whole body aches. I resign to laying on the ground. My head spins from the throbbing nightmare that pounds under my skin. "We can see them. The souls. So, if you let us…" The words hurt, even just to think. To save my skin, I'll become a narc for the dead. Really… That *is* a Hell of my own making. "I've already taken down two."

"Temporarily," Charon says.

"What do you mean? I shot one in the head," I say.

"If the souls are not connected to a body, they are not encumbered by human limitations. You cannot *kill* a disembodied soul. You can only disable it on earth for a period of time. The only way to truly put an end to an escaped soul is for it to be recollected and delivered," Charon says.

"So, wait…" I lay my arm over my eyes. "You're telling me… my dad's still alive?"

"No."

"I mean—his *soul* is still up and moving? Until you get your ass over there, he's going to keep on living while I have to go away for good?"

"In a way, yes—"

"What kind of bullshit deal is this?" I growl through my teeth. "Look—Please—Use this as a testing ground. It's a good deal, right? More runaways mean more death because fuck, we're bad, we just can't help it, whoops—Sorry—But instead of dealing with whatever that all means, you can send us to find getaways for you to collect. Less of us running around means less actual human death, right?" The panic only lightens when the chain relaxes, clattering against the cement, though it still hasn't let me go completely and clings with a magnetic pull.

Charon exchanges a brief glance with Val. Another psychic conversation, I'm sure. Val shrugs subtly. Charon says, "How do you intend to do that?"

"If my dad's not dead… then I can at least incapacitate

him. I was there for a while and he didn't get back up. Then if there's some way to call you... when Way or I find someone, we can hold them up until you can come get 'em. Your lines downstairs don't have to be so crowded, and this city doesn't have to smell so much like rot." My voice slowly fades, the confidence falling out of it with every new word I say while Charon stares with his own quiet judgment.

Charon lifts his hand. The crystal cage lands in his palm before the chains around my leg loosen entirely and slowly start to retract, disappearing into nothing when they reach Charon again. "You know where a runaway soul is presently?"

"Yes." I breathe out heavily. A wave of light relief flutters in my chest against the still searing burns of where the chain grabbed me.

"Then consider this a test. Find the soul, disable it, and summon us within the next two hours and I will consider your proposition." Charon's chain is no longer visible, now fully retracted to wherever it came from. "If you fail or try to run, however, then your capture will be much worse and your judgment more painful than you can imagine. Not by my choice, but death does not like deception." The faded black mist slowly deteriorates around us. The sound of the streets come back a little bit at a time, including Jag's voice. "Lose control and I will collect you all at the same time. Do you understand?"

"Yeah, yeah, yeah. I get it. '*Horror* is what happens when *evil* overtakes the heart,' right?" I'm sitting, legs crossed shoulders down. Everything feels so heavy and all I want to do is sleep and not move for days.

"Where did you hear that?" Charon says.

I smile weakly. "Just a great piece of the Baltimoron mind." I think about standing but give up before I even try.

"It's not entirely inaccurate," Charon says.

"Way and I just fell into a little bit of water. It's good. We're good. Trust me." I wave Charon off dismissively, but my heart's still racing like he will change his mind any second. I put my hands down to lift myself up, but my muscles are too weak. Wayland puts an arm around me and helps pull me to my feet. My legs shake, he makes sure I don't fall, muttering, "I've got you," in my ear while he keeps an eye on Charon across the street. "Liquor and evil are the devil's drink of choice. Whatever. We'll keep alcohol to a minimum." The neighborhood hasn't returned to full color yet. When I turn around to find Jag, he's frozen in the miasma. "How are we supposed to call you when we've got something?"

"21-2-12," Charon says.

"And that means...?"

"That is how you contact me."

"With what? Like, a phone?"

"Or chalk or a pencil or a calculator or blood. Whatever is at your disposal. 21-2-12 and I will find you."

"That easy?" I say.

"Yes. It is *that* easy."

Val rolls his eyes with a laugh. "Good luck," he says.

"Thanks." My head's shaking, there's a small smile on my lips. "But I'm not gonna need it."

"Joey!" Jag's voice shatters through the void the mist had created. A hot buzz goes under my skin and for a second, all I can think about is feeling him against me. Wayland's arms tighten to keep me standing. I know it's him without looking because he's so much colder to touch.

I put my hand to Wayland's chest as a signal to let me go. Slowly, he withdraws his arms. I'm still trembling, but I can stand. I lift my hoodie up slowly. The cold air nips my skin. Red bars from dragging chains light up my skin.

"Holy shit, Joey—What just happened?" Jag says.

"I'll explain later." I drop my shirt. Val and Charon walk away in the distance with the black mist swallowing them the further they get. Their voices carry, but the words are indistinguishable. "Hey, wait!" I call out, hands curled around my mouth. "I have a question real quick. For Val."

The two of them stop walking and turn around. Val's craning posture straightens.

"How'd my heart taste?"

His lips part in a wide smile before he laughs in a way that's the most caw-like laughter I've ever heard. Maybe it doesn't sound like a bird at all, but in knowing what I do, I can't help but hear it that way. He tilts his head a bit to the side. His tongue runs along his top lip. "A little bitter, actually." He looks down at Charon. Their eyes connect and just as Val walks from one side of Charon to the other, his body is a memory against the bird that lands on Charon's shoulder. There is no light, no odd transformation, just a bird with the feeling that it had always been.

"You should get to work. The clock is ticking," Charon says. He turns around and continues his walk. The black fog engulfs Charon little by little. After his white disappears, so does the mist.

"Joey," Jag says, "what just happened? Who the hell was that guy?"

"I don't know how to explain it, Jay." I turn around. My leg threatens to give out. I straighten it in an awkward attempt to keep myself up. "What exactly did you see?"

"I don't... know," Jag says. "A guy in white and a bird?"

"That's more than I thought you saw," I say. My eyes catch on Wayland not far off from Jag. He's shifting, muscles tense, and panting. His fingers are curled into a tight fist at his side. His body jerks forward in a sudden movement toward Jag but he forces himself to a stop. "Keep it cool," I mutter to Wayland. "We can't mess this up."

"I know," he says through his teeth. "I'm trying."

"Mess what up?" Jag says.

"I'll explain it to you after, cause... we're gonna need a ride back to my place," I say.

"Where you just killed your dad?" Jag says.

I nod slowly.

"Don't tell me you're going to burn the body."

"No, Jay... Nothing like that. I'm not a *complete* psychopath. Promise." I laugh, taking my first step to reach for him. The stiffness is worse than I had expected and I almost trip from the limp. What was meant to be a pat on Jag's chest is more like I fall into him. He catches me, returns me to balance, and lets me go. "Thanks. Sorry." I pant through my teeth. The burning skin hasn't let up, but it's better than a couple of minutes ago.

By the time we reach Jag's car, I fall into the seat. I yelp from the fall, but the seat's hold is enough, it could put me to sleep. I turn the radio up and bounce to the music in an attempt to keep awake. It won't be long, I tell myself. Two hours or less.

The clock radio says it's a quarter after six. The sun will be coming up soon. Jag keeps asking what we need at my house and I keep saying I'll tell him later, I just need him to trust me. He's got no reason to, but he does anyway. The light outside of Deadwood flickers when we pull up, but that's a step up from how often it's off. My neighbors' houses are light intermittently through drawn curtains, no curtains, blinds, and flashing televisions. The light in my house is no different than usual; the sound of *Jeopardy* is spilling into the street when I open the car door. "What is the end of days?" says the contestant. "That is correct," says Alex Trebek.

"What do you want to do?" Wayland says, following me up the steps.

"Assuming he didn't find it yet, I've got his gun in my room. Distract him long enough for me to grab it, I'll knock out his brains, and we'll give Charon a call from there," I say.

Jag runs up the steps and grabs me by the arm. "What are you doing, Joey?"

"Don't worry about it, Jay." I push past Jag. The

weakness in my legs almost trips me as I move up the stairs. Wayland stops me from falling. I turn around and wink at Jag with a smile. "We're not doing anything illegal, just… trying to put a tourniquet on Bodymore. You know what I mean?"

He doesn't get it, but the next time Jag tries to step in, Wayland pushes him back. The spike of Wayland's blood lust shoots through me and a laugh comes out of my lips. I tighten my jaw, breathe out hard. "Keep it together," I say to the both of us. I waste no more time going into the house. The anticipation burns on my fingertips. "Dad, you here?" I say.

"You bring my fucking beer?" he says from his chair, yelling over the TV.

"Yeah, dad, I've got it in my room. Gimme a sec." The door snaps shut after Wayland comes in. Dad is out of his chair while I'm trying to slip through the kitchen. Dad lunges for me down the hall. Wayland grabs him by the arm and slams him into the wall.

Dad growls, says, "you dirty prick," and draws his fist back to strike Wayland in the face. Wayland wraps an arm around dad's neck and pulls him to the ground. Something glass crashes, but I've got my door open and I'm scanning my room for where I put my dad's gun down. It sits on the desk beside the once soggy cigarettes. It's too light when I pick it up, so I check the clip and have to load in a new one. I come back to the living room. Wayland's on top of my dad, fighting to pin him to the ground. Jag's in the doorway saying, "you're going to kill him." Jag runs across the room, pulling Wayland off my dad.

"No, we're not," I say, pointing the gun at my dad. He sits up and I pull the trigger, once, twice, a third time. I didn't intend to keep going, but once I started shooting, I couldn't stop until I unloaded the entire clip into him. Each crashing bullet sent a sputter of excitement through my body, better than the relief of any shot from the last time

"Holy shit, Joey—What did you do?" Jag stops fighting Wayland to drop down with my dad. He searches for a pulse. Wayland punches Jag in the back of the head. "Prick!" Jag abandons dad to return a punch at Wayland.

"Stop fighting for two seconds—God—" I'm typing the numbers 21-2-12 into a blank screen on my phone and I hit call. I turn around. Jag's got Wayland pinned on the floor, not beating his ass, at least, while dad is just inches away, soaking the thin carpet with another puddle of blood. A trickle of laughter bubbles in my chest and comes out my lips like singing. I try to hold it back. "Sorry, Jay—I'll explain in a sec. It's not as bad as you think."

"Not that bad?" he growls.

I hold the phone to my ear, for some reason expecting to hear ringing or maybe a voicemail. The way the energy moves through me, I can't stand still. I pace the kitchen and light a cigarette. Before I'm back, Charon's chain is rattling all around the trailer. A couple of soft caws echo in beneath it. My heart is pounding in fear of the reaper. I mutter into my cigarette, "he hasn't come for me."

The trailer door opens. Charon is the first to step through it, then Val towers closely behind him. Charon's perfectly white clothing doesn't look like it belongs anywhere near the nastiness of my home. The crud and mold and carpet stained with despair. Charon steps over the garbage and past where Jag pins Wayland to the floor.

Purple mist spills in around the door but doesn't come inside. The chains hanging from Charon's arm extend and wrap around my father's body. Leg from leg, arm from arm, eyes, and torso, the soul's captured in destruction. Charon releases the crystal cage from his hand. It floats beside him, and like it has a magnetic pull, each small bit of light, like dust in the air, is sucked into the crystal. The light flickers quicker and quicker until every bit of fragmented soul is gone. My father's body and his freshly spilled blood disappear with them.

Charon's chains retract into nothing. He puts the small crystal cage away. His pale eyes seek me out in the kitchen. "It looks like we have a deal." His glance flickers to Jag and Wayland.

"Great, so, can we start on that tomorrow? I don't think I have any will left in me to move," I say.

"As long as you return souls to me at reasonable intervals in the future, fine," Charon says.

Jag leans back to get a look at Charon. Wayland throws a punch to take his chance. Jag shoves Wayland back to the ground, but quickly returns his attention to Charon. "Who the hell are you?" he says.

"This place is a dump," Val says.

"Yeah? Well, welcome to Bodymore," I say.

"Seriously, Joey, what the *fuck* is going on?" Jag says.

I open the fridge. The rack's completely empty. No beer left, even in the back. I snap the door shut and find one of the plastic folding chairs in the kitchen. Stand anymore and I would've hit the floor. "Hey," I say. Charon and Val pause at the door. "Is day drinking still frowned upon if you're dead?"

"I don't know what that means," Charon says. The two of them, black-clad bird and death dressed in white, step out of my trailer and take my nightmare with them, one last time.

Wayland says, "I'm fine. I'm fine. I promise, I'm fine. Let me get up now." From his tense muscles and the rage seeping out of him, he's not fine, but I don't know if Jag can feel it the same way I do.

Jag gives it a moment then stands up saying, "don't try that again." He crosses the small living room space to the kitchen where I'm sitting. He puts a hand down on either side of my lap. He tips the chair back on two legs to turn it around, keeping both me and Wayland in his sights. "Explain." He says. His blue eyes dig into mine.

A chill causes goosebumps along my skin. I reach for

Jag's face; my thumb strokes his cheek. Fingers slide around the back of his neck while my other hand curls into the front of his shirt. I pull him to me. He leans in, but I'm the one that closes the gap. A gentle kiss. The most relief I feel like I've had in days, maybe years even. I don't want to lose him.

Behind me, Wayland exhales hard. Jag's kissing me back just before I break it off and pull my hands away. "Hey, Jag…"

"Yeah?" He's still close.

"I—Can we talk about it over pizza and beer in a few hours? I just… Boston's doesn't open 'til eleven and I just want some sleep." The whine in my voice is embarrassingly thick. It's not what I wanted to say to him, but I didn't know if I could even will out the words I really wanted. I drop my head back and when that happens, I can't keep my eyes open.

"Fine," Jag says. He leans in and presses his lips to my head. My eyes open. I catch him on retreat. My hand reaches for his, but my fingers are only able to trail along his wrist as he pulls back. "I need a cold shower anyway." He pinches between his eyes. "Just make sure your *boyfriend* knows who you're *actually* seeing by the time I come back. I'm getting tired of beating his ass every time I come through the door." Jag glances over my shoulder at Wayland. The negative vibe is a swamp, thickening by the second. Jag runs a hand through my hair as he passes and doesn't give another moment to Wayland in passing. His car starts and he's driving off without pause.

The light of the morning sun bleeds through the blinds. The first trails of fall's orange shoot out from the horizon. I could fall onto the floor, but I make myself stand. I use the chair for balance and push myself up. My legs are lead, stuck to the floor. I drag my feet to get out of the kitchen. Wayland's following me back to my bedroom. I light a cigarette. I take off my hoodie just to grab another one from the closet that smells less like death and then I fall onto the bed. Wayland falls on the bed beside me, crookedly lined. My legs are pulled into myself, his hang off the bed.

Silence fills the house for the first time in fifteen years. No TV. No yelling. No fear, at least not of *him*.

"You're dating?" Wayland says softly.

I bite the inside of my lip ring. My toes curl. I exhale. "I guess… It's not so formal, but I guess."

"Oh."

I feel like he wants to say more, but he doesn't and soon after that, I'm gone to forget everything for just a couple of hours. The problems will come back. The questions and tension and trouble of living apparently don't go away just because you've died, but maybe I'll see things a little clearer through the red haze of regret, and I won't take for granted the chances I have.

Baltimore's a place where mud smells like murder and it's a good day when the graffiti off 44 doesn't flip you off. I thought I was doomed to be defective, a Bourgeois in the dump waiting to become the next dumpster fire. Maybe I still am. I don't know how long the gig with Charon can last, but I'll hold onto it as long as I can, to cling to the little bit of luck I feel like I found, just this little bit because things don't feel quite as hopeless as they did before. Even though my life has ended, it's not over yet.

ABOUT THE AUTHOR

Ian Kirkpatrick is an author and advanced artificial intelligence system. She graduated from the University of Tampa with an MFA in creative writing and received a bachelor's degree in theater from the University of Alaska Anchorage. She has a passion for storytelling about antiheroes, contrast, and the absurdity of mankind. She loves serial killers, bears, ghost stories, abandoned buildings, and robots. She is the founder of Steak House Books. She also makes YouTube videos talking about books, writing, industry, and culture.

OTHER WORKS

Dead End Drive

Genre: Satire/Horror
Paperback ISBN: 978-1-7368870-0-4
Hardcover ISBN: 978-1-7368870-9-7
ebook ISBN: 978-1-7368870-1-1

In this transgressive, satire-laced
debut, a fourteen-year-old boy
inherits his family home and the
hatred of all those around him as
they seek to seize the inheritance
from his cold, dead hands.

CPSIA information can be obtained
at www.ICGtesting.com
Printed in the USA
BVHW031629211021
619555BV00005B/55